TWO OF HEARTS

"A compelling romance supported by nuanced characters ... heartbreaking and sensitively drawn ... a well-crafted contemporary romance." —*Kirkus Reviews* on *Hearts on Fire*

"Julia Gabriel does an amazing job with this devastatingly, heartbreaking love story." —*RT Book Reviews, 4.5 Stars, Top Pick* for *Hearts on Fire*

"A heart-wrenching and emotional read, with a sweet payoff that will leave readers smiling" —*InD'Tale Magazine* on *Hearts on Fire*

"A bittersweet story about perseverance and adversity. Julia Gabriel does an amazing job of conveying the characters' feelings. The writing style is flawless, and the characters are both multifaceted and dynamic." —*RT Book Reviews, 4.5 Stars, Top Pick* for *Next to You*

"The second novel in the Phlox Beauty series, *Back to Us* is an intimate look at an unforgettable, albeit imperfect, love. Ms. Gabriel's deeply moving storytelling evokes every facet of emotion from the reader. Not only does this book have standout characters, the city of New York shines in this tale. All in all, between the beautiful settings and the sweet and satisfying ending, this book is a winner!" —*InD'Tale Magazine* for *Back to Us*

"*Back to Us* is a unique romance about falling in love all over again. Colt is a great character that readers will be rooting for throughout the book. Suffering from memory loss, he needs to recall his past in order to move on with his future. The alternation between past and present timelines works well and while the story can be enjoyed as a standalone, it is further enhanced by the inclusion of all the characters from Next to You, the first book in the Phlox Beauty series." —*RT Book Reviews, 4 Stars* for *Back to Us*

"*Drawing Lessons* is an old fashioned romance with a bucket-load of modern problems. A great read for a chilly autumn night." —*Happily Ever After Thoughts Blog*

"Gabriel paints white-hot sex scenes." —*Kirkus Reviews* on *Drawing Lessons*

"As the wife of an up-and-coming senator, Marie Witherspoon is living an enviable life. But beneath the surface she is deeply unhappy, and her creative urges and passion have been stifled by her loveless marriage and overbearing parents. When her best friend buys her some art lessons as a birthday present, Marie thinks it will help her get back to her roots. She doesn't expect that art—and her unconventional instructor, Luc—will turn her world upside down." —*RT Book Reviews* on *Drawing Lessons*

"What a sigh-worthy tale! One that isn't an insta-love relationship, it builds with each lesson, making it much more romantic ... There are twists and turns in this story that one will not expect, which is a delightful surprise. Ms. Gabriel does an amazing job of making the reader want to turn every page and savor it." —*InD'Tale Magazine* on *Drawing Lessons*

TWO OF HEARTS

A ST. CAROLINE NOVEL

JULIA GABRIEL

SERIF BOOKS

Published by Serif Books

ISBN 13: 978-0-9996548-5-9

Copyright © 2018 by Julia Gabriel

✿ Created with Vellum

CHAPTER 1

"*L*eave it to Greta to have, like, the nicest wedding ever," Cassidy Trevor said as she looked around the outdoor courtyard of the Primrose Creek Ranch. "Even with these things." She kicked out a cowboy boot-clad foot and laughed.

"Well, we're in Texas. Cowboy boots go with everything. Even bridesmaids' dresses." Avery kicked out her own matching boots.

"Even wedding gowns," Cassidy added. Beneath Greta's long white gown were the prettiest white bridal cowboy boots. Greta and Cassidy had been roommates at Talbot College. Along with Avery and the rest of the bridesmaids, they'd been a tight-knit group of friends for years. Though that was changing these days. Now only Cassidy and Avery were unmarried, which explained why they were sitting together at the bar as the assembled guests waited for Greta and her husband to clean wedding cake off their faces so the dancing could begin. The other bridesmaids were with their husbands.

"I wish I had my phone on me." Avery made a show of patting down her dress. "So I could take some photos. I'm getting so many ideas for my own wedding."

"You're getting married?" Cassidy's voice was laced with surprise. Avery engaged to be married was news to her.

Avery laughed. "No. Not yet." She pulled a wry face. "But someday, right? I mean, those paper lanterns are adorable. I'd get married just to have those."

The delicate paper lanterns suspended from the trees *were* adorable, Cassidy had to admit. As were the little tumbleweed centerpieces that were actually made of spun sugar. Everything about the Primrose Creek Ranch was gorgeous. The lush green lawn that sloped down to a small sparkling lake. The renovated barn, which stood ready in case of rain. She squinted through her glasses at the late afternoon sky. Of course, there was nary a cloud to be seen.

Even the bridesmaids' dresses were lovely, a pretty pomegranate color that matched the pomegranate martinis the waiters had been delivering on trays since "I do." It was a flattering color on everyone. One thing she had learned from Lydia's wedding last spring—chartreuse was not a good color for Cassidy. Against her blonde hair and perpetually tan skin the dress had looked like demonically vomited pea soup.

"Can't you see yourself getting married someplace like this?" Avery kept on.

"Sure. This is beautiful." In reality, though, Cassidy couldn't see herself getting married here. Or anywhere, for that matter. At twenty-seven, she should be feeling that urge to settle down. Shouldn't she? Everyone seemed to think so. Her parents, her sisters, her friends, the ladies at the quilt shop.

But she wasn't. Not even a twinge of an urge.

"So are you next?" Avery looked at Cassidy over the rim of her pomegranate martini.

"To get married?" Cassidy lowered her gaze from the eggshell blue sky and looked straight at Avery like she had temporarily lost her mind.

Avery nodded.

"Good heavens, no."

"No prospects on the horizon?"

Cass gave her friend another look. "I live in St. Caroline, remember?"

"I don't recall there being a complete dearth of men in that area when we were in college."

"There's a dearth of men I haven't known since I was in kindergarten. The summer folk come and go."

Still, it was undeniable that everyone around her was pairing off, starting families, buying houses, setting up 529 college funds. Cassidy felt pressured to start thinking in that direction too but … the thought of settling down in St. Caroline and buying a house that someone she knew had already lived in and having two point six kids felt like a lead weight on her soul.

I'm not ready yet.

"Can I ask something without you getting mad?" Avery said.

"Sure."

"Are you going to work at your mom's quilt shop for the rest of your life?"

"No. Of course not."

Avery's face was skeptical. Granted, Cassidy had been full time at Quilt Therapy, her mother's shop, since she graduated from college. That was five years ago now. *Where has the time gone?* She had worked part time for her mom before that … it was hard to say when exactly she started working at the shop. She'd grown up there, as all of her sisters had. It was a family business.

"There was a fire earlier this summer and we had to move into a new location. Mom needs the help right now." That wasn't just an excuse. The fire happened back on Memorial Day and it was now late September, but the summer had been rough sales-wise.

"But eventually, you're going to move away and do something with your degree. Right?" Avery pressed her on the matter.

"I'm thinking of going back to school, to get my MBA."

A smattering of applause broke out as Greta and her husband reappeared, their faces now clean of cake and icing, Greta's lips newly shaded with lipstick that matched the pomegranate bridesmaids' dresses and martinis. Cassidy was relieved for the distraction. She had enough trouble explaining her continued residence in St. Caroline to herself, let alone other people. On the one hand, she liked working with her mother and sisters. She'd heard enough complaints from friends about crazy bosses and passive-aggressive coworkers that she knew how good she had it with her family. They didn't always see eye to eye on things, but she never worried about her mother throwing her under the bus for some silly mistake.

On the other hand, she definitely wanted to see the world, meet new people, all that good stuff. She had a bucket list of all the places and things she wanted to see, a bucket list that grew longer every year.

"HEY. YOU OKAY, BUDDY?" The guy standing next to Matt Wolfe at the hotel bar clapped him on the shoulder. Dave, the guy's name was. Matt had met him exactly six days ago at the nearby fire training academy. Matt was in Texas taking a week-long seminar. Today was the last day and everyone in the class was out to celebrate.

"Yeah. Fine," Matt replied, squinting harder into the hotel lobby's weird orange mood lighting. It made the space look like a science fiction movie set. Or like the whole place was on fire. Maybe that was why the fire training instructor had dragged them all here.

"Because you got a weird look on your face." Dave wasn't letting this go, and Matt really wished he would. It had been a long week. Matt wanted to drink a few beers to be polite, catch a cab to the hotel where he was staying, and fall face first into bed. His flight left early in the morning.

"I think the beer goggles have kicked in," he said.

"Oh yeah? Who you checking out?"

"I see a woman over there who looks like someone I know. From back home. But I don't know what she'd be doing way out here." It probably wasn't her. It was hard to tell in the orange light, and her face was turned down toward the phone in her hands.

"Which one is she?"

"The one in the pink dress, cowboy boots. Blonde hair. Glasses. Sitting alone in one of those big chairs." Big enough for two, he thought.

"Whoa. Not bad. Well, if you do know her, introduce me." He clapped Matt on the back again.

"If that's really her, she's an ice princess. I've known her all my life and no one has ever been good enough for her."

Dave laughed. "Well, I love a challenge. Let's head over there. You can either introduce me or we'll just introduce ourselves."

For a split second, Matt considered not following Dave over to the woman in the pink dress and cowboy boots. Chatting up women used to be one of his favorite pastimes. Or, as his brother Jack was fond of saying, his only pastime. But lately, nothing engaged his enthusiasm. His mother had succumbed to ovarian cancer the month before and his older brother's wife lay in a hospital in Baltimore, comatose from a car accident. It had been a rough year and Matt was frankly exhausted. Physically, emotionally, mentally. He was wiped out.

Dave took three steps with his long legs, then turned to look back at Matt. "You coming?"

Matt pushed away from the bar and followed. "Yeah, sure." He'd let Dave do all the talking.

As they got closer to the woman in the pink dress and cowboy boots, he saw that she was in fact the person he thought she was. Cassidy Trevor. One of the Trevor girls. The sister of his brother's fiancée. The daughter of his parents' close friends.

For all those reasons—and probably more that he was forgetting—Cassidy Trevor was forever off limits to Matt. All the Trevor sisters were. As Dave strode determinedly toward her, Matt wondered whether that prohibition applied to him too.

You're not Cassidy Trevor's keeper. Plus, she really was an ice princess. In fact, that should probably be in capital letters. Ice Princess. And maybe neon lights, just for good measure. She was going to shut down Dave's advances like nobody's business.

Then he reconsidered. Dave wasn't a local St. Caroline boy. Cassidy had always turned her nose up at the guys in town. As a teenager, she had spent summers chasing after the summer kids. The rich summer kids. Which had always seemed like a losing proposition to Matt, since the summer kids all went home at the end of the, well, summer.

Not that it mattered to Matt, of course. He had been under strict orders for years to leave her alone. That was fine with Matt. There were plenty of fish in the sea, and he was an excellent fisherman. Gifted, some might say. And by "some," he meant himself.

She looked up from her phone, seeming to sense their impending arrival. Confusion darkened her eyes for a moment, then she smiled one of those big Trevor smiles. Broad with blinding white teeth. He realized why he hadn't been entirely certain of her identity from across the lobby. Her blonde hair was done up in some curlicue hairstyle. He'd never seen her wear her hair that way. Usually, it was long and loose around her shoulders or pulled back into a simple ponytail. Occasionally, a neat bun. Once in awhile, a thick braid down her back. But never this loose, curly do. He wasn't sure whether he liked it or not.

"Matt. Hi," she said when he and Dave reached her. Dave

immediately perched himself on the edge of the wide leather chair. The familiarity of the gesture rankled Matt. But Cassidy didn't seem to mind. She glanced at Dave, then looked back to Matt. "What are you doing here?"

"Training at the fire academy nearby. Since I'm taking over some of Oliver's duties while he's on a leave of absence."

Cassidy nodded somberly. "How's Serena?"

He shrugged. "The same. Ollie's too distracted to be at work right now."

"Understandable."

"Yeah. So what are you doing out here? All dressed up?" He looked down at her boots. They were a roughed-up brown leather, with pink flowers embroidered on the toes.

"My college roommate got married this afternoon." She smoothed her pink dress. "I was on bridesmaid duty."

Dave cleared his throat. *Oh right.* He wanted to be introduced.

"Cassidy, this is Dave. He's a firefighter from Kansas City."

Cassidy shook Dave's hand. "Nice to meet you."

"So you two know each other?" Dave was taking charge of the conversation. Matt was too tired to object.

"We grew up together in Maryland," she answered. "Our parents are friends."

That barely scratched the surface of their connections, Matt thought. Or maybe Cassidy didn't see them as being all that connected.

Dave reached over and lifted her drink from her hand. "Whatcha drinking?" He sniffed at the glass, another act that irritated Matt. He didn't exactly consider Dave to be a friend. It wasn't like they were going to stay in touch or anything.

"Just water," she answered, then trained a big flirty smile at Dave. "I think I had one too many pomegranate martinis at the wedding."

"Pomegranate martinis? That sounds either really good or

really awful." Dave flirted back, his hand touching her shoulder for an instant. Her bare shoulder, Matt noted, since the straps of her bridesmaid's dress were so thin as to be nearly non-existent.

"They were pretty good."

"Hmm." Dave made a show of studying the bar. "I wonder if the bartender here will make us some?"

"You should go ask." Cassidy winked theatrically at Dave. "Hint, hint."

"I think I will."

Matt resisted the urge to roll his eyes. Dave was practically puffing up his chest at his success so far with Cassidy.

"You want one, man?" Dave asked Matt.

Matt held up his near-empty beer bottle. "Nah. I'm good." He watched as Dave threaded his way through the increasing crowd and back to the bar.

"So how long are you out here for?" Cassidy asked.

"I leave tomorrow morning. And what about you?"

"I'm renting a car and driving over to Austin and San Antonio. I'm going to spend a few days checking out some quilt shops. See if I can find any good ideas to steal for mom." She flashed that blinding Trevor smile at him again, which had the same effect on him now that it had when he was in middle school and she was the glamorous eighth-grader, the "older woman" a year ahead of him.

O Cassidy, Cassidy! Wherefore art thou Cassidy?

Yeah, he remembered a few lines of Shakespeare from middle school, too.

"So how was the wedding?"

"It was good. Fine. Fun. You know." She shrugged.

Was conversation with Cassidy always this awkward? It wasn't as though they didn't see each other back home. They were friendly, if not exactly friends. But right now, he felt like he was chatting up a woman he'd just met in a hotel bar. *Look for conversational openings.* He glanced down at her short cowboy boots with the pink flowers.

"Did you wear those in the wedding?"

She twisted an ankle back and forth, and he tried to ignore the slender length of tanned leg between the boot and the hem of her dress.

"I did. We all did." She laughed. "We're out of context here, aren't we? We're not in St. Caroline anymore."

"No, we're not, Toto." That made her laugh again. Cassidy had a big, hearty laugh. She was a girl who liked to have fun. *Not a girl. A woman.* There was a straightforward quality to her that Matt had always found appealing. "You look nice," he added. "That color's very pretty on you."

"Well now, Matthew Wolfe. Aren't you just the perfect gentleman?" Her voice was suddenly soft and flirty. "Though I have to say, you look like you've been rode hard and put up wet."

It was his turn to laugh now. "It's been a tough week. With the training and all." Matt was about to ask whether she was staying at this hotel, when Dave reappeared with two martini glasses.

"Yup. Bartender hooked us right up." Dave handed a pomegranate martini to Cassidy. "Let me know if these taste as good as the ones you had earlier. If not, I'll go give the bartender hell."

Cassidy took a small sip. "Mmm. Tastes exactly the same."

"Excellent." Dave clapped Matt on the back. "Tom over there said to tell you he wants to talk to you."

Yeah, right. Matt could tell from the bemused expression on Cassidy's face that even she saw through that ruse. Dave wasn't even trying to hide it. *But fine.* Cassidy wasn't giving off any signs that she objected to Dave's interest. And Matt wasn't her keeper, he reminded himself for the second time that night. And for probably the millionth time in his life. But who was keeping count?

"Well, see you two later then." Matt retreated to the bar and to Tom, who didn't seem surprised to see him.

"Ol' loverboy, eh?" Tom laughed.

Matt didn't share the laugh. *Too damn tired right now.* The week had been nonstop work at the training academy. He drained the rest of his beer and, against his better judgment, ordered another. The thought of sleep was enticing, but he'd stay awhile longer to say goodbye to Cassidy. He half-listened to Tom's mostly idle chatter and added a few comments where it seemed appropriate or solicited. He ignored the interested stare of a woman at the other end of the bar. When his beer was finished, he turned back toward the lobby.

Dave and Cassidy were gone.

Well, can't say you didn't see that one coming. And like the world-class idiot he was, he had even facilitated it. He pulled out his phone to text his brother, Jack.

Just ran into Cassidy out here.

A moment later, a reply came. *Oh yeah? Becca says she's out there for a wedding.*

Matt stuffed his phone back into his pocket. Of course, the Trevor sisters weren't off limits to Jack. Nothing was off limits to Jack. The sky was the freaking limit for his younger brother.

For Matt, the ceiling had always been about thirty-five thousand feet lower. He was the workhorse in the family, the body that could always be counted on when another body was needed. *Old reliable, that's me.* Not that he was complaining. When his father, the chief of the St. Caroline fire department, had asked him to take over some of his older brother Oliver's training and management responsibilities at the station, Matt had stepped right up. Being a firefighter was what it meant to be a Wolfe. His father, his uncle, both of his brothers—all firefighters in St. Caroline. He wasn't taking over Oliver's job permanently. As soon as his wife was out of the hospital, Ollie would be back at the station. And Matt would step back into his old job, where he'd been since college.

He knew people tended not to take him seriously most of the

time. Yes, he liked to have a good time. And yes, he liked women. Why not? Interacting with the opposite sex had always come easily to him. Generally speaking, it had been his experience that he could have any pretty thing he wanted. As long as that pretty thing's name didn't have "Trevor" tacked on to the end.

$\mathcal{M}$att waited impatiently for the baggage carousel to spit out his checked bag, then he took his place in the long line for a cab. He was tired, but after a cramped seat on a plane it felt good to stand and stretch his muscles. His brain was tired, too, but in a good way. With his ADHD, it was hard to focus that intently for an entire week. His mind wanted to jump from fact to fact under normal circumstances. Having a large quantity of information compressed into one week and thrown at him quickly made his brain's natural inclination that much worse.

The line inched ahead and Matt periodically leaned down to shuffle his suitcase along with it. Finally, he reached the head of the line and climbed into the back seat of a cab. "Johns Hopkins Hospital," he told the driver. Oliver had dropped him off at Baltimore-Washington International Airport a week earlier before going to sit in Serena's hospital room, waiting and praying for his wife to wake up. Matt was hitching a ride back home to St. Caroline with him tonight.

He stared, unseeing, through the cab's window, remembering the day of the accident, remembering how he and his father had physically restrained Ollie while the EMTs cut Serena from the car. Fortunately, the boys weren't in the car with her. *Thank god for small miracles.* If Ollie had lost the boys, too … Matt shook his head as the cab pulled up to the hospital. *He's not going to lose Serena. She'll pull through this.* She had to. The Wolfe family had lost enough this year already.

Inside, he stopped at the nurse's station for an update on Serena's condition. He hated asking Oliver. His older brother wasn't much of a talker to begin with, even when the conversation was pleasant.

"No change, honey." The gray-haired nurse gave him a tight, grim smile.

He quietly pushed open the door to Serena's room. Ollie was there, as expected, not sitting in the chrome and vinyl hospital chair so much as he was stretched out on top of it. Only his broad shoulders and hard butt were in contact with the piece of furniture. His brother's eyes opened and he let his head roll toward Matt.

"Hey," he said quietly. "How was your flight?"

Matt shrugged. "I've been on worse." The flight had sucked. Besides the cramped coach seat that was uncomfortable even for his five-foot-eight frame, the airline had run out of the measly cheese and grapes snack boxes so Matt was starving now. At twenty-six, he still ate like a teenaged boy, something his mother used to point out was going to catch up to him "any day now." He swallowed the hard lump in his throat and looked at Serena tucked into the sterile hospital bed. He had nothing to complain about, not compared to what Ollie and their dad were going through right now. As bad as it was to lose his mother, he couldn't even begin to imagine losing a wife. Well, he couldn't really imagine even having a wife in the first place.

"You ready to hit the road?" In what looked like a stiff and painful movement, Oliver pushed his long body up off the chair. "I think dad has you scheduled for a shift tomorrow."

"Yeah. He does." Matt took in his brother's red-rimmed eyes and shaggy hair. "But there's no hurry."

Oliver drew in a deep breath and stared at his unconscious wife for a long moment. "They'll call me if there's any change. I need to get home and see the boys. They're probably driving dad crazy."

"I can drive," Matt offered.

"Thanks. I'd appreciate it."

An hour later, they were pulling into a gas station on Kent Island, the long Chesapeake Bay Bridge behind them.

"Coffee?" Oliver asked. It was the first word he'd uttered since they left the hospital.

"Sure." Matt swiped his debit card through the gas pump and begin filling the tank of Oliver's SUV. He was glad to be out of the city, glad to be headed back home where his own bed awaited him.

He hung up the gas pump just as Ollie strode out of the station's convenience store with two jumbo cups of coffee and a box of doughnuts. Matt's stomach seized up with hunger.

"I love you so much right now," he said as he got back in the truck. His words pulled a tiny smile from his brother's deep well of sadness. Oliver tore open the box and set it on the console between them.

Matt pulled back out onto the road. Less than ten miles later, the doughnut box was empty and their jeans were dusted, snow-like, with white powdered sugar. Matt licked sugar off his fingers. "I can't decide if that was the best idea or the worst idea."

"Probably six of one, half dozen of the other," his brother replied, then they both fell silent. That had been one of their mother's favorite pet phrases.

The coffee and sugar seemed to perk up Oliver as the miles rushed past. Fields of yellowing corn stalks lined the road, inter-rupted every so often by a gas station or strip shopping center. Oliver talked about Mason and Cam, his sons. Cam, the youngest, had just started kindergarten. When Matt turned the car onto another road, heading south, Oliver changed the subject.

"I need a favor from you."

Matt glanced over at his brother. "Okay. Anything. What is it?"

"Back in the spring, the Chamber of Commerce asked me to chair this new winter festival they want to do the second weekend of December."

"Yeah?" Matt was beginning to get a bad feeling about this.

"Well, I can't do it anymore. Between the drive to Baltimore and the kids, I'm out of juice, man."

"Okay. And ..."

"And the chamber said it was okay if you stepped in and did it instead."

Matt was quiet for a moment as he processed the implications of that.

"Why me?"

"You weren't there to say 'no.'"

"Thanks."

"You did ninety percent of the work on the fireman's carnival this summer. You're good at getting people to do stuff. That's the lion's share of the job. Harassing people to make sure they do what they said they would do, when they said they would do it."

"Sounds like the chamber is getting a late start on all this. It's September. The winter festival is when?"

"Second weekend of December. Friday evening through Sunday evening."

"And how much has been planned so far?"

Oliver's silence was all the answer Matt needed.

"So like nothing?"

"Sorry, man. I've been preoccupied."

"I know it." The entire family had been preoccupied for months now. But there was no way to say "no" to this. He did have experience from the carnival and he was unmarried and childless. He couldn't exactly argue that he didn't have the time.

"They said they'd find a co-chair to help you out," Oliver added.

"Like who?"

"I don't know. They hadn't identified anyone yet."

Matt could think of several likely candidates, all of them older with more pressing obligations like businesses to run and kids to raise. He would end up shouldering most of the work.

"All right. How hard can it be? Get some tourists into town to do a little holiday shopping and then eat at a restaurant while they're here. One last hurrah for everyone's business before things slow down after the new year. Right?"

"Right. That's all it is. It'll be easier than the carnival, Mattie. Way easier."

"HEY GUYS, I'm taking off. Cass, I'll see you back at the apartment later."

Cassidy looked up from the computer, where she was closing out the day's receipts for Quilt Therapy, to see her younger sister standing at the glass-paned door. At twenty-four, Natalie was three years younger than Cassidy and in possession of a far more active social life. Of course, that wasn't saying much.

"Sure thing." She waved to her sister. She and Natalie shared an apartment near Talbot College, where both of them had gone to school. Natalie tended to date grad students there. Cassidy had too, once upon a time, but she'd aged out of that. In a few more years, she'd be old enough to date the professors. *Now there's a depressing thought.*

She turned her attention back to the computer. It was a Monday, always a slow day at the shop. Slow enough that she had broached the idea a few months ago that they close on Mondays.

Her mother was still mulling it over. Financially, it was a no-brainer—especially in the off-peak winter months—but some of the customers liked to come into the shop just to chat and spend an hour or so working on whatever community quilt was set up at the moment.

"They don't spend money, but they help get those quilts done," her mother had said. "And I like the atmosphere it creates, people just hanging out and being friends. That's a big part of why our customers shop here."

Cassidy got that. She understood about intangible ROI. Return on investment. She'd been a business major in college. But she also believed that they couldn't be quite so cavalier about tangible ROI. When Michelle Trevor had opened the shop twenty years ago, Quilt Therapy had less local competition. Now there were other quilt and fabric shops in the area. People had choices they didn't have before.

The shop's front door clicked shut behind Natalie. Cassidy glanced over at her mother, who was slicing some newly-arrived fabric into two-and-a-half-inch strips for jelly roll bundles. Cassidy finished up what she was doing on the computer and shut it down. She walked over to the cutting table and ran her finger along the still mostly smooth wooden surface. The table was new, like all the furniture in the shop. Everything else had been lost to water and smoke damage in the Memorial Day fire.

"I know," Michelle said quietly. "It's not the same."

Cassidy shook her head sadly. "It's missing the character of the old table." *The history.* So much of her childhood was spent in the old shop, with the old cutting tables and quilting frame. It was hard not to feel as though a big chunk of Trevor family history was lost in the fire, too.

"We've lost some character, but gained some opportunities," Michelle added.

When they were girls, the Trevor sisters used to roll their eyes at their mother's unrelenting positivity. Cassidy was numb to it by now. Sometimes things just didn't work out no matter how positive your outlook. And it was precisely those "new opportunities" that kept Cassidy up at night. Quilter's Retreats at the Chesapeake Inn. More classes here at the shop. A wider selection of fabrics accommodated by the bigger retail space. There was even talk of expanding into a gallery that showcased quilts, and letting Becca run it.

Aye-yi-yi.

Cassidy began neatly stacking the strips her mother was cutting and rolling them up into a wheel of fabric, a "jelly roll." She tied a ribbon printed with the shop's name around each roll. That was another new expense—ribbons and bags with "Quilt Therapy" and the shop's new address printed on them. She took a deep breath to try and calm her nerves. She was the Trevor family's resident worrywart.

She rolled up more strips of fabric. If her mother's sunny optimism was borne out, the new opportunities would provide additional revenue streams for the business and even out cash flow in the slower winter months. But if they didn't pan out … what then? Her parents had never relied solely on Quilt Therapy for income. Her father and his pediatrics practice had always been the primary breadwinner.

But she and Natalie didn't have husbands who were doctors. Or husbands, period. Her mother might not be reliant on Quilt Therapy for a living, but two of her daughters were.

"So tell me about the wedding," her mother said. "I bet it was beautiful, knowing Greta."

"It was. It was good seeing everyone again."

"I'll bet. Good getting out of town, too, huh?"

Cassidy's wanderlust was a bit of a joke in the family, but she neatly sidestepped it now. "I found the most gorgeous hand-dyed fabric in a shop in Austin. I brought some back for Becca."

"That was nice of you. What did you bring back for yourself?"

"Ah, nothing." She gave a little laugh. "My stash is big enough already." Cassidy was also the fabric slut in the family. No one had a bigger collection of fabric than she did. And that was saying something, considering that her mother had a head start that spanned decades. "The stores were stocked with their holiday fabrics."

"Nat said ours will be in next week." Natalie was the shop's fabric buyer.

"Those Paris-themed fabrics looked to be popular out there, too."

"Hmm. We didn't have much luck selling those last spring. I probably would have ended up cutting them into fat quarters if ..."

There was no need for her mother to finish that sentence. The Paris-themed fabrics had been lost in the Memorial Day fire, along with the rest of the shop's inventory. Fabric, thread, notions, everything lost. They'd had to re-open Quilt Therapy in a new location—a better location that had more foot traffic because of its proximity to Main Street. But the summer was rough, both in terms of sales and the amount of work for all of them. It had been all hands on deck for months now. They were all tired.

"I hope you won't be upset ...," her mother continued.

Cassidy laughed. "That's an ominous-sounding opening, if ever I heard one." She tied off a ribbon and set down the bundled jelly roll.

"I sort of volunteered you for something."

"Uh oh." She looked across the table at her mother. "What is it?"

"I volunteered you as the co-chair for the chamber of commerce winter festival." Her mom's expression was appropriately wary of Cassidy's reaction. "They need someone to help out Matt Wolfe."

"Matt is the other co-chair?"

Her mother nodded.

"Why him?" Matt was a good time, party-all-night kind of guy —not someone Cassidy pictured as organizing anything for the chamber of commerce.

"Oliver was the original chair but with Serena in the hospital …"

"Right." No way Oliver Wolfe could handle a festival on top of that. "I ran into Matt out in Texas."

"Becca mentioned you told her that."

What Cassidy wasn't going to mention to her mother was the same thing she hadn't mentioned to her sister—that Matt had tried to set her up with his pushy buddy at the bar. Don? Dwayne? She couldn't recall the guy's name. Ugh. Fortunately, Lauren had saved her from what's-his-name's advances with a perfectly timed phone call. As twins, she and Lauren had always had a weird sixth sense about what was going on with the other. Lauren living in California hadn't changed that.

When she got off the call, what's-his-name was sucking face with a busty woman behind a potted plant and Matt was nowhere to be seen. Cassidy had gone up to her room and crashed for the night.

Michelle began folding up the fabric she'd been cutting into strips. "The chamber wants some younger people getting involved. Us old folks aren't going to be around forever."

Cassidy rolled her eyes. "You're fifty-five. You're not that old." Her mother didn't look fifty-five either, at least not in Cassidy's eyes. Forty-five, maybe. She'd put on a little weight in recent years, due to menopause, but she kept her blonde hair high-lighted to cover the grey and she dressed well—thanks to the Trevor women's love of shopping. "And when is the festival?"

"Second weekend of December. Friday through Sunday."

Cassidy ticked off the weeks in her head. "That's not much lead time. We started planning the quilter's retreat weekend earlier than that, and we still ran into a few snags."

"Well, that's why they're replacing Oliver with two of you. I don't think it will be that much work for you, given your skills, Cass. I wouldn't have volunteered you if I thought it would take up a lot of your time."

Even if it did end up taking a lot of her time, well she had the time to give, didn't she? She wasn't married. Or even dating anyone. She didn't have kids or a job with a crazy boss. Plus, she had a business degree and a natural gift for planning and organizing. Even within her own family, she was the logical choice.

"Okay," she agreed. "I'll call the chamber in the morning to get started."

At NINE O'CLOCK, Natalie still wasn't home. Cassidy cleaned up the small kitchen in their apartment, putting the rest of her kung pao chicken in the refrigerator and washing the plate and glass she'd used. The two-bedroom apartment was neat and spacious enough for them to share without tripping over each other. The living room was divided into two zones. There was a smallish area with the television, a sofa and an upholstered chair, but most of the room was given over to quilting.

Cassidy turned on the television to CNN and lowered the volume. Then she walked over to the large wooden table in the center of the room. At one end was the quilt top Natalie was working on—a nine-patch that was a riot of bright color. Natalie had an astute eye for color and fabric. She could make twenty versions of the same quilt block and every one would look entirely different. She was in charge of the fabric department at Quilt Therapy, and her popularity with customers was second only to their mother.

Scattered at the other end of the table was Cassidy's current work in progress. She made mostly scrap quilts, where a hodge podge of mismatched fabric was the whole point. It was also easier to hide mistakes in a scrap quilt. Cassidy was the least skilled quilter in the family. Oh, no one would ever come right out and say it but there it was. Becca was an awesome hand quilter and gifted at improvisational piecing. Natalie was the fabric whisperer. Charlotte was so accurate a piecer, she could practically do it with her eyes closed.

But Cassidy? She tended to cut off the points when she pieced. Her hand quilting stitches weren't a uniform length. Even Lauren was a better quilter than Cassidy, and she no longer quilted at all out in California. Face it, what Cassidy was best at was running the quilt shop.

She flipped through some odd lengths of fabric, chose a few, and began slicing them into long strips. The motion of pushing her rotary cutter through the fabric relaxed her mind, let her push away some of the stress in her life. The stress of reopening Quilt Therapy in a new location. Of seeing yet another college friend get married and move on to the next phase of life. Not to mention the stress of going through yet another holiday season as a singleton, of shopping yet again for just her parents and sisters, of smiling through all the "are you asking Santa for a husband this year" comments that every commenter seemed to think was totally original and unique.

Like no one had ever said that to her before.

Unfortunately, Santa wasn't real and thus was unable to just drop a husband for her on his way through St. Caroline on Christmas Eve. Heck, Cassidy would settle for a boyfriend but what was she supposed to do? Just somehow magically fall in love with some guy she'd known since kindergarten?

She sighed and set down the rotary cutter. She had no idea what kind of quilt she was cutting up fabric for anyway. Some sort of strip pieced quilt? She grabbed a soda from the fridge and collapsed onto the sofa. She pointed the remote at the television screen to increase the volume on Anderson Cooper. Dreamy Anderson Cooper. Too bad he was gay.

There was a category two hurricane brewing off the gulf

coast, and all the newscasters were standing in the whipping wind, their logo-emblazoned jackets shiny with rain, waves crashing white and noisy behind them. Cassidy watched for a few moments, then turned the volume back down again. She retrieved her phone from her purse, settled back on the sofa, and tapped Lauren's name on the screen.

"Hey there." Her twin's voice was soothing, like the moment you stepped beneath the spray of a hot shower and let the water cascade over your head. "Mom said you were back home."

"Yeah."

Lauren's voice softened. "What's the matter?"

"I'm back home. How's L.A.?"

"The same."

Which was to say, way more exciting than St. Caroline would ever be.

Cassidy and Lauren were identical twins, but that was where their similarities ended. Lauren had dropped out of college halfway through her junior year to move to New York to pursue acting. At the time, Cassidy thought her sister was making a dumb choice. In retrospect, though, maybe not.

"How are those business school applications coming?" Lauren asked.

Cassidy stared at Anderson Cooper's earnest face on the television, his lips moving soundlessly with the volume turned down.

"Cass?"

"I'm working on them." She could practically hear Lauren rolling her eyes on the other end.

"You took the GMAT how many months ago now?"

"The summer was busy around here. You might have heard."

"You've been talking about going back to school for the past two years, Cass. Fish or cut bait."

"Mom needs me right now."

"She'll survive. Besides, if you go to school in DC or Baltimore, you could still come home on the weekends to help with the shop. Even Philly would be close enough, probably."

"The business manager needs to be in the shop full time."

"Why? What comes up on a day-to-day basis that mom or Natalie can't handle?"

Cassidy thought for a moment, Anderson Cooper and the hurricane blurring in her vision.

"Nothing," Lauren answered her own question. "Nothing they can't learn to do. What's your hesitation, Cass?"

What *was* her hesitation?

"I don't know. I'm conflicted. I like working there, but … I can't help thinking there's more out there in the world somewhere."

"There *is* more out here in the world. I get that working with mom and Nat is comfortable. There are worse jobs, to be sure. But is that how you want to spend your life? Closing out the register every night, running ads for sales, and pulling reports on which fabric lines are selling best?"

"I'm good at it, though. What if they don't find someone else who can be trusted?"

What if you wake up one morning ten years from now and are bored out of your mind? What happens when mom retires? Or if Natalie decides to leave?

Would she like it then? If she didn't, it would be too late to do anything about it. She'd be stuck here in St. Caroline with no way to re-start a career in a different field.

"Cass, just send in the damn applications. You can decide whether or not you want to go once you find out which schools you get into. But if you don't apply, you're making the decision *not* to go."

CHAPTER 3

*T*he office of the St. Caroline Chamber of Commerce was in a street-level shop front on Main Street. The Two Beans coffee shop was to its right, Lucy Wyndham's new yoga and barre studio on the left. Cassidy sat at the long confer-ence table watching people go back and forth on the street outside. They'd pass one way and then a few minutes later, retrace their steps—with a coffee cup in hand. There was a low grade rumbling in her stomach. She had worked straight through her lunch hour so she could leave for this meeting.

She glanced down at her phone, wondering if she had time to run to Two Beans before Matt arrived for their meeting with the chamber's executive director. It was three minutes before the appointed time of two o'clock, and the director—Wilson Murray —was still in the back office on his phone. She could probably grab a coffee and make it back before Matt got here. She doubted the line was long at this time of day.

Her stomach rumbled again. Sitting here contemplating coffee wasn't exactly helping matters any. But just as she scooted back her chair to stand, the tinny chime of the front door sounded. She looked over to see Matt doing an awkward spin move through the door, pushing it open with his hip to protect the cardboard tray of coffee cups he carried. The smoky aroma of arabica tickled her nose and now her stomach was done with the polite rumbling. The hungry spasm it inflicted on her nearly made her bounce in her chair.

"I hope one of those is for me," she said as Matt walked toward her.

"Nope. They're all for me." He set the cardboard tray on the table in front of her. "You've heard of the three martini lunch? I'm having a three coffee lunch." He snorted at her crestfallen expression. "Of course one is for you." He lifted one cup and ceremoniously placed it on the table directly in front of her. "What, you think I was raised by wolves?"

Cassidy carefully lifted the lid from the cup to let the steam escape.

"Mr. Murray? I'm here," Matt called out.

Cassidy grimaced before taking a tentative sip of coffee. "I think he's on the phone."

"Oh. Oops."

He leaned around the table to peer toward Wilson Murray's office and Cassidy found herself mesmerized by the movement. It was hard not to be, given the way Matt's six-pack abs pressed against the black tee shirt he wore. She tried to focus on the words printed on the shirt—St. Caroline FD—but that just served to call attention to the distinct outline of his pecs beneath the white letters.

With that body, Matt Wolfe should look dangerous. He was shorter and stockier than his brothers, a solidly-muscled physique wrapped in a black tee shirt and dark grey cargo pants. His hair was dark and cut short, and his hazel eyes held a glint that was both watchful and opaque—like a one-way mirror.

But Matt Wolfe was also St. Caroline's resident playboy and ladies' man. If he was dangerous, it was mostly to women, Cassidy thought. She herself was immune to his charms—

completely immune. Not that she didn't get why other women weren't immune. He was a good-looking guy and could be charming when he wanted to be.

Granted, when it came to women, he seemed like he always wanted to be charming. He had even tried with her a few times—most recently over the summer at her parents' anniversary party —even though their parents were friends and they'd known each other their entire lives.

The sound of him pulling out the chair across from her pulled her attention back to the present. She took a tiny sip of coffee, mindful of not burning her tongue.

Matt leaned across the table, conspiratorially. "He's probably not speaking to anyone important anyway," he said in a low voice. "This being St. Caroline and all." Then he winked.

Yeah. Charming.

"Sorry. I'm a little punchy today," he apologized. "I've been at the station since midnight last night. I'm living on fumes right now." He lifted his coffee. "And caffeine." He leaned back into the chair.

She smiled and took another sip of coffee. "Honestly, you always seem kinda' punchy."

"Nah. Just around you."

Cassidy was considering how to respond to that when Wilson Murray emerged from his office, a yellow legal pad in hand. Mr. Murray, as Cassidy thought of him, was older than her parents—sixtyish with short grey hair and a rotund stomach. The chamber of commerce was his second career. The first had been spent at St. Caroline middle school—first as a teacher and then as the principal.

Cassidy caught Matt's eye and knew exactly what he was thinking. This meeting was going to feel just like being in school again. She bit back a smile. She didn't want Mr. Murray thinking that she wasn't taking this seriously. Nor did she want Matt thinking that she was flirting with him. Give Matt an inch and

JULIA GABRIEL

he'd probably take a mile. Plus, her sister Becca was engaged to Matt's brother, Jack. Her parents and Matt's parents had always been close friends, but the two families were now even more entwined. She would have to enforce appropriate behavior on Matt's part, if he couldn't. And she seriously doubted he could— his attempt to get her and his buddy in Texas to hook up was proof of that.

"I took the liberty of getting you a coffee," Matt said as Mr. Murray pulled out a chair and sat down at the table.

Omg, what a suck-up. Matt had been a year behind her in school, but she imagined that was how he had managed to graduate—by charming his way through. He certainly hadn't been a stellar student like Jack was.

"That was very thoughtful of you, Matt." Mr. Murray uncapped the coffee. "You missed a real nail-biter last week."

"Yeah, Sean gave me the video to watch. But Annapolis Prep's a tough team."

"Yup. No shame in that loss."

Cassidy pushed back on the bubble of annoyance welling up in her chest. She had to get back to the shop. She didn't have time to listen to Matt and Mr. Murray jawbone about the high school soccer team.

"We're going to win on Monday." Matt drained the rest of his coffee and set the empty paper cup on the table. "Now that *I'm* back in town."

"I'm glad your parents were able to spare the two of you for an hour this afternoon. We need to get going on this festival thing," Mr. Wilson said.

"Well, if I get paged I'll have to leave." Matt patted his hip and Cassidy's eyes dropped even though she knew his hip was below the tabletop and not visible. "But you're right. We do need to get started on this. I did manage to pick my brother's brain on what his original thoughts were." Matt pulled his phone out of his pocket and tapped the screen a few times. "Santa arriving on a

28

firetruck," he began to read. "Caroling through the town, ending in a singalong at the Inn's green. A Christmas light extravaganza."

"Extravaganza?" Mr. Murray lifted one bushy grey eyebrow. "That doesn't sound like Ollie."

Matt looked up from his phone. "I'm paraphrasing there. Yeah, Ollie wouldn't know an extravaganza if it bit him in the ass. He didn't really have that idea fleshed out. Just something with lights." Matt made air quotes with one hand.

"So like a contest?" Cassidy asked. "Everyone in town decorates their house? Or the shops on Main Street decorate more than usual? There's already the big Christmas tree on the square. The town does that every year."

Matt shrugged. "We don't have to do it. I'm just relaying Ollie's initial thoughts."

Cassidy caught the note of defensiveness in his voice, which wasn't a reaction she had intended to provoke. She liked to nail down the details of things without a lot of equivocation. Her mother and sisters were used to that side of her.

"I'm a sucker for lights, personally." Mr. Murray scribbled a note on his legal pad. "We'll have to think through that one, though. The chamber has some money to spend on this, but we didn't budget for it back at the beginning of the year."

"So we'll think on that some more," Cassidy said. "If the point of this is to give local businesses one last boost before winter really sets in, then we need reasons for hardcore shoppers to come." She leaned over to pull her phone from her purse so she could make some notes of her own. "Mom and I are willing to do a BOGO promotion that weekend."

"BOGO?" Matt asked. "Dare I ask what that is?"

"Buy one get one," Cassidy and Mr. Murray replied simultaneously.

"Ahh."

"We'll do a buy one yard of fabric, get one at half price," Cassidy offered.

"Can you guys afford to do that?"

Matt's question caught her off guard. Of course, they couldn't really afford it—not after the year they'd had.

"At this point, it kind of doesn't matter," she answered. "We can probably get a Christmas quilt done in time to raffle off. Plus, we should create some materials for local businesses to use. Social media graphics, an email they can send out to their customers, things like that. "

"Maybe the restaurants can do special menus for that weekend?" Matt suggested. "What do people like to eat when they're shopping?"

He looked pointedly at Cassidy, the only female in the room. She could tell he was fighting back another wink. *Jeez, he's so typical.*

"Comfort food?" he answered his own question.

"Chicken pot pies." Cassidy and Matt both turned to look at Mr. Murray. "Hearty chicken pot pies for the men while they wait for their wives to finish shopping."

Cassidy gave a little laugh. "That's a good idea, actually. My dad would be all over chicken pot pies and a cold beer."

"We'll add that idea to the list. Maybe one of the restaurants can be sweet-talked into that." Mr. Murray jotted it down on his notepad, while Cassidy and Matt did the same on their phones. "I knew you two would be a good combination."

Cassidy fought the urge to roll her eyes. This was classic Matt Wolfe. He made a great first impression but she'd bet her last dollar that she would end up doing most of the work on the festival.

Across the table, Matt started. He looked down at the pager clipped to his pants. "I gotta go. Accident out on Old York Road."

Matt ran around to the back of the chamber's office building, where he had parked his pickup in the municipal lot. He fired up the ignition and pulled out onto Main Street, rolling through the stop sign. On a Wednesday afternoon in late September, St. Caroline's business district was practically dead. The summer people were gone. Locals were at work. The wealthy folks who owned waterfront estates or gentleman's farms mostly weren't around during the week—they were off making gobs of money in Washington or Baltimore or Philadelphia.

Now that was a lifestyle Matt couldn't even begin to fathom. Sitting in a hermetically-sealed office building with stale air-conditioned air … making deals, signing contracts, running meetings … it was a good thing Matt wasn't intellectually cut out for that sort of thing to begin with. Everyone had thought his brother, Jack, was suited to that kind of life—but apparently not. Jack had moved from California back to St. Caroline almost four months ago now.

Today was Jack's day off at the fire station. Oliver was on an indefinite leave of absence, on top of the staffing problem his father, the fire chief, had been struggling with for the past year. St. Caroline was like a lot of small towns that had monied part-time residents. Those residents expected big city services, but the taxes they paid never seemed to be enough for the town to pay big city wages to its employees. Being a firefighter and EMT was a demanding job, even in a small town, and one most people weren't cut out for.

Matt sailed down Main Street toward the station, where his truck and crew would be waiting. He hoped the call wasn't bad. Everyone dreaded car accidents. Matt dreaded them even more now since his sister-in-law's accident—and if they were calling him back to the station, the call probably was bad. His father would have dispatched another crew immediately. A police car would be on the way already.

He slid the truck into a parking spot in the station's lot and ran for the open bay door. Inside, his father stopped him.

"Heath just phoned in. They've got it under control."

"What happened?" Damn, his father looked tired.

"The usual on Old York."

"Someone took the curve too fast?"

"Yeah, car skidded off the road. Driver not hurt but they're taking him to the hospital, just in case."

"Someone local?" Matt held his breath.

Tim Wolfe shook his head. "No. South Carolina plates."

"Okay, good. Well, not 'good,' of course, but—" He gave his father a long, hard appraisal. "Dad, you look exhausted."

"I am, son." Tim turned to head back into his office. Matt followed.

"Maybe you should take some time off." He could sense his father rolling his eyes, even though his back was toward Matt. Less than two months had passed since Angela Wolfe died. His father's way of coping with his grief was apparently to pretend that it simply didn't exist.

"Someone has to do my job." Tim stepped into his office, then turned to look at Matt. "I have some paperwork to complete." And he closed the office door right in Matt's face.

Matt stared at the grey steel door in astonishment. *The family is falling apart.* It was no secret that his mother had been the center of the Wolfe family, the gravity that held everything together. But Matt wouldn't have guessed that, without her gravitational pull, they would all just drift off into outer space. Separately and alone.

But that was exactly what seemed to be happening.

CHAPTER 4

The Two Beans coffee shop was the one business in St. Caroline that was busy year in and year out, seven days a week. But even Cassidy was a little surprised to see how busy it was on a Thursday morning. Normally, she didn't have time to just hang out and guzzle coffee but clearly the next several months weren't going to be "normal." If St. Caroline's first-ever Winter Festival was going to happen, a lot had to get done between now and then. And she wasn't sure how much help she could really count on from Matt.

Even if he turned out to be better at this sort of thing than she expected him to be, he had a job that was going to get in the way. That much was clear yesterday when he had to run out of their meeting at the chamber of commerce to answer a fire department call. It made little sense to Cassidy that he had been asked to take this on. It didn't make sense that Oliver had been asked to, either. She had nothing against firefighters, but they didn't have nine-to-five work schedules. Nor did Cassidy—Quilt Therapy was open from ten in the morning until eight at night—but her absence from the shop didn't pose a risk to anyone's life, limb, or property.

Case in point, Matt was ten minutes late right now—and he was the one who had suggested they meet here to discuss the festival. "The division of labor," he'd called it. *Hah.* They had to decide what the labor was going to be before they could begin dividing it up. They needed a list of events for the festival, activities and tasks for local businesses, a timeline … Cassidy flipped open the laptop on her lap and leaned back into the leather sofa that was the only open seating when she arrived.

She would have preferred one of the two-person tables that lined the brick wall of Two Beans' back room, but those were all occupied by people who didn't look as though they were going anywhere anytime soon. St. Caroline was becoming popular with retirees—people who literally had nowhere they needed to be at any particular time. It seemed like Cassidy was always getting stuck in line behind retirees at the grocery store or on the road. Life in St. Caroline was slow enough as it was.

Her eyes quickly scanned her laptop screen and the spreadsheet she had started last night. The winter festival was going to be a ton of work … but a charge of excitement was flickering in her, too. It would be a nice change of pace from the routine of Quilt Therapy, especially in the off-season months they were now in. Summer was always crazy busy at the shop, but winter not so much. Their local customers were more predictable and easier to plan around.

"Hey there."

Someone sat down on the sofa next to her. Cassidy looked up from her spreadsheet to see Mai Tran. Mai and her brother Tuan were the owners of Two Beans. Siblings from Vietnam, they'd bought the business three years ago and transformed it from a sleepy mom-and-pop operation that served drip coffee and overly sweet doughnuts to mostly takeout customers to a hipper and more inviting space that encouraged people to linger. And to spend more money, an accomplishment that warmed the cockles of Cassidy's business-minded heart.

Mai handed her a clear glass filled with a hot beverage that Cassidy recognized immediately—Vietnamese coffee, a drink Mai and Tuan had introduced to the town of St. Caroline. With its blend of strong, almost bitter coffee and sweet condensed milk, it was now practically a bonafide vice among the town's residents.

"Heard you've been tasked with the winter festival," Mai said as Cassidy took a sip of the coffee. Even though Mai was the owner, she wore the same brown and white striped apron and cap that her baristas wore.

"Me and Matt Wolfe." She took another sip, then added, "He wanted to meet this morning, but he's not here yet."

"Well anything I can do to help, just let me know."

"Thanks. But you guys are so busy all year round, I'm not sure how much benefit you'll get from it."

"No matter. St. Caroline's been good to us, so whatever you need. What do you two have planned so far?"

"We just started this yesterday, so … not much." Cassidy remembered Mai's other talent besides coffee. "Caroling has been suggested, though." Mai was well known for her pitch-perfect voice.

Mai gave a little laugh, the sound of which was just as lovely as her singing voice. "I will be all over that. And I'm happy to donate coffee and hot chocolate, too."

"Thank you. I appreciate it."

Mai waved her slender hand at Cassidy's computer. "We'll have our holiday drink menu going by then too, of course," she added. "Gingerbread latte, mint mocha, and a third to be determined. We're asking customers to vote in November on apple-honey chai tea, salted caramel cocoa, or a pumpkin cider frappe. Some people want iced coffee all year long." Mai grimaced. "Personally, once the temperature drops below fifty degrees, I don't want to see an ice cube until June."

"I'm with you there. Hot beverages only in winter." It

occurred to her that she and Mai should really be better friends. Why weren't they?

Time. They both ran businesses in town. But that was a fact that should make them good friends, as well. There was probably a lot she could learn from Mai. *If we both had time.* Which Cassidy wasn't going to have, at least not until the new year.

The front door to Two Beans opened and Cassidy sensed an immediate change in the energy. Then she heard someone call out, "Matt-tay!" Matt Wolfe had arrived.

The noise level in the coffee shop went up a notch as she watched him go from table to table, saying "hi" here and chatting there like he was the mayor of St. Caroline. He was wearing basically the same outfit he'd worn to the chamber of commerce the day before. Dark pants, dark tee shirt. He'd come directly from the fire station to meet her.

Of course, Matt didn't need to dress up to impress the ladies, even in the off hours. Case in point: the table of Talbot College girls giggling and batting their eyes at him. Cassidy wanted to throw up. She would never behave that ridiculously around Matt Wolfe. Or any other guy.

Probably why you're still single. She shushed the voice in her head. *I'm happy being single. And I'm not in a place in my life where I can get serious with someone anyway.* The laptop she was balancing on her knees contained the drafts of business school applications she had started. Lauren was right. She'd been thinking about going back to school for several years now.

Fish or cut bait.

"Looks like your date is here," Mai said.

Cassidy rolled her eyes as Mai stood up. Dating Matt Wolfe was one thing Cassidy wasn't sure she would wish on anyone. Not anyone she liked, at least.

∾

MATT SPOTTED Cassidy's blonde head the minute he set foot in Two Beans. It was just that it took him ten minutes to get a cup of coffee and finally make his way through the gauntlet of people who wanted to chat with him. Not that he minded chatting with people—more than a few of these people he'd known his entire life—but saying "no" was not his strong suit, as his mother used to say.

"Sorry I'm late," he said as he took the seat next to her on the leather sofa. Her laptop rested on her bare knees. It was still warm enough in September that she was wearing a skirt. He quickly lifted his eyes to meet hers. He wasn't here to gawk at her legs. Nor was Cassidy the kind of woman who would tolerate it.

"No worries," she replied. "I was hoping a table would open up, but no such luck today."

He looked around the back room, the newer addition Mai and Tuan had built. They'd done a nice job, with the exposed brick wall helping to disguise the fact that this section was newer than the front room. Brick was fire-retardant, too. It was a shame so few buildings were built with brick anymore. Oh, he understood the reasons. Brick wasn't cheap. But it bought him and his colleagues at the fire department more time to get a fire under control. If he ever built a house for himself, it was going to be brick all the way—

"... so I can create a timeline for all of this, once we nail down exactly what we're doing."

She paused and looked up at him and ... shoot. He hadn't heard a word she'd said. But apparently she assumed he had, because she kept going.

"I was thinking about this last night, and I think we should kick off the festival on Friday night with the arrival of Santa. Out of town folks probably won't come in until Saturday, but Santa is really more for the local kids anyway. He can ride one of your fire trucks ..."

Matt was trying his damnedest to focus on what Cassidy was

saying. It helped if he kept his eyes locked on the eyes of the person who was speaking to him. But Cassidy's eyes were a distraction. He associated blonde hair with blue eyes but all the Trevor women—except Becca—had blonde hair and brown eyes. As a kid, he had been fascinated by Cassidy's coloring, by those eyes that were like pools of milk chocolate.

"... and then caroling at the tree on Main Street. How does that sound to you?"

Focus, man, focus. Caroling. Fire truck. Santa. He retraced her words.

"What if Santa arrives by boat and one of our trucks picks him up at the pier? I mean, he wouldn't fly into town and ditch his sleigh at the station. I can ask Oliver if we can use his boat." What else had she mentioned? "And is caroling at the tree just on Friday?"

She shrugged.

"Do you think we could get the out-of-towners to join us for caroling on Saturday?"

"We could try."

"Who should be Santa this year?" Matt's brain circled back to the big man.

They were both silent for a moment. John Matthew, the former owner of the Chesapeake Inn, had played Santa for years. Everyone Matt and Cassidy's age had grown up sitting on his knee every December and confessing their most hoped for gift. But John had passed away the year before.

"Well, Sterling did it last year," she pointed out. Sterling was John Matthew's son and the new owner of the Inn.

The lack of enthusiasm in her voice pinned down Matt's thoughts precisely. "He wasn't that good at it."

"Yeah, he wasn't comfortable around the kids."

"Do you think he'll expect to be asked again?"

Cassidy bobbed her head back and forth, indicating that she was weighing the idea. It was a gesture Matt had seen her do dozens of times over the years. No, make that hundreds, probably. Not that he was supposed to be noticing Cassidy Trevor's gestures.

"I'm guessing he'll be relieved. I can ask Lucy, though." Lucy Wyndham was Sterling's fiancée.

"We definitely need someone who's comfortable with kids." Matt took a deep slug of coffee. "What about your dad? No one's more comfortable with kids than a pediatrician."

"I think he was asked a couple times in the past. But he thought too many of the kids would recognize him."

"Yeah, he might slip up and say, 'Don't forget to pick out a sticker on your way out.'" Matt could feel a stupid-ass grin spreading across his face, but was powerless to halt it.

Cassidy snorted milky coffee onto her keyboard. "Oh shoot. Don't make me laugh." She hurried to mop it up with a brown and white striped napkin.

Matt wanted to make her laugh again. It was his tried-and-true way to distract women's attention away from his other, less stellar qualities. Like the fact that he was a terrible listener, and women always wanted terrific listeners. He'd had more than one date go south when the woman in question discovered he wasn't paying attention to a word she was saying. Not because he didn't want to pay attention … he just simply *couldn't.* It was like he couldn't hold his brain still for very long.

"Yeah, probably don't want to get the guy who brings you presents confused with the guy who jabs a needle in your butt," Cassidy continued.

Matt's heart skipped a beat at the realization that he might have missed something she said while he was pondering the fact that he was a terrible listener. This wasn't a date where it didn't matter so much if the woman got pissed at him. This was a business meeting, and Cassidy was treating it as such. He needed to, as well.

She bent her head to her laptop and, with a few staccato clicks of the keyboard, typed in a note. "Okay well, we'll have to come up with a short list of names for Mr. Claus."

"We'll need someone to lead the caroling, too, I'd imagine." *Try to contribute something productive here.* "But not me. I can't sing to save my life."

"Me either."

She smiled at him, but it was a split smile. Her lips looked genuine. Her chocolate brown eyes less so.

"I could ask my dad. He's a frustrated opera singer," she suggested and added that to the list on her computer. "All right. Other things we need to do. We need to go around to retailers and restaurants. I think most of them know about the festival from the chamber of commerce, but we need to try and get commitments on sales and special menus. What else did Oliver have in mind originally?"

Matt forced his brain back to the conversation with his brother. "Holiday light displays."

"Who would do those? Residents? The Inn? Businesses?"

Could they really rely on residents to put up lights? Plus, visitors who were in town to shop and eat might not see lights on private homes. The businesses on Main Street always put electric candles in their windows and other holiday decorations. Those were nice but not a destination event … there was something niggling at the back of his mind, if he could just slow down his brain long enough to reach out and snag it.

"Matt? Am I losing you?"

Cassidy's voice was gentle, pulling him in, but he resisted. If he could just reach that thought …

"Do you want to move on to my marketing ideas? That's more my field of expertise."

Field! He snagged the thought.

"I saw this thing on the news last year where a farmer set up a huge holiday light display in his field. People could walk through it."

Cassidy nodded thoughtfully. "Did he charge people to go through it?"

"Mmm, I don't know that. Maybe if we google it, we can find out?"

Her fingers flew over her keyboard, then stopped. "It didn't sound like the chamber had any real money budgeted for this. So I'm not sure how we'd afford something like that."

"Good point." Matt's attention was drawn to Ian Evers ordering something from one of the baristas.

"We may have to be content with the Christmas tree on the square, unless one of us wins the lottery."

Ian had his coffee, but was still chatting with the barista, a young woman. Too young for Ian, Matt thought. *Focus.*

"What's next on our list?" he asked. "Marketing the festival, you said?" She *had* said that, right?

"I don't think we should leave that up to the individual chamber members. I think we should create a standard email they can send out to their customer lists, as well as some graphics they can use on social media."

"I can help with that. I made some graphics over the summer for the fireman's carnival. I have a pretty good eye for that sort of thing."

"Okay, you're hired."

Shoot. Why'd I volunteer for that? Did he really have that good an eye for artistic stuff? Surely not a better eye than she probably had. *I did the graphics for the carnival. They don't have to be fancy.*

"So I'll write the email and you can do the graphics. I'll also see about reaching out to churches and senior centers within a reasonable driving distance."

"Why?"

"They often do bus trips for shopping and sightseeing. If we could get a couple of those from Baltimore or DC, that would be great."

Damn. She knows her stuff. How much was he really going to be able to contribute here? *You'll be the body. Like usual.* Legwork, Matt was good at that.

"I can go talk to the businesses about the festival, get them thinking about running sales and stuff," he offered. "I have plenty of time for that."

"We can divvy up those, if you want," she said. "Why don't I do the retail shops and you do the restaurants? And I'll go talk to Lucy about whether Sterling wants to be Santa again. We can regroup next week at some point and see where we are."

"Sounds like a plan."

He watched as Cassidy snapped her laptop shut and stood. His eyes followed her as she made her way through the front room of Two Beans, with only one person stopping her to chat. She pushed open the coffee shop's front door and disappeared into the bright light outside.

Inside, Two Beans seemed a little dimmer to Matt. The electricity that was Cassidy Trevor was gone now. She was smart, organized, thoughtful. *Beautiful.* He reached out and yanked his mind back. No point in wandering down that neural pathway. Cassidy was out of his league.

He had never needed his family to point that out, either.

CHAPTER 5

"You got up early."

Cassidy started at the sudden appearance of her sister in the doorway to their apartment's kitchen. She'd been so engrossed in what she was doing—staring intently at a draft of her resume and wondering how to spin the fact that her job experience was limited to one job and a couple of internships—that she hadn't even heard the shower turn off down the hall. It was Saturday morning and both of them were scheduled to work at Quilt Therapy that day.

"I woke up early and couldn't get back to sleep."

"Totally unfamiliar with that problem." Natalie walked over to the coffee maker and poured herself the last cup.

Yeah, Natalie rarely went to bed before midnight. Little chance of her waking up before dawn the way Cassidy did these days. On the whole, she liked living with her younger sister. They knew each other's habits, knew which buttons not to push. But increasingly her sister's lifestyle, which entailed more parties and less worry, made Cassidy feel just a wee bit older.

"Whatcha doing?" Natalie headed toward Cassidy. Cassidy closed her laptop as nonchalantly as she could.

"Just surfing." She stood and dumped the remains of her third cup of coffee down the sink. "Can you drop me off at Lucy's studio on your way in? I signed up for the eight o'clock class."

Her sister's eyes dropped to take in Cassidy's yoga pants and tank top. "Sure thing. Better if you're all yogified before you get to the store."

It had been their mother's idea for Cassidy to begin taking yoga classes "to relax." After spending an hour and a half trying to make her resume sound more impressive to business schools, she needed a yoga class in the worst way. Heck, she hadn't even written a resume since her final semester of college and only then because one of her classes had required it.

Cassidy Trevor, Business Manager, Quilt Therapy LLC.

It would be a lot easier if she actually had something to put on her resume. Maybe her mom would let her be the "vice president of business operations," just for the purposes of her resume. She had done well on the GMAT. Her grades in college were excellent. But her work experience was thin, and there was no real way to spin that. She worked at a small family-run business—a quilt shop, no less. And yes, Lauren was right, she had more responsibility in her job than a lot of twenty-seven-year-olds did. It just didn't look that way on paper.

Twenty minutes later, Cassidy hopped out of Natalie's silver Honda, her rolled-up yoga mat and a bag filled with a change of clothes slung over her shoulder. "See you in an hour," she said, waving as her sister drove off.

Inside Studio L Yoga, students from the previous class were slipping feet into flip flops, readjusting ponytails, and sucking water from water bottles. Cassidy signed in on the iPad, then threaded her way down the hall to the storage cubbies, where she stashed her purse and work clothes. She kicked off her slip-on sneakers and headed into the studio. She liked to snag a spot in the back of the room.

She unrolled her mat next to Ashley Wardman, who was gently stretching.

"Hey there, Ash."

Ashley twisted her torso to look back up at Cassidy. She looked even thinner to Cassidy than she had two weeks ago—and at this point, it was hardly possible for Ashley to lose any more weight.

"Hi. Long time no see." Ashley untwisted her body and leaned back on her hands.

"I was at a wedding in Texas," Cassidy replied.

"Ah. Was it fun?"

Cassidy nodded. "My college roommate got married." The studio was filling up with more students, mostly younger. On Saturdays, the classes were attended by more of the students from Talbot College and St. Caroline High School. Another thing that was starting to make her feel old.

"How's Ben?" Cassidy asked quietly.

Ashley gave her a tight, sad smile. "The same. Thanks for asking."

Cassidy knew Ben Wardman wasn't the same. She'd overheard some women in the shop discussing him the other day. Ben's brain cancer had been diagnosed over the summer, and the prognosis wasn't good. But before she could dwell on that, Lucy glided into the studio and closed the door behind her. "How is everyone?"

Lucy took her spot at the front of the room, looking impossibly put-together even though she'd been teaching classes since six that morning. Her brown hair was pulled up into a perfect ballet bun with barely a single strand of hair loose. Her dusty purple leggings with the strippy cutouts along the calves and her Studio L tank top looked fresh and pristine. Cassidy could swear the woman didn't sweat.

"It's the weekend, right?" Lucy went on, "We're here to relax and re-center. Whatever happened this week at work or at school, that's all outside this room." She gestured toward the ceiling. "Let it all go. Set your intention for the next sixty minutes."

Cassidy closed her eyes and searched her brain. After four months of yoga, she still didn't have an "intention" for her "practice." The best she could hope for was to not topple over during class and knock everyone else over too, like a row of dominoes. And hair? The class hadn't even begun, but already her ponytail had lost any pretense to tight sleekness.

All the same, it was hard to resist Lucy's enthusiasm and her sincere interest in everyone leaving Studio L Yoga feeling better than when they walked in. So Cassidy took a deep breath and then exhaled, letting go of her inability to unearth an intention inside herself. If she could manage to forget about her to-do list for the next hour, that would be enough.

Finish resume.

Create short list of schools to apply to.

E-mail copy for winter festival social media to Matt.

Nail down mom on Black Friday hours.

Normally, her mother liked to keep Quilt Therapy closed on the day after Thanksgiving. It was a day people should spend with their families, she believed. But it was Cassidy who spent more time poring over the shop's finances, and she was arguing for being open on Black Friday this year. They could use the sales.

"Let's get started, shall we?" Lucy was sitting on her mat at the front of the room now, her legs folded in.

Focus. Cassidy hadn't even noticed when Lucy sat down. *Live in the moment. That should be my intention.* She glued her gaze onto Lucy, following her every move. But when she twisted into a torso stretch, she couldn't help but notice Ashley again. She could see the outline of the other woman's ribs beneath her thin top. Ben Wardman was only in his thirties. He wasn't supposed to get sick. *But it happens.*

"Exhale and twist a little deeper." Lucy's voice was soothing, but Ashley's ribs were still there and Cassidy couldn't pull her eyes away from them.

What if I get in an accident like Matt's sister-in-law did? She pushed the breath from her lungs and twisted her body half an inch further. *Next week? Today?* There were so many things she hadn't done yet. Places she hadn't seen. People she hadn't met yet. She'd never been in love. *How will I do that if I never leave St. Caroline?* It was rare for new people to move to town and, even if someone did, what were the odds he would fall in love with her? Or her with him? Yeah, she could "lower her standards," as everyone told her to, but …

I don't think my standards are that unreasonable. Gainful employment. A sense of humor. A nice smile. How unreasonable were those? She was pretty flexible on body types, too. No one ever gave her credit for that. She found lots of body types to be attractive. Tall and thin. Short and muscled. Even a few extra pounds wasn't a dealbreaker for her. And of course, she wanted some chemistry with a person. *How is that too much to expect?*

She unwound her body and followed Lucy and the rest of the class into a locust pose on her stomach. She lifted her shoulders and feet off the mat.

"Don't forget to breathe," Lucy reminded.

I want a man who will make me forget to breathe.

Okay, so that was probably too much to ask for.

When class ended, Cassidy rolled up her mat and tried to restore some semblance of order to her ponytail. She hung back while the other students said goodbye to Lucy, some of them lingering to chat. Normally, Cassidy was one of the first out the door, rushing off to the shop, but she needed to talk to Lucy today.

At last, all of the students were gone except for Cassidy and Ashley, who was still lying on her mat, eyes closed, her chest rising and falling with her repeated deep inhales. Ashley ended every class that way, an hour's worth of yoga not enough to counter what was happening in her life.

"Lucy, do you have a minute?" Cassidy took a few more steps toward the door, to give Ashley her privacy.

"Sure. What's up?"

"So you've heard about the winter festival that the chamber is putting on this year?"

"I sure have."

"Matt Wolfe and I are the co-chairs."

"I did hear a rumor to that effect." Lucy smiled. "Just so you know, Sterling is champing at the bit, ready to put something up on the Inn's web site. And I'm going to offer discounted class packages from Thanksgiving right up to Christmas Eve. I've even ordered some nice red and gold gift boxes to make the gift cards easier to wrap."

"Wow. You are on top of things." Not that Cassidy ever doubted that Sterling and Lucy would be. "So … Matt and I were wondering whether Sterling was planning to play Santa again this year."

"Oh good heavens, don't even ask him. He was awful last year." Lucy laughed out loud. "I love the man, but he still has way too big a stick up his ass for that."

"Okay. I'm sure we can find someone else—"

"I'll ask Douglas. He'd be perfect to play Santa."

Cassidy didn't know Doug Preston that well, other than that he was the director of the Kids Kamp at the Chesapeake Inn.

"Do you think he'll do that?" she asked Lucy.

"Oh of course. I'll twist his arm, for good measure. I'll call him tonight and then let you know tomorrow. You don't need to know before then, do you?"

Cassidy shook her head. "No rush. That would be awesome, Lucy."

"I can do the photos again this year." Ashley's voice came from the back of the room, quiet but strong.

"Oh Ash, don't worry about it," Lucy answered. "We can find someone else."

"I'd like to do it again."

There was a moment of awkward quiet. Cassidy didn't know what to say. Ashley had enough on her plate this year already. It was going to be the last Christmas she and Ben had together.

Ashley broke the moment for them. "Doing it was so much fun last year. I need a little fun in my life right now." She stood and rolled up her mat. "I know everyone means well by treating me with kid gloves. But I'm not that fragile, guys. Let me have some normalcy in my life. Please."

Cassidy mustered a wary smile. "Well then, consider yourself hired."

THE RADIO in ladder truck 7 squawked. Matt listened as the mutual aid call went out. St. Caroline's fire department was requesting help from other departments in the area.

"That's not good," Jack said, from the driver's seat of the truck.

"Nope."

They were headed for the Lighthouse Apartments, on the western edge of the Talbot College campus. Until three years ago, the building had been a dormitory. Then the college sold it and built a newer, more modern dorm.

"We inspected this building when it was converted to apartments," Matt added. "Dad recommended a new sprinkler system and new smoke detectors in every unit."

"Think the new owner did any of that?" Jack asked, taking a wide turn onto Main Street, the fastest route across town to the college.

"No idea." From the corner of his eye, Matt spotted three women standing on the sidewalk in front of Studio L Yoga. Lucy Wyndham, Ashley Wardman, and Cassidy. Cassidy was wearing some loose off white blouse and a pair of skinny pink jeans.

Cotton candy. Pink lemonade. Pink flowers.

He tore his gaze away. He couldn't afford to be distracted right now by the thought of burying his face in all that blonde hair and taking a deep inhale … he'd bet she used some flowery-smelling shampoo. She seemed like that kind of girl.

Soft. Pretty. Feminine.

"Hoover *dam*," he heard his brother mutter as the truck began to slow. Jack was turning into the apartment building's parking lot. How'd they get here already?

Focus.

The call had said smoke was spotted coming from several second floor windows, alpha-delta corner—the front and right side of the building. From the looks of it, the fire had spread. A wall of smoke blanketed that entire corner now, from the second floor to the fourth, broken only by streaks of orange flame. Matt was out of the truck before Jack even set the brake.

"Weston FD is working the fire." Heath, another St. Caroline firefighter was suddenly by Matt's side. "We're doing search."

Matt headed for the building, running through the floor plan in his head. He'd been in the building only once, but he had a near photographic memory for stuff like that. He couldn't focus on the present worth a damn, but if it happened in the past he could call it right up.

Jack caught up to him. "So you've been in here before?"

"Yup. First floor hallway runs parallel to the front side of the building. On the upper floors, though, the hall runs perpendicular to the front. Two stairways at alpha-delta and alpha-bravo. No elevator."

"I'll follow you then."

"We'll go alpha-bravo first."

Inside, thick noxious smoke filled the hall. Visibility was zero, so Matt zeroed in on the picture in his mind. The units on the first floor were larger than the ones upstairs, so the doors were farther apart. He tapped his fist along the wall until he hit the first door. His hand slid down to the doorknob and turned it. Fortunately, it was unlocked. With any luck, that also meant the occupants were already outside. Matt had a vague memory of people milling about at the far edge of the parking lot. But he couldn't focus on that particular picture right now. There were twenty-four units in the building, and they all needed to be checked.

He pushed open the door and entered the apartment. Even in the pitch black, he sensed his brother's presence behind him, following closely.

"Fire department! Anyone in here?" he shouted. No answer. The lack of a response didn't mean the place was empty, necessarily. Someone could be asleep or overcome already with smoke inhalation. A small child could be hiding beneath a bed or in a closet.

He and Jack quickly but methodically checked the apartment —first the living area and kitchen, then the two bedrooms and the bathroom. Closets, too.

"This one's clear," he said.

They checked the other apartments on the ground floor before heading up the stairs. They passed Heath on the second floor landing.

"We've got this floor. Go up to the fourth," Heath said.

They searched three units on the fourth floor before coming to one that was locked. Matt ran his hand over the round doorknob, matching what he felt beneath his palm to the picture in his brain. The building's new owner hadn't upgraded the doors or locks.

"Stand back," he said to Jack. He stepped away from the door, then hit it with a hard kick from his boot. It took two tries but the lock gave way and the door opened.

"Fire department! Anyone in here?" he shouted inside.

"It's getting hotter up here," Jack pointed out.

"I know it. You take the kitchen and living room. I'll check the bedroom. This is one of the smaller units."

Matt felt his way in the dark toward the bedroom, stumbling loudly over a loose rug on the floor.

"You okay?" Jack called out.

"Fine!" Matt shouted back.

He kicked the rug out of the way with his boot, so he wouldn't trip over it on the way back. His hand found the bedroom door. He turned the knob and pushed it open, listening carefully as he moved into the room, counting each step. His knee hit the edge of a mattress. He bent over the bed, patting the surface. His hands hit a lump beneath the covers. There was a person in the bed.

"Got someone!"

CHAPTER 6

"You're gonna do what?" Matt stared at his brother's back. Jack was standing at the stove in their dad's kitchen, flipping pancakes. From the dining room came the sound of flatware and plates clinking as Mason and Cam helped Becca set the table.

"Paint your room pink." Jack flipped the pancakes onto a large plate, then poured more batter onto the cast iron griddle.

Matt thought on that for a minute. Jack had moved out of Matt's cabin and back into their childhood home to keep their father company after their mother's death. Becca had moved in, too. But it hadn't occurred to Matt that they would materially change the house in any way.

"Not immediately," Jack clarified without turning around from the griddle. "Just wanted to let you know. In case you want to take any final pictures."

Matt knew his brother was smirking down at the pancakes. He was about to make some smart ass remark, when Mason and Cam clattered into the room. They'd spent the night here with his dad, Jack, and Becca after the hospital called Oliver with the news that the nurses had seen a slight improvement in Serena's condition. Oliver had wanted to be there in case she woke up.

"Uncle Matt! Were you at the big fire yesterday with Uncle Jack?" Mason asked.

"I was." Matt leaned over and ruffled Cam's hair. Cam was the shyer of his two nephews, and about as different from Mason as Matt was from Jack. No one had ever accused Matt of being shy, but he felt a distinct affinity for his younger nephew. Cam was going to spend years in the shade of Mason, just as Matt had grown up in the long shadows cast by Jack's intelligence and potential.

As if on cue, Cam drifted away as Mason began to grill Matt on the details of the fire.

"What was the cause? Arson?"

"No, bud. Looks like it was a kitchen fire."

"They didn't have a fire extinguisher in the kitchen?"

"Fire extinguishers don't do most people much good," Matt replied as he watched Becca move around his parents' kitchen, gathering napkins and the butter dish. She appeared to know exactly where to find everything. That shouldn't surprise him, given that she was living there now, but it did anyway. It was his childhood home and seeing someone else living there made it feel less like … home.

"Why not?" Mason was asking. "Dad says to always keep a fire extinguisher handy in the kitchen."

"That's the smart thing to do, buddy," Matt acknowledged. "It's just that most people don't know how to use one quick enough and well enough in the event of an emergency. I always tell people to use one only if the fire is small enough to be put out in a matter of seconds. Otherwise, it's better to evacuate the building and call the fire department."

"Your Uncle Mattie's right." Jack turned around, holding a plate heaped high with fluffy pancakes. "Anybody hungry?"

"The table is set," Becca said. "Mason, why don't you grab the maple syrup from the fridge?"

Matt held the refrigerator door open behind Mason and reached in over his nephew's head to grab the jug of milk. It wasn't Becca who had changed the feel of the house for him, he thought.

It's that mom's not here.

He tried to yank his brain back from the next thought, but it was no use. His brain had a mind of its own. *This house will never feel like home again. Not without her.*

When they were all seated around the dining room table, Becca said grace in her soft, clear voice. It was different from his mom's voice, but all the same it was probably good to have a female in the house. Otherwise the Wolfes were nothing but a pack of men and boys. At least until Serena came home.

But what if Serena didn't come home? *Shut. Up.* What Matt wouldn't give to be able to turn off his brain once in awhile. Just flip a switch and let all the junk swirling in his head settle to the bottom for a few minutes. How nice that would be—a few blessed moments of peace and quiet in his mind.

The pancakes were passed around the table, followed by the butter and syrup. The look of concentration on Cam's face as he carefully handled the bottle of syrup nearly broke Matt's heart. Here he was, feeling sorry for himself because his mother was gone and his nephews—who were all of five and seven—had to man up every day without Serena. Without Oliver too, a lot of days. His older brother spent as much time as possible at the hospital.

Mason was still going on about the fire, in between bites of pancake. How many gallons of water did Jack think they used? How many departments responded to the mutual aid call? Did everyone have to move out?

"Yes, everyone moved out," Matt answered. There had been no injuries, thankfully, but the property was a total loss.

"How will Santa know where to deliver their presents?"

Matt turned to look at Cam, who had just thrown that question out there. Behind Cam, Mason's mouth was open to speak. Matt silenced him with a look that said *don't you dare*. Mason had stopped believing in Santa last year. That seemed early to Matt. Mason was only seven. Matt was pretty sure he and Jack had still believed at that age. At any rate, he didn't want Mason popping the Santa bubble for Cam. Not yet. Not with everything that was going on.

"He'll know," Becca said. "The elves keep him up to date on everyone's whereabouts."

"That's their job, buddy," Matt added quickly, before Mason could get a word in edgewise.

Becca redirected the conversation by asking the boys how school was going. But Matt's brain was stuck back at *how will Santa know where to deliver their presents?* He thought of the kids standing outside the Lighthouse Apartments, watching their homes go up in flames and water damage. The Lighthouse wasn't exactly a luxury building. For some of those kids, Santa probably wouldn't be coming this year.

There was an idea struggling for air in Matt's brain but every time he thought he had a hold of it, the breakfast conversation swirling around him swatted it away. *Cam liked his kindergarten teacher. Mason's favorite subjects were gym and recess. Cam was tired of getting off the bus at the fire station each day. He wanted to go straight home after school.* He had no choice but to give up after awhile.

When the boys finished their pancakes, they helped Becca clear the table. Matt felt Jack's gaze on him.

"You okay?" his brother asked. "You've been awfully quiet."

"What are those Christmas trees called where kids hang their wish lists and then people take the lists and buy the stuff?"

"You mean a giving tree?"

"Yeah. That's it."

"We used to do one at the company in California," Jack added.

"I'm thinking about those kids at the Lighthouse Apartments yesterday. You think dad would allow one of those in the station?"

Jack shrugged. "You could ask. He puts up a tree in there every year anyway."

"I guess I could ask the Inn to put one there, but ..."

"Those kids might not feel comfortable going to the Chesapeake Inn."

"That's what I was thinking. The station feels like a better fit."

"I can ask dad when he gets home, if you want," Jack offered.

"Sure, if you think about it. If not, I'll ask tomorrow when I go in."

Jack pushed back his chair. "Are you okay with us painting your room?"

Matt pushed back his own chair and stood. "Yeah. I don't care. Whatever you guys need to do. I'm cool with it." He *was* cool with it. More or less. He hadn't lived at home in years, so it could hardly be called his room anymore.

He followed Jack into the kitchen, where Mason was supervising the loading of the dishwasher. With Serena in the hospital, the boys were having to grow up a bit and help out their dad more. He watched as Becca good-naturedly followed Mason's direction on loading flatware.

"Dad says tines up."

Becca flipped a handful of forks right side up. She was a good woman. Maybe a better woman than his brother deserved. She was certainly a better woman than Matt deserved. Which reminded him—it had been two months since he'd had a date. Well, that hadn't really been a date—more like drinks and a hookup the last time he and his buddies spent the weekend in Dewey Beach. It was the kind of date he preferred though. No commitment, no expectations beyond a good time. If there was one thing Matt Wolfe was good at, it was showing a woman a good time.

~

IN THE BACK room of Quilt Therapy, Cassidy was lost in thought as she helped Natalie and Becca unwrap bolts of newly-arrived holiday fabric. There were the usual novelty prints of candy canes and snowmen. There were also some stunning floral patterns in deep, rich reds and golds, vines and blooms inter-twined. She could envision buying a few yards of that. Not that she had time to start a new quilt.

She glanced up occasionally as her sisters also held up bolts they particularly liked. It was no surprise that Becca liked the small batch, hand-dyed fabrics. She was the art quilter in the family. Natalie, on the other hand, was partial to the more contemporary, abstract patterns in lighter reds and greens.

Cassidy's brain kept circling back to her ever-growing list of things to do. Every bolt they unwrapped had to be put into the shop's computer system before it could go on sale. That was her job, and she'd be here tonight long after Nat and Becca went home. They really should have had the holiday fabrics for sale earlier. September was kind of late for someone to begin a Christmas quilt.

And then she had the winter festival to work on. And her business school applications. Those she had to work on when Natalie wasn't in the apartment. She took off her glasses and rubbed her tired eyes, not caring that she was smearing mascara around her eyes like a raccoon.

"Was Jack at the apartment fire?" Natalie's question broke through the to-do list in Cassidy's brain.

"Yes, he was," Becca answered. "Took them most of the day to get it under control."

Cassidy shook her head sadly. She and Natalie drove past the building—or what was left of it—on their way to the shop. "Looked like they'll have to tear it down," she said.

"That's what Jack said," Becca replied. "Total loss. No one got hurt though."

"Was Matt there, too?" Cassidy asked.

Becca looked up from a bolt of fabric and nodded. "Yeah, he's still training Jack. Jack said he was glad he was with Mattie in there."

"Why's that?"

"Matt had been in the building before and he has an almost photographic memory. Jack doesn't have a lot of experience in multi-family buildings. He said Matt knew where all the stairs were and how the apartments were laid out."

"I guess that would help, huh?" Cassidy pictured Matt and Jack feeling their way through a smoky building. "Never really thought about that aspect of it before."

Becca picked up another bolt and began unwrapping it. "Yeah, I'm learning a lot about firefighting these days."

"Is Matt good at it? Has Jack ever said?"

Becca nodded her head vigorously. "He says Matt's an amazing firefighter. You wouldn't think he would be, with his ADHD and all. But Jack says it's like the only place where he can really focus is in a fire."

"That's odd," Natalie said.

Cassidy picked up another bolt. "I never knew Matt had ADHD."

A look of alarm flashed briefly across Becca's face. "I probably wasn't supposed to share that, so don't spread it around."

"I would never do that." Cassidy frowned at her sister.

"Not saying you would," Becca backtracked, unwinding a few lengths of fabric from the bolt to take a closer look at the pattern. "I probably shouldn't have said anything."

The three sisters worked quietly after that, no one saying a word. Cassidy thought about the revelation that Matt had ADHD. She'd had no idea.

Natalie broke the silence. "Mark's band is playing next Saturday. Do you guys want to go?" Mark was Natalie's on-again, off-again boyfriend.

"Sure." Becca perked up. "I'm not sure what Jack's schedule is for next weekend, but I'd love to go."

"How about you, Cass?"

Cassidy shook her head. "I'll be in Annapolis that day." She had accepted an invitation to speak at the retailers association there, about holiday social media for retailers.

"That's next weekend?" Natalie gave her an incredulous look. "Didn't realize it was that soon."

"Well, holiday marketing starts ramping up now. That's the first part of my presentation. You can't wait until Thanksgiving to start thinking about it."

Natalie shook her head again. "I don't know how you keep all that stuff straight."

"Spreadsheets, my dear."

"Yeah well, don't ever leave Quilt Therapy because I do not want to inherit that job. Ugh." Natalie slapped a palm onto a stack of holiday fabric bolts. "Looks like we are finished here, ladies."

Don't ever leave *Quilt Therapy*. An hour later, her sister's words still sounded in Cassidy's brain. She leaned back in the used office chair, took off her glasses, and rubbed her tired eyes. A familiar feeling of guilt washed over her. If she got into business school, she would be leaving Quilt Therapy—and it would be just Natalie left here to help their mother. Charlotte was looking for a job in Washington, DC. Lauren, Cassidy's twin, had moved to California ages ago. Becca had moved back to St. Caroline a few months ago, but her time was split between a large quilt commission project and Quilt Therapy. Besides their mother, only Cassidy and Natalie were full time employees.

She can hire someone outside the family. Lauren had said that so often to Cassidy, it was practically a mantra by now. But it wouldn't be the same for their mother with non-family employees. Quilt Therapy wouldn't be the same.

She leaned back into the computer. She needed to maintain her focus on the task at hand. If she could get all of the new bolts entered into the system tonight, Natalie and her mom could shelve them all tomorrow morning. She squinted at a label, then typed the multi-digit code into the computer. Squint, type and repeat.

She carried a stack of bolts out to the cutting table in the showroom and picked up a new batch to enter. She sat her butt back down in the chair.

If I don't make a change soon, I'll still be sitting here ten years from now. But how do I tell everyone I don't want to work here anymore? She liked working with her mother and sisters, she really did. The Trevors weren't some dysfunctional family like you see in the movies. On the contrary, the Trevor family was eminently functional. That was what made this all so hard. She loved her family with all her heart. But it felt like she had a second heart, too—and that one was filled with wanderlust.

She pushed that thought away. *If you don't get this done soon, you'll still be sitting here when the sun comes up.*

By ten-thirty, she had all the new fabrics in the system. Her eyes were bleary and her fingers stiff from hours of typing, but the sense of accomplishment felt good. She shut down the computer and was turning off the lights in the back, when a sharp rap sounded on the door. Her heart jumped into her throat. She patted the phone in her pocket, then slid it out. St. Caroline was a safe place, especially in the off season. But who would be knocking on the shop's door at ten-thirty at night?

She held her breath as she slowly walked into the front room. She could make out a dark figure on the other side of the glass-paned door. A man's figure. The figure leaned in to peer through the glass.

She was about to tap 911 on her phone when she heard, "Hey, Cassidy? Are you still here?"

She nearly fainted with relief. It was Matt's voice. She took a deep breath, trying to re-oxygenate her brain, then hurried to the door and unlocked it.

"Hey there. I thought maybe I'd missed you," he said.

She stepped back to let him enter, then laughed—partly from relief and partly at the sheer ridiculousness of the situation. "What are you doing here?"

He held up a paper lunch bag. "I brought you a snack." He reached into the bag and pulled out two smaller, plastic sandwich bags.

Cassidy's stomach growled at the sight. She *had* skipped dinner. "Um, that's nice of you?"

He let a dark canvas gym bag slide off his shoulder. "Peanut butter and jelly was the best I could do, with the resources at hand. Nothing open in St. Caroline this late on a Sunday night." He unzipped the bag and pulled out a skinny quart jug of milk. "I appropriated some milk from the station fridge, too."

She couldn't help herself. At the sight of a well-muscled fireman and notorious ladies' man holding peanut butter and jelly sandwiches and milk, a wide smile spread across her face. He grinned back, clearly pleased as punch with himself. And damn if it wasn't the cutest thing Cassidy could recall witnessing in who knew how long. Matt had never struck her as cute before —certainly not with that body, which his dark cargo pants and long-sleeved tee shirt were doing nothing to conceal. But there was a boyishness about him just now that was very appealing.

She remembered what Becca had accidentally revealed about him. *ADHD.* Cassidy didn't know much about ADHD. Weren't people with it supposed to be hyperactive? Bouncing off the walls? Matt certainly wasn't that way. Happy-go-lucky some-times, sure. But there was also something about him that was ... contained. Like he was holding himself in.

"I forgot cups," he said, snapping his fingers. "Sorry."

The sound snapped her back to the present. "We have glasses in the back." She turned and headed for the small kitchenette. He followed.

"Can I ask what made you do this?" She reached up and pulled two short glasses off a shelf in the shop's kitchen. "I mean, I appreciate it. Don't get me wrong. I'm starving right now, actually. But ..." It was a little puzzling. Bringing a late night snack was the sort of thing one did for a friend, but she and Matt weren't that kind of friends. She wasn't even sure Matt had any platonic female friends. That didn't seem to be the way he rolled.

"Becca stopped in at the station with doughnuts for everyone. She mentioned you were working late." He gave a wry twist of his mouth as he held out a sandwich to her. "I'd have brought you doughnuts but they lasted about two point four seconds in the station."

She took the sandwich he offered and patted her hip. "That's okay. The last thing I need are more empty calories going straight to my hips."

"What are you talking about? You have a great figure."

Then he seemed to remember where he was. *Or who he's with.*

"Sorry. I mean, you do. But maybe I shouldn't have said that." He leaned back against the kitchenette's counter and busied himself with opening his sandwich, not looking her in the eye.

"Thank you for the compliment," she said quietly, keeping her own eyes on her sandwich.

He ate half of his before speaking again. "You guys have a lot of fabric out there. No wonder every closet in my parents' house was filled with it."

It was an awkward segue to a new topic of conversation, one Matt certainly wasn't interested in. Fabric.

"We're like drug dealers, I know."

Matt's loud laughter cracked the uneasy tension in the room.

"Oh, I wanted to tell you," she added, "Douglas Preston agreed to play Santa."

"That's great. Check that off the list, right? And Sterling wasn't bent out of shape over being fired?"

Cassidy shook her head. "Not that Lucy said, no."

Matt popped the last of the sandwich into his mouth and swallowed. "Dad agreed to put up a giving tree at the station. Is there a way to wrap that into the festival?"

She thought for a long moment. "Hmm. Might be hard to get out-of-town visitors to take a list and then bring the gifts back to town."

"What if we put up donation boxes in some of the businesses? I could probably get some of the guys to help shop for the gifts afterward."

Cassidy nodded. "That's a good idea." She washed down one last bite of sandwich with milk. "Or we could have a few people walking around downtown with donation buckets."

"People dressed as elves."

Cassidy coughed, pressing her lips together to keep from spewing milk. "That would be perfect, actually," she said when she could finally come up for air.

Matt grinned. "I'm sure I could blackmail Jack into it."

"He'd be a pretty tall elf." Matt's brother was six foot five.

"He'd be impossible to miss, the giant elf."

Cassidy laughed again. "Well, if you can't get him to do it, I'll see if Becca can talk him into it."

Matt rolled his eyes theatrically. "He would do literally anything for your sister."

"Well, I like the general idea of the giving tree and donations." Cassidy washed out her glass in the small sink, then washed

Matt's too. "I guess we should get together sometime to go over things."

"We should. I've got a crazy schedule this week. Couple guys are out for training, so I'm filling in everywhere."

Cassidy turned off the light in the kitchen. Matt followed her out to the cutting table, where she'd left her purse. She turned out the lights in the front room, set the building alarm, and locked the door behind them. Out on the sidewalk, the night air was noticeably cooler than it had been the week before. Winter was around the corner.

Matt fell into step beside her as she walked the half block to where her car, a sensible Honda Civic, was parked on the street. She pressed the button on her key. The car beeped and flashed as it unlocked.

"Thanks for the sandwich," she said, turning back to Matt. "Let me know if you have some time this week to talk about the festival."

"Will do."

But he made no move to leave. She looked up at him. Growing up, Matt and Jack had seemed almost like twins. Everyone thought of them in the same breath. The two younger Wolfe boys, "Mattie and Jackie." But really, they were almost as different as two people could be. Jack was tall and lanky, whip smart, with blonde hair. Matt was a good bit shorter with a chest that looked like it might have been carved from stone. Not that she was paying any mind to his chest. Because she most definitely —oh hell, she was totally noticing his chest and the way the cold night air was making his nipples poke through his shirt.

Nor could she interpret the look she was seeing in his eyes right now. It was the look of a man who was about to kiss her, but that didn't make sense. Matt wouldn't want to kiss her. They weren't on a date. Though at the moment, it definitely felt like the end of a date. It felt like that moment where she always began to worry about her glasses getting in the way of a kiss. Should she remove them? Would he remove them? Would they just get awkwardly mashed between their faces?

Questions that didn't need to be answered right now, because she and Matt were not going to kiss.

He reached down and opened her car door for her. "Drive safely."

Yeah, definitely not the words of a man about to kiss her.

CHAPTER 7

"That's how it's done!" Ben Wardman's voice rang out as the ball sailed in a smooth—almost slow motion—arc toward the goal. Matt saw it as clearly as Ben did: there was no way for the other team's goalie to stop the shot. He just stood there at the end of the bench and enjoyed the sight of the white soccer ball against the brilliant blue of the cloudless sky, backlit by late afternoon sun.

"Way to go, Danny!" When the ball hit the ground behind the goalie, Matt added his own voice to the cheer engulfing the sidelines. The St. Caroline players were up off the bench, jumping and high-fiving each other.

"Those kind of goals are a thing of beauty, eh Mattie?" The St. Caroline athletic director was standing next to Matt. Half the teachers in town still called him "Mattie." Of course, he just called Dan Conway "Danny."

Carrying on the tradition.

Matt smiled as he watched the players jog back to midfield. Then he glanced over at Ben, wrapped in a heavy wool blanket in his wheelchair. A knit cap covered his head. Ben's wife, Ashley, stood behind him, her posture and gaze alert and watchful.

Matt couldn't imagine how hard this season must be for Ben. For years, Ben had served as the head coach of the soccer team at St. Caroline High—in addition to being a popular science teacher. Now he was relegated to the role of spectator, while the head coach position was filled by Sean Crane, the industrial arts and technology teacher. Matt was filling in as a volunteer assistant.

Play on the field had begun again, and Matt forced his attention back to the game. He followed the ball as it was passed from player to player, intercepted, passed and intercepted again. Matt had been a good soccer player in high school, always able to see several plays ahead. If he'd been a better student, academically, he could have been a college player, too. Alas, he hadn't been a good student. Not like Oliver. Not like Jack, boy genius. Matt had gone to community college and earned an associate's degree in fire administration. He knew his mother had been disappointed that he never went the two additional years and earned his bachelor's.

Mom had a freaking Ph.D.

"Coach!"

It took a moment for Matt to realize the players on the bench were yelling at him. He looked at them and one of the freshman cocked his head toward a soccer ball sitting in the grass a good fifty feet beyond the field. *Oh right.* As the assistant coach, he was supposed to chase down balls that went out of bounds.

"Got it," he said and jogged off to retrieve the ball. Ashley Wardman met his eyes as he passed. He could practically see the pain around her, like an aura. *What was in the water in St. Caroline these days?* He'd asked Dan Trevor that question at the Trevors' anniversary party over the summer. The doctor's reply was simple. People get sick. That was just one of the many pithy sayings to assault Matt's ears over the past year.

No one is guaranteed a tomorrow.

Into every life, a little rain must fall.

Life goes on.

Live for today.

Shit happens. That was how he paraphrased them all in his head. But there was a grain of truth to each one of them. You never know what's going to happen tomorrow. Or five minutes from now. He scooped up the runaway ball and dribbled it back to the sidelines. Ben was the perfect example of that. A healthy, athletic guy in his early thirties—not the sort of person who was supposed to get sick and die. Yet that's exactly what was happening, and they were all watching it happen week by week. Ben got weaker and frailer. At every game, there seemed to be less of him left.

The other team's bench erupted into cheers. They'd scored, and Matt had completely missed it. *Focus focus focus.* It was so much easier to hold his mind still when he was playing soccer or coaching. But standing still on the sidelines, watching? His thoughts bounced around more than the ball on the field.

He found it easiest to focus when his body was engaged. Responding to a call with the fire department? He didn't have to think twice about his attention span. It was just there. Ditto playing sports or … having sex. If it involved his body, his mind behaved just fine.

"Subs!" Sean Crane yelled out and Matt snapped to attention.

"Alex! Rafael! Erik!" Matt lined up the subs until the ref halted play. He glanced down at the sports watch on his wrist. "Seven minutes!"

He watched the subs run in. St. Caroline was up by two, but he'd seen games turn in less time than they had left on the clock. He shifted his weight from foot to foot and forced himself to concentrate on the game until the final whistle. St. Caroline won, four to two. He turned to say something about the game to Ben, but Ashley was already pushing the wheelchair toward the parking lot. A familiar sadness coursed through him, a slow heaviness that clogged his veins.

He got in line behind Sean and the kids, to shake hands with the other team. The other team's head coach had been a teammate of Matt's at St. Caroline.

"Good game, Mattie," the guy said as he gave Matt's hand a strong squeeze. "Glad to see you're back involved in soccer." He looked over Matt's shoulder. "Ben already gone? I said 'hi' before the game but I was hoping to talk to him again."

Matt gave a little frown. "He tires out pretty quickly these days, Ash says."

As the kids wandered off to meet their parents, soccer bags slung over their shoulders, Matt and Sean gathered up balls and forgotten water bottles. When the last player was gone, they carried the balls to the storage shed.

"Want to grab a burger at Nick's?" Sean asked as he closed the padlock on the shed's door.

"Sure." Matt had been waiting for this question. He and Sean always went to Nick's Burger Barn after a game. "Meet you there."

MATT BIT into his cheeseburger as Sean read his current online dating profile out loud. Fortunately, no one else was sitting within earshot of their table. Matt preferred the off season in St. Caroline. There was less traffic on the roads. More parking in downtown. And a shorter wait for your food at Nick's.

"So I rewrote it last night," Sean was saying. "Now it says, 'Ready to find love, settle down and have your babies! I am a 36-year-old teacher, never married, gainfully employed and not too hard on the eyes. I am looking for that one woman with a big smile, kind eyes and a beautiful heart. I am more spiritual than religious. I find all kinds of women attractive, so I'm not looking for any one type. I promise to help do the dishes, change the diapers, and vacuum up the dust bunnies. I'm also a good kisser (references available). Respond with where you want to honeymoon in the subject line so I know you're real.'"

Matt lifted one eyebrow. "You're getting serious."

"Yeah well, most of the replies to my old profile were from college girls looking for a sugar daddy. I figured maybe I wasn't being clear enough."

Matt clapped a hand over his mouth to avoid spitting chocolate milkshake all over the table. "You're not old enough to be a sugar daddy, are you? I'm picturing a sixty-year-old."

"Not rich enough either. I'm a teacher. I'll need a wife who works, too."

Matt nodded toward Sean's phone. "Maybe better put that in there."

"You think so?"

"No." Matt chuckled. "You can probably hash that out on the first date."

"But what do you think? Will this version work?"

Matt shrugged and swirled a crispy french fry in the ketchup on his plate. "I don't know, man. I try not to target the marriage-minded females."

"I can forward the sugar babies on to you."

"I'm not flush enough for them either, but I'm happy to waste their time while they wait for the nursing home to call."

Sean scrolled through his profile again. "Picture or no picture?"

"Picture, but fully clothed. No dick pics. And no pictures with you holding a fish you just caught or standing in front of someone else's private plane." Matt rolled his eyes. "Don't know what some of those guys are thinking."

"How about you? How's your profile working these days?" Sean crumpled up the paper wrapper his burger had come in, and dropped it onto the table.

"I dunno. Haven't logged in for awhile."

"Seriously? You don't check every day?"

"Nah. I haven't had time lately. Or the energy."

"When was the last time you had a date?"

Matt looked up at the wooden rafters of the Burger Barn. Nick had been lucky so far with kitchen fires. His restaurant really was a barn. Nick had found it while on a trip to Vermont, bought it, and shipped it to Maryland. A really bad kitchen fire though, and the place would burn to the ground in minutes.

"Weren't you dating a nurse from Annapolis in the spring? Whatever happened to that?" Sean wasn't letting this go.

"Yeah. That ran its course. I guess that was the last time I had a proper date."

"Hookups?"

Matt felt his face warm. Sean always seemed to want to live vicariously through Matt's exploits. Or Matt's exploits as Sean imagined them. But Matt wasn't one to brag about his conquests. He'd been raised better than that. He took another long slurp of milkshake. "A woman in Dewey Beach over the summer. Met her in a bar and went back to her condo."

"She lived there?"

"She owns a summer place. Just a one-bedroom. Not one of those big homes on the water."

Sean let out a low whistle. "Still. Any place at the beach. That's not cheap real estate. How old is she?"

Matt shrugged again. "Forties maybe? Older."

Sean waggled his eyebrows. "Mrs. Robinson?"

"I'm a little older than Benjamin Braddock." Matt wanted to change the subject. He wasn't exactly proud of his love 'em and leave 'em behavior, and he'd been trying to cut back this year. Successfully, he might add. But the thought of dating someone seriously—or heaven forbid, settling down for good—filled him with a terror darker than any smoke-filled burning building.

As the child of a firefighter, he'd spent his whole life watching people lose everything in a heartbeat—a home to a fire or a loved one to an accident. It was breathtaking how quickly it could happen. Look at Oliver. One day, he woke up with a terrific life—a job he loved, a beautiful wife, two adorable kids—and when he went to bed that night, that life was in tatters.

Or take his dad. He lost the love of his life this year.

It seemed foolish to get too attached to people or things. You were going to lose a few of them eventually. No two ways around that, as far as Matt could see. That was why he rented a cabin, bought a used pickup truck, kept his heart out of anything concerning women. That way, if something bad happened, it wouldn't bother him as much.

In his peripheral vision, he saw the neon sign in the restaurant's window flicker and he remembered the favor he wanted to ask of Sean.

"Hey, so have you heard about this winter festival the town is doing?"

Sean nodded. "Briefly. Heard they made you president or mayor or something."

Matt fired a french fry across the table. "I had to take over my brother's role in it. Though apparently they don't trust me entirely, because they asked someone else to help."

"Yep. Cassidy Trevor. Your life is rough, my friend."

Matt rolled his eyes. "Anyway. We've been bandying about the idea of a big Christmas lights display somewhere in town. We don't have a location yet, but I was wondering whether some of your students could help build some frames to hold lights. You know, like giant presents or a forest of candy canes. Just some things to hang the lights on."

"Sure. We can do that. I'll offer them extra credit. They'll do anything for that."

SEAN CRANE and his students can help us with the lights display. He tapped "send" on his phone. Immediately it occurred to him that

Cassidy might not know Sean. She didn't socialize with the teachers, as far as he was aware. *Sean is the industrial arts and technology teacher at SCHS.*

He stared at the phone for a good thirty seconds, waiting for a response. When nothing came through, he set it down on the coffee table in his cabin and clicked on the television. She was probably busy. She worked late last night. She also hadn't been overly thrilled to see him when he showed up with milk and peanut butter and jelly sandwiches. That was clear.

He clicked through the channels, stopping when he found the football game. He leaned back into the sofa. He was just trying to be nice, bringing her a sandwich. Maybe she was used to men making more of an effort around her. Grander gestures.

Not that a "grand gesture" had been his intention. That implied more cunning and strategy than he was capable of. Last night's intention had been about as simple as one could get. She was working late. He thought she might appreciate a bite to eat.

On the screen, the home team's quarterback threw an interception. Flags were thrown on the play. Matt wasn't rooting for either team, particularly. The camera cut to a shot of the cheerleaders on the sidelines. Their purple pom poms reminded him of the smear of grape jelly on Cassidy's lips last night, and how badly he had wanted to kiss it off.

When the game cut to a commercial, Matt leaned over to pick up his phone from the coffee table. He wasn't checking for a reply to his text. Not at all. He hadn't even asked a question, to begin with. He'd simply relayed some information that required no immediate response from Cassidy.

A few swift taps on the screen and he was logged into his dating profile. Months had passed since he last checked this site. His inbox was filled with messages and winks and photos. He began to scroll through them. Life was too short not to enjoy yourself while you were here. He wasn't in the market for a serious relationship the way Sean was, but he liked the company of a beautiful woman. It filled the time. And when it came to focusing his mind, the only thing more effective than firefighting was sex.

He remembered Cassidy standing in front of the yoga studio, wearing those pink jeans. Who knew pink jeans were even a thing? She looked good in them. She was probably good at yoga too, he imagined. As far as he could tell, Cassidy Trevor was good at everything she did—dating all the way back to childhood. She was like Jack that way. They both had the Midas touch.

Matt's touch, on the other hand, was not quite so golden. He was good at things that were down and dirty. He wondered whether Cassidy knew about his ADHD. Her father did, since Matt and his brothers had been patients of Dr. Trevor when they were kids. There was that whole doctor-patient confidentiality thing—in theory. But living in a small town rendered lots of theories moot, in Matt's experience. Like his own personal theory of dating. You meet a woman you're attracted to and you ask her out. She says "yes" or "no," and you go from there.

But in a small town like St. Caroline, not all women were on the approved list of eligibility. Cassidy was not, even though he could swear she'd been waiting for him to kiss her last night when he walked her to her car. He had come within mere seconds of doing it, too. Faced with those soft lips and all that blonde hair, his fingers had itched to plunge into. It took all his self control to hold back.

He knew his reputation was that he had no self control where women were concerned, but that simply wasn't true. He'd been crushing on Cassidy for years, but had he ever made a serious play for her? No, he had not. His parents did not want him breaking her heart—not that Matt dated women long enough to break their hearts—and he respected their wishes. He might be terrible boyfriend material but he was a good son.

CHAPTER 8

"Studies have shown that social media absolutely influences consumers' purchasing decisions. In one study, over half of the respondents said they had discovered a new-to-them brand or product via a social media post." Cassidy was wrapping up her presentation to the retailers association in Annapolis. She clicked through to her final slide. "So even though we are trying to get consumers to do more of their shopping offline, we still have to be online ourselves because that's where people are today."

She smiled at the group of fifty or so people sitting in an overly bright meeting room at one of the downtown hotels. As they began their applause, the association's executive director, Kellie Brownington, approached the lectern.

"Thank you, Cassidy. And thanks to all of you for coming out on this rainy Saturday. Next month, we have Joel Lederer to talk to us about financing expansion. I know you won't want to miss that."

Cassidy shut down her laptop as the attendees gathered up their jackets and bags, preparing to head out into a rainy early evening. Despite the weather, she felt wired. Energized. She liked public speaking. Even as a child, she was always the one who volunteered to read in front of class, do the presentation part of group projects, get up in front of the entire school to introduce assembly speakers.

"Can I treat you to dinner before you head home?" Kellie asked. "Maybe the rain will stop before you hit the road."

"Oh, I'm staying here at the hotel tonight. I'll drive home in the morning."

"So much the better." Kellie smiled. "I can buy you a drink then, too. I was really impressed with your presentation, Cassidy. I've got another opportunity I'd like to talk to you about."

After Cassidy stashed her laptop in her hotel room, she and Kellie took a cab to Brix Wine Bar. The streets of downtown Annapolis were filled with people, despite the rain. Cassidy watched through the window of the cab as people ducked into bars and restaurants. She loved cities, even small ones like Annapolis. She fed on the energy, the people, the diversity. The novelty. She liked her hometown well enough, but there were so many other places to see.

New York. Boston. San Francisco. Chicago. London. Paris.

The cab pulled up to Brix and she and Kellie got out. Inside the wine bar, it was dry and warm. They followed the hostess past the bar and a massive floor-to-ceiling wine rack filled with dark bottles of wine. They passed cozy two-person tables, all of which were filled, and a large velveteen sectional designed for lounging. On the sectional sat clusters of friends and couples, drinking and talking. Cassidy's eyes skimmed over them before settling on a beautiful redhead and the man sitting next to her … Matt Wolfe. Her eyes widened at the sight, then she looked away quickly—but not quickly enough to avoid Matt's notice. From the corner of her eye, she caught a flash of his quick smile. Then she followed Kellie and the hostess into a back room filled with more small tables.

As she pulled out her chair and sat down, her heart pounded

with the shock of seeing Matt here—on a date, obviously. A date with a drop-dead gorgeous woman. *Of course.* Matt wasn't the only "ladies' man" in St. Caroline but he was the only one she was friends with. Or not friends. They weren't really friends, were they? If she had met Matt in college, they wouldn't have been friends. He wouldn't have looked twice at her.

She picked up the wine list and gave a silent prayer of thanks that she and Kellie were seated in the back room, where she couldn't see Matt and the gorgeous redhead. Not that it mattered to her that he was here on a date. That was none of her concern. But he might find it awkward to have someone from St. Caroline watching him. It might constrain his behavior, and Cassidy didn't want to be responsible for altering the trajectory of Matt's evening in any way. If he wanted to go home with a gorgeous woman? Again, not her concern.

A waitress sidled up to their table and Cassidy ordered the larger glass of merlot. "Since I'm not driving tonight, I might as well live it up, right?" she said to Kellie, who ordered a chardonnay.

Live it up. Right. As she sat in a hip wine bar with a business contact, while Matt Wolfe was here on a hot date. Cassidy couldn't remember the last time she'd been on a date, hot or otherwise. *No point in dating right now, anyway.* Not until she submitted her business school applications and learned whether she was accepted anywhere.

The waitress returned with the wine. They had no sooner clinked their glasses together in a toast than Matt appeared in the doorway of the dining room. Cassidy watched as he scanned the room. When his eyes spotted her, a smile lit his face and he headed their way. Cassidy was shocked to the core when he leaned in and pressed a warm, friendly kiss to her cheek.

"Hey there, Cass," he said.

She barely noticed him reaching over to shake Kellie's hand

and introduce himself. She was still stuck on "Hey there, Cass." *Cass.* No one except her parents and sisters called her "Cass."

"You never said anything about being in Annapolis tonight." His words yanked her back to the moment.

"Um yeah. I was here speaking to the retailers' association." She gestured toward Kellie, sitting across from her.

"Oh? What about?"

Cassidy stared at Matt's face, not comprehending why he was interested in what she was doing in Annapolis—and distracted by the sexiness of the dark stubble shadowing his jawline.

"Cassidy gave us tips on how to use social media to increase holiday sales," Kellie jumped in with the answer.

Cassidy shot her a grateful look.

"She knows her stuff," Kellie added.

"I guess we need to get started on that for the festival, huh?" Matt said.

Cassidy nodded. "Maybe we can meet next week some time."

"Sure thing. Sounds good." Matt was about to say something else when the waitress reappeared. "See you back home," he said.

Cassidy watched him walk away, then gave the menu a hurried once-over. "The steak salad, please," she ordered.

"Somebody from St. Caroline?" Kellie asked, when the waitress left.

Cassidy nodded and took a tiny sip of wine, enjoying the merlot's spiciness as it trickled down her throat.

"He makes you uncomfortable."

Cassidy gave a little laugh. "Oh no." She noted Kellie's skeptical expression. "Our parents are friends. Matt and I are just—" She added a little wave to her little laugh. "—very different people. And we're co-chairing a winter festival in town so we're spending more time together than we normally would."

"It doesn't surprise me that you would be co-chairing an event. Have you heard of the Northeast Retail Show in Boston?"

Cassidy shook her head.

79

"I went to school with the guy in charge of speakers. I'm putting together a panel discussion on retail and tourism. I'd love to add you to the panel, if you're interested."

It took Cassidy just over a nanosecond to decide she was interested. "How many attendees are there?"

"Close to a thousand last year."

Cassidy's eyes widened. "I've never spoken in front of a big crowd before." She munched on her salad while thinking about the idea. "When is it?"

"Mid-February."

"I could do that, I'm sure. We're slow for a few months after the holidays."

Kellie laughed. "Aren't we all? The show closes on Valentine's Day, but the panel is scheduled for the day before."

"I doubt that would be an issue for me." The odds of Cassidy having a date on Valentine's Day? Slim and none. But the thought of speaking on a panel at an industry event was oddly more exciting to her than a date. *Boston!* She could check that city off her bucket list.

Their entrees arrived and they dug in, eating quietly for awhile. Cassidy hadn't realized how hungry she was until she took the first bite.

"How did you end up in Annapolis?" she asked after a few minutes. She knew Kellie had graduated from Harvard Business School—the web site for the retailers association included Kellie's bio.

"I fell in love with an academic who was offered a tenure track job at the Naval Academy."

"How do you like it here?"

Kellie's long silence was telling. "I like it." She pushed her fork through the remains of her dinner. "I don't quite have the career I envisioned for myself but ... love, you know? An MBA can get a job anywhere. An academic has to go where that year's openings are."

Try as she might, Cassidy couldn't imagine moving for someone else's job. Even for someone she loved. Oh, Cassidy wanted to fall in love someday. The operative word there being "someday." But not before going to business school and seeing more of the world. Once you fell in love and had to start coordinating your life with someone else's, your horizons got a lot narrower. You had to take into consideration another person's career. Their interests. Their friends. Their bucket list. Cassidy wanted to check off more of her own list before merging it with someone else's.

MATT SUNK into the weird low couch thing next to Marina. Marina? Or Maria? Or maybe it was Maura. *Shit.* He couldn't remember. Seeing Cassidy had flustered him so, now his date's name was lost in the recesses of his pathetic brain. His date—Marina, he was *pretty* sure it was Marina—handed him back his glass of wine.

"Sorry about that," he said. "If I had ignored her, I would never hear the end of it."

"Oh? Why's that?"

"My parents are friends with her parents. And we're working on a business event together."

"I thought you said you were a firefighter." She lifted her wine glass to her lips as she coolly regarded him. It was impossible to miss the wariness and skepticism in her voice.

Matt didn't fault her for that. People weren't perfectly honest in online dating profiles. Sean had learned that the hard way a few times.

"I am. But St. Caroline's a small town. Everybody has to chip in on chamber of commerce projects."

"I see. Well, that sounds interesting." She took another drink of wine. "What kind of project is it? An event, you said?"

He took a tiny, almost imperceptible, sip of wine himself. He didn't even like wine. Why had he agreed to come to a wine bar? *Because you were trying to look like a sophisticated, urbane man online.* Yeah, about that. He was a firefighter. He had man cuts all over his hands. His—what had Becca called them? Oh yeah, his *cuticles* were a mess.

And for what? Marina was undeniably even prettier than her pictures online, and she was smart and funny, yada yada yada. She was an associate at a law firm in Annapolis, had rowed crew in college, played guitar in a local country band. Totally interesting.

And yet, Matt didn't want to be there right now. His head just wasn't in the dating game. The flesh was willing, but the spirit was weak. What he really wanted to be doing was talking social media for the festival with Cassidy. How crazy was that? He'd gone over to say "hello" because he had wanted to, not because he'd never hear the end of it from his dad.

"It's for a winter festival in December," he answered her question. "Santa for the kids and a big Christmas lights display. The shops will have sales. That sort of thing."

"I love Christmas lights." She smiled.

"Well, you should come see them. Second weekend in December." He faked another sip of wine. "I really am a firefighter," he smiled back. "Not an ax murderer."

Her smile widened. "You never know online."

"That's true."

They ordered appetizers—oysters and some bruschetta thing —and Marina became noticeably flirtier. Suggestive, even. Weren't oysters supposed to be an aphrodisiac? Apparently, they were working on her. It was clear to Matt that he could go home with her if he wanted. But he didn't want that. Oh, he wouldn't mind getting laid that night. Even Jack had responded to an episode of Matt's grouchiness the other day with the suggestion that he needed to get laid. But despite Marina's attractiveness and apparent eagerness, the idea of hooking up with her held surprisingly little appeal to him.

She leaned into him in such a way that her blouse gapped open, affording him a clear glimpse of her cleavage. Ample cleavage, in fact. And at some point, she had kicked off her heels and folded her legs up onto the sofa. She had nice legs. Slender ankles. Smooth calves.

Normally, his body would respond to such an obvious invitation. But not tonight. *I mean, nice legs aren't that uncommon.* Cassidy had killer legs. *A killer body.* It wasn't as though he hadn't seen her at Secret Beach over the years. She could rock a swimsuit with the best of them. A very clear picture of her lying on a big striped beach towel came to mind.

"Will you excuse me for a minute?" he said, setting his wine glass down on the tray that served as their table.

He wound his way through the bar until he found the men's room. Inside, he made a beeline for a stall and locked the door behind him. He didn't need to use the facilities. He just needed a moment to think, and he couldn't do that out there with Marina batting her eyes at him and shifting her legs every so often to draw his attention to them.

He closed his eyes. When he woke up that morning, he'd been all gung ho for this date. Now it was the last place he wanted to be. He'd almost rather be inside a burning building than spend the next hour pretending to like wine and then going back to Marina's apartment to pretend to make love to her. Well, he'd never really "made love" to anyone, given that he'd never been "in love" with anyone.

He reached into his pocket and pulled out his phone. He tapped Jack's name in his contact list and waited until his brother picked up.

"Hey there." Jack's voice was chipper. In the background were the usual noises of the fire station. "What's going on? Thought you had a date."

"I do."

"Get stood up?"

Matt heard the choked laugh on the other end.

"No. We're here at the bar."

"Okay. So why are you calling me?"

"I need you to do me a favor."

"What, you're drunk and you need a ride?"

"No. I've had about two mouthfuls of wine."

"You hate wine. So what kind of favor do you need?"

"Page me."

"Come again?"

"Can you page me? Like it's a call."

"It's a slow night here. Don't worry about things."

Matt sighed. For a smart guy, Jack could be remarkably dense sometimes. After another beat of silence, there was a short laugh of comprehension from his brother.

"Ahh. Date not going well? Did she misrepresent herself online?"

"No. She's fine. No chemistry, you know?" He waited for Jack to make a joke about Matt never needing chemistry before. Which totally wasn't true—but Matt's reputation as a ladies' man had gotten out of hand. "I want to leave, but I don't want to be a dick about it."

"Faking an emergency call is only slightly less dickish," Jack pointed out.

"Yeah, I know that. Can you just do it for me? Please? I'll owe you one."

"Alright. I'll add it to your tab."

"Thanks."

Matt shoved his phone back into his pocket and contemplated what favor Jack would later extract from him. On his way back to Marina, he glanced into the back dining room. Cassidy and her colleague were gone, a busboy wiping down the table they'd been sitting at. He missed the chance to say goodbye because he'd been hiding out in the men's room.

It's not like you'll never see her again. Disappointment weighed heavy in his chest, anyway—a fact that made absolutely no sense to him.

Marina smiled brightly when he returned to the sofa. She handed him back his glass of wine, and he took another pretend sip from it. Jack hadn't paged him yet and it was entirely possible that his brother wouldn't. Other people were constantly second-guessing Matt. Hell, he was starting to second-guess himself here. He took a larger swallow of wine—liquid courage. If he got home and regretted his decision to leave, he could always ask Marina out again. He had the distinct impression that she was the sort of woman who gave men too many second chances. Even smart, beautiful women were not immune to that. Not that Matt intentionally tried to lead women on. On the contrary, he tried to be very upfront about the fact that he didn't want to get involved, not seriously.

Finally, his phone vibrated. He gave Marina a wide-eyed look of alarm before looking at the screen and reading the message. *EMERGENCY! REPORT TO THE MOTHERSHIP IMMEDIATELY!* He grimaced sheepishly.

"I have to go. I'm being paged by the fire department. I am so sorry." By the sympathetic look on her face, he knew she was buying the regretful expression on his. His conscience bitch-slapped him as he shoved the phone back into his pocket. This was totally a dick move, but it was easier than waiting another hour and then declining to go back to her place. "I'll settle up the check on my way out."

CHAPTER 9

*C*assidy clicked off the television in the hotel room and flopped back onto the bed's overstuffed pillows. She turned her head to look at the laptop lying on the blonde wood hotel desk. She could work on her business school applications, but she didn't much feel like it at the moment. Two glasses of wine and her brain was foggy. It kept circling back to the weirdness of running into Matt at the wine bar.

She leaned over toward the nightstand, picked up the glossy corporate hotel magazine, and began to flip through it. It was one of those magazines designed to promote the hotel's locations in other cities and Cassidy perused the articles, imagining trips to Seattle and Sydney and … Boston. She stared at the photograph of Faneuil Hall with its wide brick facade and arched windows. She'd love to go to Boston, even in February when it would be ungodly cold. Quilt Therapy was always slow right after the holidays. The shop could spare her for a few days.

She pushed herself up off the bed and retrieved her phone from the desk. Her mom picked up on the second ring.

"How'd your talk go?" Michelle asked. "What did you do for dinner?"

"It was fine. I went out to eat with the executive director afterward."

"To a nice place?"

"A wine bar here. Brix."

"Sounds sophisticated." Her mother laughed softly. "Not my speed, of course."

Cassidy bit back the impulse to mention seeing Matt. "The executive director invited me to be on a panel with her at a retailers' conference in Boston."

"Oh? Is that something you'd like to do?"

"I think so, yes."

"When is it?"

"February."

"Well, that's a no brainer then. We won't be busy in February. What's the panel about?"

"Retail and tourism."

"Well, that's certainly a topic you know something about. If you want to go, that's fine."

The more Cassidy thought about it, the more she did want to go. She wanted to see Boston. She wanted to meet new people. She liked sharing what she knew with peers.

As soon as her mom hung up, her phone rang again. Cassidy turned back from the bed to answer it, expecting it to be one of her sisters. Instead, the screen read "Matthew Wolfe." She hesitated a moment before answering.

"Hey there, Cass."

"Hi ...?" Her voice drew the syllable out to a question.

"Are you on your way home?"

"No. I'm staying in a hotel tonight. Driving home tomorrow."

"Are you hungry?"

There was a mirror on the wall across from the bed, and Cassidy watched herself frown in it. "Um, I had dinner at the restaurant." Then her stomach growled. Apparently, the salad wasn't as filling as she'd thought. "Aren't you on a date?"

"I was. It ended, though."

She glanced at the clock on the nightstand. *That was fast.*

"Which hotel are you at?"

Without thinking, Cassidy told him.

"Nice."

She looked around the room. It was definitely one of the nicer hotels she'd ever stayed in. Not that her experience was all that wide. Her stomach growled again, louder this time.

"Are you still in Annapolis?" she asked.

"Yep. But I didn't eat at the bar."

"Are you drunk?"

"No. I'm not slurring my words, am I?"

"No." Cassidy watched her reflection in the mirror go from frowning to puzzled. "I'm just not sure why you're calling me."

"I'm starving and I'd rather not eat alone."

"Why didn't you eat at the restaurant?"

"We didn't hit it off. The chemistry just wasn't there."

She watched her reflection lift a skeptical eyebrow. *Since when do men need chemistry to hook up?* Whatever "chemistry" was. Cassidy wasn't sure she'd ever experienced that particular concept.

"Cass? Are you still there?"

And why was he calling her "Cass" again?

"Yeah. I'm still here. Why don't you come over and we can order room service?" The words were out of her mouth before she could stop the thought. "I'd meet you somewhere, but I don't want to go back out in the rain."

Huh. Matt Wolfe struck out on a date, she thought as she set down the phone. *That must be a first.*

MATT FLOPPED BACK onto the bed in Cassidy's hotel room,

causing the topmost pillow to topple over and land on his face. He batted it onto the floor.

"I'm stuffed," he groaned.

"Me too," Cassidy groaned back.

He peered over at her lying on the other side of the bed, the silver room service tray between them. There was only half a chicken finger and two french fries wallowing in ketchup left on the platter. Before he arrived, Cassidy had changed out of the suit she was wearing in the restaurant. Now she wore grey sweatpants and a red Talbot College tee shirt. Her feet were bare, her toenails painted a bright blue shade.

Four empty beer bottles stood like sentries on the desk at the foot of the bed. The two Matt drank had him feeling pleasantly warm and relaxed. But he could tell Cassidy was a little buzzed. Good thing she didn't have to drive anywhere tonight.

He wished he didn't have to drive anywhere tonight, either.

"You awake over there?" He nudged her gently with his elbow.

"Mmm-hmm."

He snuck a peek at the clock on the nightstand. It was nearly eleven. With an hour's drive ahead of him, he should be hitting the road. He stood and lifted the room service tray from the bed, hyper-aware of Cassidy's eyes on him. He set the tray down onto the wheeled cart and took it out to the hall. When he returned, Cassidy was on the phone to the front desk asking for housekeeping to come pick it up.

Even dressed in sweatpants and a tee shirt—and blue toenails, musn't forget those—she gave off an air of efficiency and control. Unlike his own evening, which had veered completely out of control at some point.

This was how his evening was originally supposed to end— lying on a bed next to a beautiful woman. But somehow he had gotten both the bed and the woman mixed up. The bed wasn't supposed to be in a hotel room, and the woman wasn't supposed to be Cassidy Trevor. But the original impulse still coursed through his veins loud and clear. His body was dying to get laid. But now he was next to a woman he couldn't get laid with.

What had happened? If he had just gone home with Marina, everything would be copacetic right now. Wouldn't it?

He stood at the foot of the bed and waited for Cassidy to hang up the phone.

"They said someone will be right up." She turned around just in time to catch him running his hand through his hair.

"I should get going."

She glanced at the alarm clock behind her. "Are you okay to drive?"

He nodded. "Sure. I'm fine." Two beers and not enough sleep —but other than that? Totally fine.

"The weather's still crappy out."

He nodded again. "I'll be fine." The thought of driving home to St. Caroline in the driving rain and dark did not overly thrill him, but what other choice did he have?

Cassidy scanned the room, a tiny frown creasing her fore-head. "I wish I'd gotten a double room instead of this king bed."

Was she suggesting …? No. Matt shoved that idea right back out into the crappy weather where it belonged. He followed her gaze to the upholstered chair and ottoman across the room. Her suitcase was splayed open on the ottoman.

"It's late," she pointed out. "Maybe you should stay and drive home in the morning."

They looked at each other for a long moment—a long, awkward moment—until Matt had to break eye contact.

"We don't have to tell anyone," she hurried to clarify. "So no one gets any ideas."

She tucked her feet up beneath her hips, causing those blue-hued toenails to disappear from sight. Suddenly Matt wanted to see her toes again. Wanted to push those soft sweatpants up her calves and …

She laughed softly. "Not that anyone would probably get any ideas about *us.*"

He lifted his eyes from her legs to her face. Her long blonde hair was messy and her skin was washed clean of makeup. He hadn't noticed that until now. Most of his body was bone-tired, but certain parts buzzed with attention. Parts that weren't supposed to be interested in Cassidy Trevor. No one would get any ideas about him and Cassidy ... *except for me.* That near kiss—or near miss—had occupied a good share of his attention over the past week.

She swung her legs over the edge of the bed. "You can think about it while I brush my teeth." At the door to the bathroom, she turned and looked back at him. "You don't want to have an accident driving home."

The door closed behind her and Matt listened as the water turned on. *An accident.* That was a good point. The last thing his family needed was another accident. He felt fine enough to drive —he thought, anyway. But who knew? The cause of Serena's accident still had not been determined. As far as anyone knew, there'd been no other cars around. Her car had checked out, mechanically. No obvious malfunction or failure there. Maybe an animal had run out into the road. Maybe she'd fallen asleep for a moment, or let her mind wander.

God knew, Matt's attention wandered all the time. His parents hadn't let him even test for his driver's license until he was nearly eighteen. They had been too worried about his ADHD. That didn't trouble him at the moment. His driving record was spotless. But he had responded to enough accident calls—he knew better than to trust his own sense of invincibility.

He heard the water in the bathroom shut off. A moment later, Cassidy emerged. She flashed him a silly, "all clean" smile—and he wanted to kiss that silly grin right off those soft, minty fresh lips. He sucked in a long, slow breath. *Wherefore art thou Cassidy?* And in that instant, it hit him—he hadn't gone home with Marina because he didn't want Cassidy to see him leave the bar with her. Or leave with any woman, for that matter. *But why?* What did it matter if she saw him leave with a woman? There was no gossip value in that. Jack already knew he was planning to hook up tonight. And no one else would be surprised to hear of it either.

Cassidy's grin faded and she returned to the bed, chucking him lightly on the arm as she passed. She set her glasses on the nightstand, then pulled the covers up to her chest. She squinted up at him, a gesture that struck him as way more adorable than it should. "If you get in an accident, I'll have to do the winter festival all by myself. And that will be a disaster."

"Doubtful."

She shrugged. "Suit yourself. But I'm calling it a night. I have to be home by ten tomorrow morning."

He walked over to the upholstered chair and moved her suitcase from the ottoman to the desk. Then he flipped off the light switch, shrouding the room in darkness. He lowered his body into the chair and stretched his legs across the ottoman. It was going to be a restless night for him, with precious little of anything resembling sleep.

But if this was the closest he was ever going to get to sleeping with Cassidy Trevor, he'd take it.

CHAPTER 10

*C*assidy slid the needle and thread into the quilt top, pulling the knot through to bury it in the cotton batting beneath.

"What possessed Natalie to piece this yesterday?" she asked Becca, who was sitting right next to her at the quilting frame.

"Fabric possessed her. Isn't that always the case?"

Cassidy had come into Quilt Therapy that morning to find a new quilt on the shop's quilting frame. The top was done in the style of a traditional Amish bars quilt—alternating stripes of solid scarlet and kelly green surrounded by a wide border of dark forest green. It was simple and striking, reminiscent of an abstract painting. The plan was to hang it in the shop's front window over the holiday season.

It needed to be quilted, though, so Cassidy and Becca were working on that until the shop opened at eleven, Sunday hours.

"Do the Martin sisters know about this?" she asked Becca. A quilt like this was a hand quilter's dream come true—lots of open, solid fabric with few seams to get in the way of tiny, immaculate stitches.

"They will soon, I'm sure. Word spreads fast." Her sister's laugh was gentle and sweet. Like Becca herself.

Cassidy and Becca rocked their short, thin quilting needles in and out of the fabric, picking up several stitches then pulling the thread through. They fell into an easy rhythm that Cassidy found comforting, especially after the strangeness of the night before in Annapolis. It had totally made sense for Matt to spend the night instead of driving home late at night in the rain. But the optics weren't good, if anyone found out about it—which eventually someone would. That kind of news would spread like wildfire in St. Caroline, and everyone would assume she had slept with Matt. Because when had a woman ever spent the night with Matt Wolfe and not slept with him? Who would believe that she was the lone exception, the one woman Matt wouldn't want to hook up with?

Even though she apparently *was* that lone exception.

She pushed her needle back into the layers of fabric and batting, and pushed thoughts of Matt from her mind. "I'm glad you're back home, Becs. I don't think I ever said that." She pulled her needle out. "I should have said it before, I guess."

Becca bumped her shoulder gently into Cassidy's. "I'm glad to be home."

Becca had lived in Ohio so many years, Cassidy had assumed she wasn't ever moving back. But here she was, home in St. Caroline again, her life coming together at last. Cassidy would be lying if she said she wasn't the teensiest bit jealous of her sister's newfound happiness. Not that Becca didn't deserve it, because she so totally did. Her life had been rough in Ohio—rougher than she had let anyone else know.

"How was your talk?" Becca asked.

"Good. The woman in charge wants me to be on a panel discussion at a retail show in Boston."

"Oh yeah? That's awesome. When?"

"After the new year. February."

"You must have knocked their socks off last night."

Cassidy laughed. "You know me. I can talk about business stuff until the cows come home. Makes me feel smart."

"You *are* smart. You and Charlotte got all the brains in the family." Becca made a mock pout. "So not fair." She winked at her sister.

"Don't let Nat hear you say that."

"I'm sure she'd agree. Speaking of sibling rivalries, Jack said Matt was in Annapolis last night, too. He had a date."

"Oh yeah?" Cassidy hoped her voice conveyed utter cluelessness. She also hoped that Matt hadn't spilled the beans on where he spent the night.

"... he called Jack from Annapolis ..."

Cassidy caught the tail end of her sister's words. "What?"

"Matt called Jack from the restaurant last night and asked him to page him so Matt could pretend he had a call to go on."

"Why would he do that?" Cassidy lost her rhythm and her needle plunged too deep into the quilt. "Shoot." She carefully drew the needle and thread back out.

"He wanted to leave." Then Becca laughed. "That sounds like something Charlotte would do, call and ask to be rescued from a bad date."

Cassidy jerked her hand out from beneath the quilt. "Ow." A bright red dot of blood bubbled on her fingertip.

"Stab yourself?"

"Yeah." She anchored her needle in the fabric with her other hand and stood up. "I don't want to bleed all over the quilt."

"Well, the backing's red so no one will notice."

She snorted as she retrieved a tissue and cleaned off her finger. "Nat would notice a spot of blood on red fabric. She has x-ray vision for that stuff." She took her seat at the quilt again. "That was kind of a jerk thing for Matt to do, leaving a date."

Hmm. He left that part of the story out when he called. She held her breath as she waited for Becca to elaborate and reveal whether she knew Cassidy had been at the same restaurant … or what happened later.

"Yeah, Jack was surprised too. He said Matt's been so stressed over everything—their mom, Serena—and he's been watching Cam and Mason a lot while Oliver's at the hospital. He told Matt he needed to just go out and get laid."

Cassidy's eyes widened. *"Jack* said that?"

Becca laughed again. "I know. Mr. Straight and Narrow."

"Well, apparently Matt didn't take his advice."

"No! That's what Jack said. Matt always does the opposite of what he suggests."

Cassidy began to breathe easier. Maybe Matt hadn't said anything to Jack about seeing her in Annapolis. "Is Jackie coming for a visit over Halloween?"

Becca shook her head, sadly. "No. Christmas. She'll be here for an entire week then."

Cassidy laid her head on her sister's shoulder. "Sorry."

"No worries. She wanted to go trick-or-treating with her friends. I totally get that." She sighed. "We're all making this up as we go."

Cassidy lifted her head. "You two are doing a great job with everything."

Becca shrugged, took one last needleful of stitches, and then stood to unlock the shop's front door. It was almost eleven o'clock. She flipped around the shop's "Open" sign and turned back to Cassidy. "The firehouse is doing their trick-or-treat party for kids again this year. Why don't you stop by after you close up? We could use all the help we can get."

Cassidy didn't miss the use of "we" by her sister. She and Jack were quickly becoming a single unit. Or the way she deftly steered the conversation away from her and Jack's daughter. Moving back to St. Caroline hadn't magically fixed everything in her sister's life.

"Sure. I can do that."

MATT WATCHED as the EMTs gracefully lifted the stretcher into the back of the ambulance. An elderly gentleman had run his car off the road. No damage to the car, save a flat tire, and seemingly no damage to the gentleman either. But the EMTs were taking him to the hospital to be checked out, just in case.

"Wonder what happened?" Elliott Parker said as the doors to the ambulance closed.

Matt turned toward the man standing by his side. Elliott Parker was an artist who owned a "gentleman's farm" in St. Caroline. Word was that he grew organic vegetables that he then made paintings of. Matt couldn't vouch for the accuracy of that rumor. Seemed a little silly to go to all the trouble of farming just so you could paint produce. But who knew? Rich people bought paintings and, as far as Matt could tell, many of them had more money than sense.

"I don't know," he answered the other man's question. "Might have fallen asleep. Distracted driving. At least he didn't run into one of your lampposts over there." He nodded toward the twin brick columns that flanked Elliott's long and winding driveway. At the head of the driveway rose an old stone farmhouse. Off to the right stood a cluster of small red barns beneath a cloud-dappled sky.

"Is your house on the historic register?" Matt asked.

"Nah. Old enough to be, I guess."

Matt's brain ran into a dead end on that conversational thread. Normally, one thing automatically sparked another thought, but old houses … *I got nothing.* He glanced over at his partner, Heath, who was leaning against the fire engine and talking on the phone. Heath had asked out Cassidy once, but she turned him down apparently. Heath was a decent enough sort but she had a reputation for turning up her nose at local guys.

Matt glanced back at Elliott in his paint-stained khaki pants, wrinkled button-down shirt, and leather flip flops. Elliott was a few inches taller than Matt and lean like a runner. Messy dark hair, blue eyes. He wondered whether Cassidy would go out with a guy like Elliott. He wasn't a local. He was from California.

"Heard the town's holding a winter festival," Elliott said. "Anything I can do to help? I did pencil portraits at the summer festival."

"You did?"

"Yup."

"You should probably talk to my co-chair, Cassidy Trevor, about something like that." Matt gazed out over the acres of Elliott's property as he mentally kicked himself for bringing up Cassidy. *Why not just give him her phone number, idiot! Make it real easy.* He squinted at a small grove of trees in the distance. *What you really need to do is stop thinking about Cassidy, period.*

The night in Annapolis was five days ago already, but his mind insisted on revisiting every little detail. No matter how hard he tried to refocus his attention, every damned thing reminded him of it. The bay doors at the station lifting made him think of the hotel's noisy air conditioner kicking on. His uncomfortable cot at the station took him right back to the uncomfortable chair and ottoman. He'd spent half that night awake, just watching her sleep from across the room.

Even the blue of Elliott's rumpled shirt reminded him of her blue toenails. Marina probably didn't have blue toenails. He'd bet his last dollar that she painted her toes that purplish-black shade so many women thought was chic and sexy. *That you used to think was chic and sexy.* The thought of Cassidy's blue toenails filled him with a crazy urge to rub her feet, kiss her instep—and he had never once wanted to kiss the arch of a woman's foot—slide his hands up her toned and tanned calves.

"I'll do that then," Elliott said. "Is she one of the quilting Trevors?"

Matt nodded. There was no reason for him to care if Cassidy

went out with Elliott Parker. She was an attractive woman and Matt was appreciative of that. Nothing more. Besides, he was supposed to leave the Trevor sisters alone.

The ambulance began to pull away, its lights flashing silently. *Lights.* Matt scanned the acres of land around Elliott's house.

"Actually, I do know a way you could help out with the winter festival."

CHAPTER 11

Cassidy parked her car in the long driveway of Elliott Parker's house and got out. She'd been past this old stone farmhouse hundreds of times in her life, but never closer than the road. At some point, the property must have belonged to someone who lived in St. Caroline full time—but not in Cassidy's lifetime. For as long as she could remember, it had belonged to one summer resident or another. Now it belonged to an artist whom she knew by sight from seeing him around town, but hadn't otherwise met.

She didn't pay much attention to summer residents anymore. As a teenager, she'd been borderline obsessed with them. Not their enviable lifestyles so much—although those were undeniably exotic and intriguing to a small town girl. What had fascinated Cassidy was their almost alien-like status, emissaries from "out there." What was also undeniable was the way she'd made an utter fool out of herself mooning over the teenaged sons of the summer families, hanging around the marina where their parents docked their boats and doing her best to dress like she was headed to Georgetown or William & Mary instead of Talbot College.

Lauren, on the other hand, had been more interested in the kids who attended the Chesapeake Inn's summer camp for disadvantaged kids. Lauren was always drawn, like a moth to flame, to the bad boy types. And wasn't it ironic that Lauren was the one who moved away from St. Caroline while Cassidy had been the one to stay?

"Hey Cass!"

She turned toward the sound of Matt's voice. Elliott Parker's house was surrounded by acres of lawn and field. A dozen or so people were convened over where the road wrapped around the corner of the property. A figure recognizable, even at that distance, as Matt stood waving his arms at her. She waved back and started off in the group's direction.

Matt had excitedly called her one evening last week to tell her that he had found the perfect location for the Christmas lights display. Right here, Elliott Parker's property. As she strode toward the yellowing field, she had to agree. This was a fantastic spot—far enough outside town to not bother any neighbors but easily accessible. The road that hugged the north and east sides of the property was flat and straight. The light display would be easy to see from the comfort of a car.

When she reached the group, the high school industrial arts teacher and his students were discussing materials. Looking at their bright, enthusiastic faces Cassidy's heart sunk anew. When Matt called last week, she didn't have the heart to tell him about her conversation with Mr. Wilson. There was no money for a lights display in the chamber of commerce budget. She was dreading this conversation, dreaded it so much she had dragged her feet on leaving the shop and driving here.

"Hey, there she is," Matt said, standing next to Elliott Parker.

Both men were dressed identically in jeans, running shoes and dark fleece jackets. As a cool late afternoon breeze blew across the field, Cassidy realized she had left her own jacket in the car. It was too far to bother going back for. But then both

Matt and Elliott took off their jackets and offered them to her. She looked back and forth between the two jackets, and the men laughed. She grabbed Matt's and slid her arms into it.

"Thanks."

Elliott put his back on, then held out his hand in greeting. "Elliott Parker. I've seen you around town, but I don't believe we've ever officially met."

Cassidy shook his hand. "I don't think so, either. Nice to meet you."

"So Sean and the kids have some great ideas." Matt cocked his head toward the teacher and his students.

"Like what?" Her heart sunk further. He was so enthusiastic about this, and she was going to have burst that bubble. And soon.

"The kids think they can build a Santa's workshop display. And Sean suggested a sort of lovers' lane walk beneath—" Matt stretched his arms above his head. "—a canopy of lights sort of thing. Plus an assortment of other lights. Trees, snowmen, gift boxes. What do you think?"

She sighed. "Umm ..."

"What?" Matt frowned.

"I spoke to Mr. Wilson. The chamber doesn't have a budget for something like this." She looked away to avoid the disappointment she was sure she'd see on Matt's face.

"Oh. I forgot about that." She didn't have to look at Matt to hear the wind rushing out of his sails.

"I can pay for it," Elliott offered. "It'll be my contribution to the festival."

Cassidy tilted her head as if she hadn't heard correctly. "But there won't be any ROI for you." She didn't see a way a Christmas lights display in a field would translate into painting commissions for him. If that was even how he made his money. Cassidy wasn't sure, now that she thought about it. Maybe he was just plain wealthy.

"Not everything needs a return on investment." Elliott's voice was soft but the note of reprimand in it raised Cassidy's hackles.

"The businesses in town need one."

"I'm not a business." Elliott glanced over at Sean and his students. "I can afford to donate building materials and lights. It would be my pleasure to do so."

"Well, thank you then," she said. "Certainly, a nice drive-by lights display will be a good draw for visitors."

Sean and his students walked them through some of the ideas they had. The students were confident they could recruit enough classmates to provide live elves in the Santa's workshop display.

"Lot of elves in town this year," Cassidy joked and nudged Matt with her elbow. He nudged her back. She caught the look that passed between him and Sean, just for a moment.

The meeting wrapped up after a short discussion on the need for generators to power the lights. Cassidy waved goodbye and headed for her car. It wasn't until she was halfway home that she realized she was still wearing Matt's fleece jacket. She muttered an unsavory swear word and pulled into a driveway to turn around.

MATT HANDED a twenty-dollar bill to the pizza delivery guy. "Keep the change."

He turned to carry his large pepperoni-sausage-mushrooms-olives-and-tomato pie inside when the glint of headlights caught his peripheral vision. He peered down the gravel road leading to his cabin. A moment later, a dark grey compact car pulled up. Cassidy's car. Not an unwelcome sight. Not at all. He had no idea what she was doing here, but at least she hadn't driven back to Elliott's place. The artist's discreet interest in her had not escaped Matt's notice.

She waved and crossed what passed for his front lawn, a few

JULIA GABRIEL

yards of scrubby grass with no walkway. The cabin he rented had been a duck hunting camp in years past. Due to St. Caroline's population and real estate growth, it was too close to town to serve that purpose anymore.

"I forgot to give you your jacket back," she said, unzipping it and shrugging the fleece material off her shoulders. "Here." She held it out, then noticed the pizza box in his arms. "Oh sorry. I'll carry it in."

Matt held open the cabin's screen door with his hip and allowed her to enter first. She draped the jacket over the arm of his couch.

"You didn't have to bring it back tonight," he said.

He set the pizza down on his beat-up wooden coffee table. *Distressed*, Becca had called it once.

"I wanted to do it while I was thinking of it," she replied. "But you've got company coming so I'll skedaddle." She turned toward the screen door.

"I don't have anyone coming."

She looked pointedly at the large pizza on the coffee table. "That whole thing's for you?"

"What? You don't think I can eat that whole thing by myself?"

"I ... I'm sure you can."

She was missing the joking tone in his voice, which didn't entirely surprise him. Cassidy was as buttoned up as his brother, Jack. Really, the two of them were the perfect couple. Two peas in a pod, as his mother used to say.

"I was joking, Cass."

"Oh." She looked momentarily confused before recomposing herself. "Sorry. It's been a long day."

"Hey, no worries. Why don't you stay and have a slice? Or two?"

"You can spare two slices?" Now she was teasing him.

"I always order a large so I have leftovers. I'm a bachelor guy. It saves me the trouble of trying to cook." He walked the ten feet across his small living room to the kitchen. He opened the refrigerator, then turned to her. "Beer? Soda? Or water?" He shrugged. "That's the extent of our options tonight."

He inwardly held his breath, fully expecting her to leave despite his invitation and offered refreshments. He didn't want her to leave. In fact, he had wanted to walk her back to her car at Elliott Parker's property, but Elliott kept talking and talking and talking …

"Beer, I guess."

Her words surprised him. She was going to stay. He pulled two bottles from the fridge and returned to the living room. He set one bottle on the coffee table, then used the hem of his shirt to twist off the cap of the other. He handed it to her.

"Here." He lifted the lid of the pizza box. "We should eat while it's hot." He looked back toward the kitchen. "Plates. We need plates. Sorry. I usually just eat from the box."

"Eating from the box is fine." Cassidy sat down on the couch.

"You sure? Because I can get plates." He probably had two clean plates. Probably. *Pretty sure.* Paper plates, maybe. He didn't generally entertain women at his cabin.

He watched as she neatly lifted a slice of pizza from the box, careful not to let any toppings slide off. He slowly lowered himself to the floor on the other side of the table, mesmerized by the slow, careful journey of the pizza to her lips. The sight of the tip of the pizza disappearing into her mouth was so freaking sexy, he could barely sit still. He wanted to grab the slice from her slender fingers and feed it to her himself. And he had no idea where that idea was coming from. Matt could be charming in the presence of women. Sexy, no doubt. Maybe even charismatic. But he didn't do romance. He didn't sell what he wasn't offering.

"So we should start getting active on social media right after Halloween," she said after half a slice.

"Okay." He pictured a calendar in his head. "Today's October nineteenth. I need to get cracking on that then."

She nodded and took a long swig of beer.

"Cass, you can tell me I need to hurry the hell up on stuff. I won't get upset."

"Why do you call me 'Cass?'"

"Doesn't everyone?"

"My family does."

He thought for a moment. "That's what Becca refers to you as. Cass. But I can call you whatever you want." He took a long drink of beer, too. "What's your middle name?"

"Ann."

"Cassidy Ann?"

She nodded. "I like that."

She laughed. "I'll let my parents know you approve. What's your middle name?"

"Dean. Matthew Dean Wolfe." He picked up a second slice of pizza. "So when I did the social media graphics for the fireman's carnival over the summer, I found a web site that has stock photos and templates. Okay if I use that again?"

"Sure. Winter photos? Holiday images?"

He nodded. "Maybe the chamber of commerce has some photos of St. Caroline I can use."

She smiled as she lifted the beer bottle to her lips. "Good idea."

He felt unaccountably pleased that she liked his idea. He watched as she downed another slice. Normally, he felt intimidated around really smart people but the more time he spent around Cassidy, the more comfortable he felt with her. In fact, three hours passed in as easy a time as he could remember experiencing. They ate more pizza. She drank another beer. He switched to soda. He got out his laptop and they worked on social media graphics together, sitting side by side on the couch. She helped him wrap up the leftover pizza in foil, then opened a third beer.

He'd never seen Cassidy this relaxed before. Had never even

imagined such a woman existed beneath her businesslike exterior. On second thought, maybe she and Jack weren't two peas in a pod after all. Maybe Becca managed to get his brother to let down his hair, so to speak, but Matt had never witnessed it.

Maybe she needs someone who can help her let down her hair.

Matt frowned and glanced down at the beverage in his hand. Yep. Soda, not beer. He shook the echo of the voice from his head.

"Are you okay?" Cassidy asked.

"Yeah. Sure." He looked at the screen on his laptop. "We got a lot done tonight."

"We did."

She leaned back into the sofa and Matt twisted his body to look at her. The urge to lean over and kiss her had his lips tingling.

Not after three beers.

There was that voice again. *Wasn't planning to,* he answered back. Good grief, he was talking to himself. *I need to get my medication checked.*

Yes, how long has it been since you saw Dr. Smythe?

"I can't believe you did that," Cassidy said.

"Did what?" Matt's heart skipped a beat at the possibility that he had said all that out loud. Living alone, he did sometimes just talk to himself.

"Had your brother page you in Annapolis so you could ditch your date."

"How'd you find out about that?"

"Becca told me."

Of course, Jack had mentioned it to Becca. "Great. So much for sibling loyalty." He was acutely aware of Cassidy studying him.

Lovers share things.

Matt scrubbed his hands over his face. What was going on here? His medication was off? He was having a bad reaction to something he ate? Or was it just that Cassidy Trevor was sitting next to him on his sofa, a place he'd never expected her to be?

"I didn't want to hurt her feelings," he explained.

Right on cue, the pager on his belt loop began to buzz. Mortified, he glanced down at the message.

"If you want me to leave, you can just say so. No need to fake a call."

"This is a real page. I wasn't on call tonight but someone just went home sick. I have to go in. I'm sorry."

"I should be getting home anyway."

She pushed herself up off the couch, then wobbled unsteadily on her feet. He reached out to grab her arm. Matt looked at the empty beer bottle on the coffee table. Her third.

"You're in no shape to drive home," he said.

"I'm fine."

He gave her an exasperated look. "Just stay here," he added. "Sleep it off. I'll be back around six."

"I can't stay at your place." She looked around for her purse.

"Why not? It's not like I'm going to be here." He followed her gaze to where her purse lay on the floor by the front door. She took three unsteady steps toward it, then Matt wrapped his arms around her waist and hoisted her up over his shoulder. He headed toward the short hallway that led to his bedroom.

"What are you doing?" she shrieked.

"You're staying here tonight. I don't want you having an accident on the way home. I do not want to answer that call."

He carried her to the bedroom and flipped her onto the bed. When she tried to get up, he pinned her with a glare. "If you're not here when I get back at six, I will be livid. Liv. Id." He repeated the last word, enunciating it clearly for effect.

"I can't spend the night here."

"Why not? We spent the night in a hotel together and nothing happened. And that was with me *in the room*."

A pained look flashed through her dark eyes.

Easy, boy.

"Because you'll tell Jack I'm here and then Jack will tell Becca and then everyone will think …"

"I won't tell Jack. I promise. I don't tell my brothers everything. Far from it, in fact." The pager vibrated on his belt loop. "Look, I have to go. Please just stay here until I get back. Don't make me handcuff you to the bed."

She rolled her eyes. "You're a firefighter. You're not issued handcuffs."

His eyes darted toward the bedside table. "There's a pair in the nightstand. Don't make me use them."

A short laugh burst forth from her lips, but she let her body flop back against his pillows. The realization that his pillows were going to smell like her hair bloomed in his brain.

"I've got to go, Cass. Use whatever you need. Toothpaste, whatever. I'll see you at six."

CASSIDY LISTENED to Matt's truck start up, then the gravel of the road crunching beneath his tires as he drove off. She was lying in the dark on Matt Wolfe's bed, certainly not the first woman to find herself here. She stared at a shadowy water stain on the ceiling, her brain too fuzzy to even contemplate moving her muscles. She'd had too much to drink—three beers, which was two more than her normal limit. Matt was right. She was in no shape to drive home and she was an idiot for even arguing the point with him. With an EMT, for pete's sake. He got to see firsthand the aftermath of people drinking and driving.

Still, spending another night with Matt was not a good look for her if anyone found out. Of course, strictly speaking, she was simply spending the night at Matt's place tonight. He wasn't here, a verifiable fact that anyone could double check with the fire department. *Still.* She sighed. This was how rumors got started and the last thing she wanted was for people to think she was now another notch on Matt Wolfe's bedpost.

She lifted her head to peer down the length of the mattress. Not that his bed had bedposts. In the dim light leaking in from the hallway, she could tell the room was pretty utilitarian, really. Mismatched furniture. Plaid curtains that looked like they'd outlasted several renters, not to mention several decades. Her head swooned as she peered over the edge of the mattress to check the floor for dirty laundry. There was nothing on the oak floor except a throw rug. It was your basic bachelor pad, but neat and tidy. It was hard to imagine Matt's mother raising sons that weren't neat and tidy.

Cassidy had known Angela Wolfe for years. Besides being a long time customer of Quilt Therapy, she'd been a close friend to her own mom. Of the three Wolfe boys—Oliver, Matt, and Jack—Matt had always been the wild child.

Speaking of wild child ... she remembered Matt's warning. *Don't make me use them.* She rolled her eyes, then rolled her body toward the nightstand. No way he owned a pair of handcuffs. This was St. Caroline. People weren't that kinky here. Not even Matt. She tugged on the drawer. Inside was the usual assortment of loose change, receipts, condoms, and ... a pair of handcuffs.

Whoa. That wasn't just an idle boast, after all. She lifted them out of the drawer, gingerly, like she was handling a live snake. She lay back on the bed and held them over her head, running her thumb over the soft purple velvet lining the interior of each cuff. These weren't standard issue police handcuffs. These were ... kinky sex handcuffs. Did Angie Wolfe know *this* about her middle child?

She held the cuffs against her wrist, imagining Matt using these on a woman. The gorgeous redhead from Annapolis came immediately to mind. Or ... she giggled at the next thought—of Matt himself handcuffed to his bed. Although ... she looked back toward the head of the mattress. There was nothing to attach the cuffs to, since Matt's bed had no bedposts.

She turned them around in her hands one more time, then set them down on the mattress beside her and closed her eyes. She'd take a quick nap—that would probably leave her okay to drive home.

Four hours later, she was awakened by her ringtone. She rolled over and swatted her hand about on the nightstand. Her hand came up empty. Confused, she sat up and looked around. *Oh right.* She wasn't at home.

The ringing started up again and she stumbled sleepily out to the living room. She grabbed the phone from her purse.

"Hello?" she mumbled into it.

"Cass! Omigod where are you?" It was Natalie. "Are you okay?"

"I'm fine—"

She was cut off by her sister's avalanche of concern. "Are you at the hospital? Where are you? You didn't have an accident, did you?"

"No, I'm not at the hospital. I'm at—" She slowly scanned Matt's spartan living room, realizing how bad the answer was going to sound. "I'm at Matt Wolfe's." She flinched in advance and waited for Natalie's reaction, which was delayed. Delayed a lot.

When her sister spoke again, all concern had vanished from her voice. "You slept with Matt Wolfe." It wasn't a question.

"No!"

"Then what are you doing at his place at three in the morning?"

"We met yesterday after work to go over some stuff for the festival. I ended up having too much to drink over pizza and ..."

"Uh huh."

"He's not even here, Nat. He had to go into the station hours ago. I was too buzzed to drive home so I stayed here to sleep it off." The buzz was totally slept off now, she thought. She couldn't be more wide awake if there was an intravenous line of coffee flowing into her arm. "I'm heading out now."

"Are you coming into work today?"

"Of course I am. Why wouldn't I? Mom has me on the schedule for today." She leaned over and picked up her purse, then looked around the room for her shoes. "I'll see you there."

CHAPTER 12

It was nearly eleven o'clock before Cassidy's mother spoke to her. Natalie was out in the main showroom, helping two regular customers choose fabrics for new projects. Becca was upstairs slicing Halloween novelty prints into long strips for the Girl Scout troop she was teaching quilting to. Cassidy was in the small office, finalizing numbers on the two quilting weekends they had scheduled for next year, when her mother appeared in the doorway. Cassidy looked up.

"Do you want to eyeball these numbers before I head over to the Inn?" she asked.

"Sure, I'll take a quick look." Michelle leaned over her daughter's shoulder and squinted at the computer screen. "Who are you meeting with?"

"Cassandra and Gina." Cassandra was the Chesapeake Inn's marketing director. Gina was the Inn's long-time pastry chef, newly promoted to catering manager. "Sterling wants them getting event details into the system earlier."

"I can understand that. We sprung last summer's event on them at the last minute We were lucky they could do it." Michelle scrolled down to the bottom of the document. "You're figuring on a hundred and twenty-five people again?"

Cassidy nodded. "That netted us about nine thousand dollars when all was said and done. We have more lead time on marketing this year, so I'm confident we can hit that attendance level again."

"Okay. That was a comfortable turnout for the Inn's reception room."

"Depending on how these two go, we could shoot for filling the ballroom the year after. Plus, the Inn's rates have gone up a bit."

Michelle straightened and stepped away from the desk. "Better to play it safe. We've only done one. The first might have been beginner's luck." She started to leave, only to turn back at the door. "You spent the night with Matt Wolfe, I hear."

This was her mother's real reason for coming back to the office. And the reason she hadn't spoken to Cassidy until just five minutes ago.

"At his house. Not *with* him. He was at the fire department. I had too much to drink. That's all." Cassidy was furious with her sister for ratting her out.

"That doesn't sound like you, having too much to drink."

Cassidy sighed audibly. "No. But it happened."

"It's a bad idea for you to get involved with Matt."

"I'm not involved with him."

"Maybe call someone for a ride home next time."

"There won't be a next time, alright?" Definitely not. She thanked her lucky stars that no one apparently knew about the night in the hotel. Matt was more discreet than Natalie, obviously.

"If the two of you break up, it will make things awkward for Becca and Jack."

"We won't be breaking up because there's nothing going on between us. Seriously, mom. I've known Matt my whole life. If he were going to be attracted to me, it would have happened by now." The look on her mother's face was still skeptical. She held up her hands as if in surrender. "I won't mess up their relationship. I promise."

At noon, Cassidy printed out her event projections and set off on the walk to the Inn, still fuming over Natalie stirring up a hornet's nest that didn't need to be stirred. Not to mention her mother's little lecture. Cassidy rolled her eyes at no one in particular as she turned into the Inn's long driveway. Of all the people in the world, she was the last person who needed to be warned about interfering in someone else's relationship. She was the responsible one in the family—the person who made sure the shop was stocked with merchandise in a range of price points, the person who negotiated harder with the Inn on dessert options, the person who worried about taxes and retirement account contributions until three in the morning.

And on top of all that? She was the last person in the entire town who was looking for a relationship right now. She had a crazy-hot date tonight—with her computer and her business school applications.

CHAPTER 13

$\mathcal{T}$he spacious community room at the St. Caroline fire station had been invaded by a horde of tiny aliens for the Halloween party. Also stormtroopers, superheroes, princesses, and witches. And a few costumes Cassidy couldn't identify. Herding the aliens and their brethren were zombie firefighters, their turnout pants and clunky boots topped with ripped and torn shirts. Some of them—Matt, for example, whom Cassidy was pointedly trying to avoid—wore shirts that were more shreds than actual fabric. There was also one zombie dalmatian mascot, Jack.

Cassidy stood behind the pumpkin golf game, where kids had to putt a golf ball into a jack o' lantern's gaping mouth. She sipped at a red plastic party cup of cider and surveyed the room. She, Becca, and a crew of firefighters' wives and girlfriends had spent three hours decorating the place. Tendrils of filmy white fabric dangled from the ceiling. Strategically placed fog machines hissed out grey steam beneath a soundtrack of creaking doors, howling wolves, and ominous-sounding footsteps. The zombie firefighters were enthusiastically hamming it up. Even Matt.

Cassidy wasn't paying any attention to Matt though. Absolutely not. It had been a week and a half since she'd spoken to Matt face to face, the night she spent at his cabin. Since then, they had communicated about the festival via text and email. That was proving to be sufficient—the festival planning was moving right along.

By eight o'clock the party was winding down. Halloween fell on a school night this year and eight o'clock seemed to be the witching hour, judging by the way parents were beginning to shepherd their kids—laden with their trick-or-treat bags of candy—toward the exit. Cassidy looked around for Becca and spotted her, in her Renaissance faire-style maiden costume, standing by the apple bobbing station. Natalie was off at a Halloween party with friends of hers, which was just as well. The atmosphere in their apartment was still a little frosty. In fact, Cassidy was still waiting for her sister to apologize for her loose lips.

She joined Becca at the giant apple bobbing pail. Only two apples remained floating in the water, suspicious bite marks marring the red skin, evidence of unsuccessful attempts to snare them.

"I'll stay and help clean up," she offered. She knew her sister was driving to Washington, DC in the morning to meet with a woman for whom she was doing a large quilt commission.

"Thanks."

Cassidy turned back to the pail of water. Just as she reached into it to grab the apples, she felt the weight of a head on her shoulder and warm breath on her ear.

"You're supposed to dunk your face in, not use your hands." Matt's words sent a puzzling shiver down her spine.

You knew you wouldn't be able to avoid him all night.

She held up one of the apples. "Looks like many people have tried to get this one and failed."

She felt his fingers weave their way into her hair, and the sensation was so delicious it took all her willpower not to lean back into his body. It had been ages since someone had touched her.

"Aww, come on."

His hand gently pushed her head toward the pail. Instinctively, her body froze. She dropped the apple and used her hands to brace herself against the table. In a flash, she was taken back to a long-ago day at the beach in Ocean City. She was eleven years old and happily swimming in the waves when she noticed how far she suddenly was from the shore. She swam toward the sand but with every stroke, she ended up further and further away. She was caught in a riptide. Her strokes grew more frantic as she tried to overcome the pull of the current. Her muscles burned with exhaustion and she slipped beneath the waves. Once, twice, a third time …

Matt's fingers slipped from her hair and his hands grasped her upper arms, the way the strong arms of the lifeguard that day had yanked her from the riptide and pulled her to shore. "Hey. I'm just playing. I wasn't going to really dunk you."

She nodded quietly and quickly plucked the apples from the water again. "I told Becca I'd help clean up so she can go home."

"I'm on cleanup duty too. Drop those apples back in there and help me carry this thing into the kitchen."

Together they lugged the heavy pail into the station's kitchen and dumped the water into the sink.

"Well, we got all but about three gallons of it." She looked ruefully at the puddle of water on the floor at their feet.

She yelped as Matt suddenly lifted her up and sat her on the countertop. He proceeded to mop up the water with a handful of paper towels.

"I'm still a little pissed that you left my place before I got home." He stood and tossed the soaked wad of towels into the trash. "And you didn't put my handcuffs away either." His smile softened the stern tone of his voice.

"Sorry. Natalie called in the middle of the night, frantic because I wasn't home and then ..."

"And then what?" He stood in front of her, but made no move to help her back down off the counter.

And then everyone got mad because I spent the night at your place."

He frowned. "Why would they get mad? It was the prudent thing to do."

Cassidy couldn't bite back her laugh in time. "Prudent, eh?" She took a long, deep inhale, then shook her head. "My mother is convinced I slept with you."

His eyes widened in surprise, then narrowed in mirth. "Oh the horror. Sex with Matt Wolfe. What could be worse?"

"Ruining Jack and Becca's relationship, apparently."

Now it was Matt's turn to laugh. "Okay, Jack and Becca weren't there. That's way too kinky."

Cassidy flicked her fingertips at his hard bicep. A bicep that was covered only with shreds of fabric. In fact, his entire chest ... and shoulders ... and abdomen ... hard abdomen ... were barely covered by his zombie tee shirt. "Says the guy with handcuffs in his nightstand," she joked, to cover up the effect his barely-covered body was having on *her* body.

He grabbed her flicking fingers. "But seriously, how were you going to ruin their relationship?"

"You'd dump me or I'd dump you, and that would make things awkward for them ... something like that."

Matt snorted and laced his fingers into hers, a gesture that wasn't exactly tamping down the simmering chaos in her body. "Pretty sure that if Jack had to choose between me and Becca, I'd be on the losing end. Becca, on the other hand, might very well choose you."

"I think the point that was pressed home to me was to not make that choice necessary."

Heavy footsteps sounded outside the kitchen and Cassidy

snatched her hand back. Matt quickly lifted her off the countertop and set her on the floor. Chief Wolfe poked his head into the room.

"Oh there you are, Mattie. The guys ordered pizza, if you want some. You're welcome to have some, too, Cassidy."

Cassidy shook her head. "I need to get home, but thank you."

"Thank *you* for helping out tonight. We appreciate it."

When his father was gone, Matt turned his attention back to her. "We're allowed to be friends, Cass. If Jack and Becca's relationship can't withstand someone else's friendship, then there's not enough there to begin with."

She started walking toward the door. He fell into step beside her, then reached out and stopped her. "Hey. What happened out there when you thought I was about to dunk you? Which I wasn't, by the way. I would never do that to someone."

"I almost drowned when I was a kid. I got caught in a riptide and didn't know how to get out. I can't stand having my face under water."

He cupped her face in his palms. "You have to tell me this stuff, Cass."

"Why?"

"Because we're friends."

Cassidy hurried through the community room, past the zombies scarfing down pizza. Matt kept up with her, stride for stride, following her all the way out to her car in the station's parking lot.

"We are friends, right?" he asked.

"Yes. Just friends." She unlocked her car and got in. Matt waved as she backed out of the lot and pointed the car toward home.

Just friends. Except there was a very un-friend-like vibe humming through her veins at the moment—and the utter pointlessness of that couldn't be clearer.

A year from now, she wasn't going to be here in St. Caroline.

She'd be in business school somewhere, wherever she got in. She had her short list of schools. North Carolina, Texas, Indiana, Tennessee, Michigan. She'd get her mom and sisters through the peak summer season at Quilt Therapy next year, but then she would head off for the fall semester. And she wasn't sure she'd be coming back.

BACK INSIDE, Matt grabbed the last two slices of pizza and a paper plate, then cornered his brother. "Did you know Cassidy almost drowned when she was a kid?"

Jack plucked a salty slice of pepperoni from his own plate and popped it into his mouth. "Yeah." He chewed and swallowed. "We asked her to go kayaking with us one weekend, but she declined. Becca says she's terrified of water."

"Huh. I would never have guessed that."

"Me either. She always seems so in control." Jack bit off the tip of his slice. "Becca worries about her, actually."

"Why's that?"

"She says Mrs. Trevor and Natalie rely on her too much to run the shop."

Matt thought for a moment. "Yeah, she doesn't seem to have much of a life outside of their business, does she?"

CHAPTER 14

$\mathscr{T}$he night of the conference soccer championship was as damp and chilly as the mood in the stands at St. Caroline High School ... and on the field. It had drizzled on and off throughout the afternoon. Even now, the dark sky beyond the bright temporary stadium lights was shadowed with ever darker clouds.

Matt and Sean watched the team warm up on the field. Anyone, including the opposing team, could see that their hearts weren't in it tonight. Conspicuously absent from the St. Caroline sideline was Ben Wardman. His absence was so strongly felt by everyone on the team that there might as well have been an empty wheelchair sitting there.

Ashley Wardman called yesterday to say that Ben was transported to a hospice facility. There was no hiding or sugarcoating what that meant. The end was near. As he watched the boys make half-hearted shots on goal, Matt wondered whether any of them had ever lost anyone close. He doubted it. He certainly hadn't, at their age. His Uncle Jack, a firefighter, had died on the job before Matt was born. Uncle Jack was often an invisible presence in the Wolfe household—his death had always colored his mother's view of firefighting. And after Matt's ADHD was diagnosed at the age of eight, his mother suspected that Uncle Jack—her twin —had also suffered from ADHD. But Matt had no personal memories of him.

He knew what these boys were about to go through, however. Since his mom's death, his own heart felt glue-sticked together.

He turned to Sean. "Let's call them in. Time for a pep talk."

"St. Caroline!" Sean shouted. "On the sideline!"

The team began a slow jog toward them.

"Faster! Come on, guys!" Matt added.

"So," Matt began when the boys were huddled on the sideline. "Coach Ben is not with us tonight. How do we feel about that?"

The boys spent a long moment looking at their knees, their cleats, at anything but Matt. Finally, there was a quiet "sad." Some murmured agreement and nodding, then came a louder "mad."

"I'm mad, too," Matt said. "Mad. As. Hell. This sucks, doesn't it?"

"It's not fair," another boy added.

"No, it's not fair. Not at all." Matt looked each boy in the eye, in turn. "Coach Ben deserves to be at this game. He deserves to *win* this game. *I* don't deserve this championship. Coach Sean here doesn't deserve this championship. It's Ben Wardman who has put years of time and effort into the St. Caroline soccer program." He could see some chests begin to swell with pride. "I want you to go out there and channel all your anger, all the unfairness of this suck-ass situation, into winning this title for Coach Ben. Leave it all out there on the field tonight."

Heads were nodding, slowly at first and then more vigorously.

"Alright everybody," Sean chimed in. "Coach Ben on three. One, two, three!"

"COACH BEN!"

The first half of the game proved to be one step forward, two steps back. The boys would play brilliantly for awhile, then the weight of what they were trying to do seemed to drag them back into some sporting quicksand. One mistake, one bad pass or missed shot, and they fell apart for minutes on end before pulling it back together. Matt and Sean paced the sideline, shouting encouragement and direction.

When the other team called for subs, Sean came up next to Matt and said in a low voice so the boys on the bench wouldn't overhear, "Ashley's here."

Matt lifted his gaze from the field for a moment to scan the St. Caroline half of the stands. Sure enough, there was Ashley Wardman's dark head partially obscured by the video camera she held, following the ball as expertly as any coach. *Of course.* She was filming the game for Ben. *No pressure.*

Matt looked back at the field just in time to see St. Caroline block a shot with less than a minute to go before halftime.

"Yes! That's the way, St. Caroline!" Sean shouted.

But Matt saw the next play unfolding in his head as soon as it began. The blocked shot bounced off the heel of Danny Conway and right onto the foot of an opposing player. Two neat passes later and the ball swished into the goal, St. Caroline's goalie staring dejectedly at it. The ref blew the whistle, signaling the half was over. St. Caroline was down by two.

"We got to get them focused," Sean muttered as the boys came off the field.

Focused. Not exactly Matt's forte.

"If we don't send Ashley home with the championship ball, I will drink myself into a stupor tonight," Sean added.

The championship ball.

"Guys, gather round!" Matt yelled as the players grabbed their water bottles and guzzled. "We're down by two," he continued. "We are not out of this." He paused a moment to give the boys a moment to hydrate. "Okay everyone, put down your bottles. Hold your hands out." He mimed the gesture. "Close your eyes. Pretend you're holding the championship ball in one hand. In the other hand, you have a marker. With that marker, you are signing your name on the championship ball." He watched as the boys signed their names in the air. "Do it again. *Feel* what that's like, because forty minutes from now we are signing that ball and sending it home to Coach Ben."

The ref tooted his whistle. Halftime was over. The boys ran onto the field with new energy.

"You are a genius," Sean said to Matt.

"Tell me that when the game's over. And cross your fingers." But Matt had a good feeling about things. When he needed to focus, it helped to visualize what he wanted to happen, to imagine it in his muscles.

Forty minutes later, the St. Caroline parents and fans erupted into a giant cheer as the ref blew the final game-ending whistle. The boys had pulled off the win, seven to six. Matt watched the boys celebrate, jumping and high-fiving each other in jubilation. He hung back, allowing them their well-deserved moment in the sun. He remembered being their age and living completely in every moment. There was no rush to get to the next day or next week. At twenty-six, Matt found it difficult—no, make that damn near impossible—to live in the present that way.

He watched the boys sign the game ball, then Sean inked his name on it. Sean held the ball and marker out to Matt, so he could sign too. As he scribbled his signature across the scuffed white leather, he thought back to the things he had wanted when he was in high school. To be a firefighter. To be good at something that wasn't a constant struggle between distraction and attention. To kiss Cassidy Trevor.

He handed the ball and marker back to Sean. The boys were dispersing to parents and friends. Life looked a lot shorter to Matt these days, and the idea that you could want things without ever getting them was all too real.

He gathered up the forgotten water bottles, emptied them, and stuffed them into the big team duffel bag while Sean carried the championship ball across the field to Ashley. He knew Sean would want to go out for a burger and beers to celebrate. Matt preferred to go home, but it was the last game of the season and he had no good excuse for bailing. So he closed his eyes for a moment and visualized having a good time. When he opened them, Sean was back.

"Ready to celebrate?" He clapped Sean square between the shoulder blades. "I think there are some beers with our names on them."

CHAPTER 15

"Whoa. That's a lot of food." Cassidy looked at the two bags in Matt's arms. "Trying to fatten me up for Thanksgiving?"

Matt kicked the door of her apartment closed behind him and followed her into the small kitchen. "Well, I know a few ways to help you burn off the calories later."

Cassidy's eyes widened and then she laughed. "Did you just make a sexually suggestive ... suggestion to me?"

Matt set the two bags onto the counter. "I did."

He casually tapped the smaller of the two bags, as though making a sexually suggestive suggestion to her was just par for the course. And maybe it was these days. Certainly, they were spending a lot of time together, working on the winter festival—enough time that it felt like they were friends. Or something close to friends.

"This needs to go in the freezer. Dessert." He opened her freezer door like he lived there, rearranged a few plastic containers of frozen leftovers, and then slotted his bag into the newly open space.

"What? You're not even going to show me what it is?" She stuck out her lower lip in a playful pout. "What if I don't like it?"

"I have it on good authority that it's one of your favorites." He mocked her pout, then made an exaggerated show of checking out her outfit. "Glad to see you dressed up tonight."

Cassidy looked down at her outfit—black leggings and an oversized Talbot College sweatshirt—and then at his. *Oh.* Matt wasn't wearing his usual ensemble of dark grey cargo pants and black St. Caroline fire department tee shirt. Instead, he was wearing nice jeans, a plaid shirt, and docksider shoes. She was about to comment on it, but then swallowed the impulse. She wasn't sure what to make of the fact that he was a little dressed up tonight. She didn't want to embarrass him or come across as though she were complaining. Because she most definitely was not. He looked very nice.

"What?" Matt said. Then he rubbed his jaw with his thumb and forefinger. "Oh, you're staring at this." His chin and jawline were covered with a day's worth of stubble. "I'm not on call tonight so I didn't have to shave."

"It looks fine. I mean, it's just … different. That's all." It was a good look on him, she thought. A sexy look. It was the way he had looked in Annapolis, when he'd been on a date. When he'd slept across the room from her.

He began pulling boxes and containers from the other, larger bag—releasing the delicious aromas of ginger and curry and rice. Thai food. "I love Thai food." Had she told him that? She didn't think so. "How'd you guess?"

"I didn't guess. Becca told me you'd do almost anything for green curry." He waggled his eyebrows.

"*Almost* anything. But the only Thai place I know of around here is Lotus Thai on Kent Island."

"Yep. That's the only one I know of, too."

"You drove that far to get this?"

He shrugged. "Plates?"

She pulled two clean plates and some flatware from the dishwasher. That was a non-answer if ever she'd heard one.

"Your sister not here tonight?" He looked around.

"Nope." She pulled apart the flaps of the cardboard rice container. "She and Charlotte went to Philadelphia for the weekend. They have tickets to the Simone Adkins concert there." She scooped rice onto one of the plates and then pushed the container toward Matt.

"Am I going to get you in trouble being here unchaperoned?" He scooped rice onto his plate, too.

"I haven't told anyone you're here but if they find out, we're working on festival stuff. We have a lot to nail down tonight. If we met at Two Beans or a restaurant, we'd take up a table for hours." She shrugged. She and Matt had been meeting in public places twice a week since Halloween. There were a lot of moving parts to the festival, and she wasn't sure her mother really appreciated that. This wasn't just a weekend quilting retreat at the Chesapeake Inn where the Inn's events manager handled most of the details. Cassidy was even starting to take a certain perverse pleasure in all of the details of the festival. She was good at this sort of thing, and it was a welcome change of pace from the sameness of Quilt Therapy. There were so many things her mom and Natalie could be doing differently—more profitably—but it was as though moving the shop to a new location was as much change as the two of them could handle in one year.

Cassidy, on the other hand, loved change. Relished it. In the Trevor family, she was the "efficient but easily bored" daughter—also the one who didn't understand why being easily bored was a bad thing.

She picked up her plate and headed for the coffee table, where her laptop sat open amidst printouts of calendar pages and to-do lists. "We'll have to eat here," she said apologetically. "We use the dining room table for quilting." She nodded toward the table covered with Natalie's cutting mat and stacks of fabric.

"No worries. The coffee table is where I eat at home, too." He took a seat on the sofa next to her. "Though not because I quilt."

"Some men quilt," she pointed out.

"I'm all thumbs." He wiggled his fingers in the air. "It's my poor ..." He stopped.

"Poor what?" she pressed.

"Oh ... never mind."

But she knew what it was. After Becca mentioned that Matt had ADHD, Cassidy had done a little online research into the condition. Fine motor skills could be a challenge for people with ADHD.

"What's that?" he asked, leaning in to peer at her laptop screen. "College applications?"

Shoot. She hadn't closed out her business school folder.

"Yeah. I'm applying to business schools. You can't tell anyone, though."

"You mean like getting an MBA?" He turned his head to look at her.

She nodded and pulled the laptop closer, clicking the window shut. "But you can't tell anyone," she repeated.

"Why not?" He bit into a crispy spring roll.

"Because no one knows yet. I don't want to spend the next six months having everyone try and talk me out of it."

He chewed and swallowed. "Why would they do that?"

She pushed curry-covered rice around her plate with her fork. "Because I won't be around to run the shop."

"Well, how complicated is that?" he said, then quickly back-tracked. "I mean, I'm not trying to say your job is easy or anything ..."

"It's not that it's complicated. It's that no one else likes to do the part that I do. The accounting, the marketing, the making sure we're making money in any given month." She gave a rueful grimace, then opened one of her festival spreadsheets.

"I think it's great that you want to go back to school, Cass."

She shrugged, a gesture he mimicked in an exaggerated motion.

"Why are you shrugging off my compliment?" he asked, popping the rest of the spring roll into his mouth.

"I'm glad you think it's great, but no one else will feel that way."

"So? You get to decide whether you want to go back to school or not." He looked over the calendar printouts scattered across the coffee table. "Is that why you don't date anyone in town? Because you know you're leaving?"

"Mostly, yes," she admitted, lifting a forkful of curried rice to her lips, then enjoying the burn of the spice against her tongue. "What's the point of getting serious with someone in St. Caroline if I'm not going to stay? That would just be one more person trying to talk me out of leaving."

"You need a friend with benefits," he mused, still poring over the notes she'd scribbled on the calendar pages.

"Yeah well, not a lot of people have volunteered for that job." She brushed off the suggestion, then changed the subject. "So I got commitments from the middle and high school chamber singers—plus about half of the choir at the Episcopal Church—to lead the caroling on Friday evening. Are we still using your brother's boat to bring in Santa?"

They spent the next two hours going over the festival's schedule in minute detail, making lists and more lists, jotting down things to double-check and blanks to be filled in. But for the most part, things were coming together. The flyers he had designed were back from the printer and hanging in shop and restaurant windows all over town. Advertisements had been submitted to newspapers in all of the surrounding towns and press releases sent to all the local radio stations. A file of social media graphics had been uploaded to the chamber of commerce web site.

At eight o'clock, Cassidy took off her glasses and rubbed her tired eyes. "What are we forgetting?"

"Besides dessert?"

"Oh!" She jumped up off the sofa. "Sorry! I forgot that you brought dessert."

Matt stood, too, and placed a hand on her arm. "I'll get it."

She sank back into the sofa and craned her neck to watch Matt retrieve his mystery dessert from the freezer. He pulled a round cardboard container from the white paper bag. "Is that ice cream?" she called over.

"Hey! No peeking."

He angled his body to block her view of what he was doing. When he turned around, he was holding two cereal bowls filled with ice cream, a spoon nestled against the scoops in each. As he got closer to the sofa, Cassidy could see the small chocolate chunks in the ice cream.

"Is that mint chocolate chip?" she asked, her mouth watering.

"It is, ma'am." He held one bowl out to her. "Becca said you would absolutely put out for this flavor," he added and then laughed at the momentary look of startlement on her face. "I'm just kidding, Cass. You know she'd never say something like that." He slid a spoonful of ice cream into his mouth. "But watching you blush was totally worth it."

She smiled and shook her head at him, then dug her spoon into the cold ice cream in her own bowl. Matt's joking nature often took her by surprise, but she liked it all the same. Increasingly, she was able to relax around him and she was self aware enough to know that was a good thing for her. It was no secret to her that most people thought she was way too uptight.

She downed her bowl of ice cream, enjoying the contrast between the sharp mint flavor and the sweetness of dark chocolate. She felt his eyes on her, close and intense. Sometimes she saw the evidence of his ADHD—in the way his attention was easily diverted or when she realized he had completely missed the last several minutes of a conversation—but there was often a watchfulness about him, too. He might only be paying attention to what was going on around him fifty percent of the time. But when he *was* paying attention, it seemed as though not much escaped his notice.

"So when was the last time you had a date?" he asked.

And then there were the times when he seemed to pay too much attention to things. Like right now. She laughed off his question to cover up the fact that she really didn't want to answer it.

"I don't know."

"Guesstimate."

She thought for a moment, counting back the months. *Whoa.* There were a lot of months to count.

"It's been that long?" he prodded, his voice dipping back down to what she recognized by now as his joking register.

She rolled her eyes in response. "At least a year."

"A year?" His eyes widened in surprise—mock or genuine, she couldn't tell. "What about Dave?" he added.

"Dave who?"

"In Texas."

She frowned, then her memory kicked in. "Oh. Dave, your buddy? The one you tried to foist off on me?"

"I wasn't trying to *foist* him off on you. He asked me to introduce you. The two of you disappeared after awhile."

"We didn't disappear *together*." She studied Matt's face, trying to read his thoughts. "Seriously? You thought we hooked up? He went to the men's room at one point and I used that as my opportunity to escape."

"So it's been a year since you had a date. How long since you slept with someone?"

"And are you going to answer these same questions?" Though Cassidy wasn't sure she wanted to know the answers.

"If you want to know. I'm an open book."

133

Cassidy couldn't hold back the snort of laughter. "People always say that. 'I'm an open book. Ask me anything.'" She shook her head. "I'm not an open book." In fact, she couldn't think of anyone she knew who fit that description. Certainly no one in her own family was an "open book."

"So you're not going to tell me when you last had sex?"

"It's been about two years, okay?" She struggled to keep the note of exasperation from her voice. It was embarrassing to admit how pathetic her social life was.

Matt let loose with a long, low whistle. "Two years? Don't you miss it?"

She thought for a long moment. *Did* she miss it? It was a question she was generally too busy to ponder. She missed that feeling of being attracted to somebody. She missed having someone to do things with, someone who wasn't one of her sisters. But did she miss sex? It had always seemed like so much anticipation with never quite the payoff she wanted.

"Not really," she answered. "I think it's probably overrated."

Matt's eyes widened again in surprise, and this time she could tell the shock was genuine. "Really? I love sex." He looked at her like she was an alien species.

"Of course you do. You're a man."

"I have some buddies who don't think it's all it's cracked up to be. It depends on whether you've had a good lover or not."

"So are you a good lover?"

His grin stretched from ear to ear, exposing his canines. She'd never noticed that he had "fangs" before. Her tongue ran over the points of her own fangs. She was the only Trevor who had them.

"Well, not to brag or anything, but I haven't had many complaints."

Cassidy laughed loudly. "Well, not to burst your bubble or anything, but I've never complained directly to a man about the quality of the sex we just had." She let her body sink back into the cushions of the sofa. "It's easier just to fake it and let him think he's a stud."

"You wound me, Cassidy Trevor."

She was back to being unable to tell whether the look of mild injury on his face was real or feigned. "Well, I do miss kissing," she said, by way of rerouting—and softening—the conversation a bit. "I really miss kissing."

"I could kiss you. End your dry spell."

She looked at him, looked at his lips. She'd be lying if she said she hadn't spent any time in recent weeks thinking about what it would be like to kiss Matt. He was an attractive man and she was a woman. A woman starved for affection and male attention. Just because sex was overrated didn't mean her body didn't crave a man's touch.

"Sure," she heard her voice saying. "Sure, loverboy. Show me what you got."

He hesitated for a moment—just long enough to make Cassidy think he wasn't actually going to do it—then leaned over and gently cupped her cheeks in his hands. She could feel the calluses on his palms. Matt was a man who used his hands for a living. Used his entire body, for that matter—and the thought of that sent a slow rolling shiver down her spine.

"Relax, Cassidy. I don't bite."

She wasn't so sure of that.

He brushed his lips against hers, so lightly it barely registered in her consciousness—although it was registering in lots of places outside her consciousness.

"I'll stop. Just say the word." His breath was warm on her ice cream-chilled lips. Another thing that was registering in all sorts of places that really should remain unregistered. Unregistered with Matt Wolfe, at any rate.

"If you stop, I'm going to spontaneously combust."

"Where's your fire extinguisher?" He pressed his lips just a degree more firmly against hers.

Cassidy let her lips part. "No idea."

His lips nudged at hers. "Most people don't know how to use one anyway."

"Are you implying that I don't?" She felt her lower lip catch in his front teeth.

"You're kissing a fireman. If you catch on fire, I'll put you out." The pressure of his lips was harder now. "Just not right away."

The full-blown kiss that followed proved to be the most expert kiss Cassidy had ever experienced, a kiss that somehow managed to make itself felt over every inch of her skin. When he was through, even her pinky toes were tingling.

"Dry spell officially over," he whispered as he pulled his lips away.

Over indeed.

She heard a soft buzzing, one that was distinct from the buzzing in her ears.

"Shoot," Matt muttered and leaned over to glance at his phone, lying on the coffee table. Cassidy spotted the name on the screen as he picked it up. Tim Wolfe. His father.

"Hey dad."

Cassidy stacked his empty ice cream bowl inside hers and carried them to the kitchen, to give him privacy for his conversation. She was a little dazed by what had just happened. It was a wonder she didn't pass out on the tiled floor. Matt was a certified EMT, of course, so 911 was sitting in her living room.

As she bent to load the bowls into the dishwasher, she suppressed a tiny smile. There were probably plenty of women who would fake passing out just so they could call 911 and have Matt Wolfe show up to rescue them. After that kiss, Cassidy was contemplating the idea herself. When she straightened back up, Matt was standing right there. She let out a startled yelp.

"I have to go. I'm sorry," he said. "Email me a copy of the festival schedule so I have it, okay?"

Gone was the teasing, flirty Matt of a few minutes ago. She began to wonder whether she had imagined the kiss, even.

"Will do." She watched as he walked to the door of her apartment. His movements were quick, but he wasn't moving like he was rushing out to a fire. "Is everything okay?"

His hand was on the doorknob, rotating it. Several inches of light from the hallway beyond spilled into her apartment. He turned to look back at her, his face practically a blank mask. "Serena woke up."

THE GARAGE DOOR on Oliver's house was open when Matt parked his truck at the curb. He and Serena bought the house two years ago, a freshly-built three-bedroom Cape Cod in this suburban-style subdivision on the edge of town. Even in the dark, Serena's influence was evident. Window boxes hung on the porch railing, their glossy white paint matching the porch swing that creaked gently in the night's cool, dark breeze. A crafty wooden sign hung on the front door, the words "bless our home" painted in fancy letters. In the back, hidden from Matt's view at the moment, was a small fenced yard with a wooden playset he had helped Ollie assemble for the boys.

From the shadows of the open garage emerged his brother's tall form. At thirty, Oliver was the eldest Wolfe brother. He was only four years older than Matt—still, Matt had never felt particularly close to him. He had always been much closer to Jack. Oliver was the strong, silent type. He kept his own counsel. The consensus in St. Caroline was that if anyone could withstand the stress of a situation like the one Ollie found himself in, it would be Ollie.

Matt wasn't so sure. Everyone needed an outlet for stress, and he'd never been able to tell what Oliver's outlet was.

He strode up the gently inclined driveway to meet his brother. "Good news, eh?" he said.

Oliver shrugged. "Maybe. Closest thing to good news we've had so far."

Matt gave his brother a quick man-hug, as quick as Ollie would tolerate. "Give her our love. Do the boys know?"

Oliver took a step back toward the garage. "No. I don't want to get their hopes up. I want to see how she's really doing first. They're asleep, though."

"Makes sense, man. Well, get going. I'll hold down the fort here." Matt stood along the edge of the driveway as Oliver backed his SUV out of the garage and into the street. When the red taillights disappeared at the end of the block, Matt went into the house through the garage, closing the door behind him.

As soon as he stepped into the kitchen, he could tell the boys were not asleep. The house crackled with their energy. He hung his jacket on a wooden peg, kicked off his shoes, then took the stairs two at a time to the second floor. Cam and Mason shared a bedroom at the end of the hall. He paused outside the partially open door. Inside, Cam's sobs were punctuated by gasps of "I want to go with da-a-a-d ... I want to see momm-y-y-y."

The sound of Mason, only two years older, trying to comfort Cam broke Matt's heart.

"Shhh, Cammie. We'll get to go in a few days. Tomorrow, maybe. Shhh."

Mason sounded way older and far more mature than any seven-year-old should. Matt knew he wouldn't have been capable of comforting Jack when they were kids. Hell, he wasn't capable of comforting Jack—or anyone—now, and everyone in the Wolfe family was grieving hard over the loss of Angie Wolfe.

Matt pushed the bedroom door completely open to find both boys snuggled into Cam's twin bed. He took in Mason's worried expression and Cam's tear-streaked cheeks. "Is there room in there for me?" He expected Mason to shoot him a skeptical look, but instead his older nephew scooted back toward the headboard and flipped the covers open.

Matt climbed in and tucked the sheet and quilt—made by his mother—around the three of them. "This is cozy."

"Cam likes it when I sleep in his bed," Mason explained.

Cam sniffed and Matt couldn't discern whether the noise was one of protest or acquiescence to his brother. Probably a little of both. They were brothers, after all. Most things required at least a token protest. He wondered whether Cassidy and her sisters were that way.

"Did mom wake up?" Mason asked.

"I don't know," Matt lied, respecting his brother's desire not to get the boys' hopes up.

"Because dad left here like a bat outta hell."

"Excuse me?" Matt lifted one eyebrow and glanced at Cam, who was trying hard not to giggle. "Who uses that phrase around you?" Though Matt knew exactly where they'd heard it.

"Nana used to say that," Cam rescued his older brother. He nodded his small head emphatically. "Like, all the time."

Matt gave a wry smile. His mother had been known for her salty language sometimes. For an instant, he could almost hear her rolling laugh, faint in his memory. "Yes, she did. I just didn't realize she said it around you two."

"Mommy liked Nana," Cam continued. "I think she's visiting her now. Is that why she's asleep? She's visiting Nana?"

Matt thought for a moment, wondering what Oliver had been telling the boys about Serena. It seemed unlikely he had equated their mother's situation with the death of their grandmother. Oliver's head was all over the place since the accident, which was why he was on a leave of absence from the fire department, but Matt couldn't imagine his head was that out of whack.

"No, your mom isn't visiting anyone." Matt took a quiet, deep inhale. "She's just been sleeping so her body can heal." He decided to change the subject. "Thanksgiving is coming up. You know what that means."

Mason looked at him with squinted eyes, as if trying to gauge whether this was a trick question or not. "What?"

"After Thanksgiving, you need to get your list for Santa together."

That perked up Cam.

"And you know what else?" Matt continued. "When Santa comes to St. Caroline this year to pick up the lists, he's coming in on your dad's boat."

"Seriously." Mason's response was as flat a statement of skepticism as Matt had ever heard.

"Yup. Seriously."

"Will Jackie be here to see Santa?" Cam asked.

"I don't think so. It would be a long trip for her before school is out."

"What about Christmas?" Mason asked.

"It is my understanding that she is coming over Christmas, to stay with Uncle Jack and Becca." Mason and Cam had happily and readily adopted their new cousin.

"When are you going to have kids?" The tone of Mason's voice made his question sound more akin to an accusation.

"I don't know. I should probably get married first, huh?" Marriage. Matt had no idea if that would ever happen. Women generally wanted children at some point after "I do"—and Matt wasn't sure that was a good idea in his situation. Not that he didn't like kids. He freaking *loved* kids. He spent as much time with his nephews as he could. As much as they would tolerate, anyway.

But ADHD could be inherited, and Matt hated the thought of passing it on to children of his own.

"Mom said you're a playboy." Cam's unexpected words yanked Matt back into the present and out of his uncertain marital prospects.

"She did, eh?" What was he supposed to say to that?

"I want to be a playboy," Cam elaborated. "Instead of having to go to preschool all the time."

Matt chuckled. He could tell by the look on Mason's face that his older nephew had a better sense of what a playboy really was.

"Well, school is important. So is sleep. Nana used to tell me that the sooner I went to sleep, the sooner morning would come."

"Dad uses that line on us, too." Mason shifted on the pillows, yawning.

Matt read the boys a bedtime story, a book about cheeky train engines. The lights were off in the room and the dim light from the hallway wasn't enough to read by, but Matt had this particular story memorized from all the time he'd been spending with the boys lately. The boys had the story memorized by now too—a comforting and familiar ritual between the three of them.

He could tell Mason was bored, but restraining himself for the sake of his little brother. This wasn't the first time Matt was impressed by Mason's behavior as a big brother. He'd rather be listening to a story about superheroes or light sabers. Not that Matt could blame him. Matt and Jack had played out some epic light saber battles when they were Mason's age. *Lose you will.*

By the time he turned the last page, Cam was fast asleep, his small body heavy against Matt's chest. Mason reached over to support Cam's head while Matt eased out of the bed. Together they laid Cam back onto the smushed pillow. Mason pulled the covers more snugly over himself and his brother.

"I'll be downstairs," Matt mouthed to him. "Goodnight, buddy."

Mason nodded at him solemnly, as though they were peers when it came to taking care of Cam. Sadly, they probably were, Matt thought as he gently closed the boys' bedroom door. Mason was shouldering more responsibilities than a normal seven-year-old should. Maybe the news about Serena really was good this time. He hoped that it was.

Downstairs the house was as neat as a pin, except for ... *ouch.* Matt bit back an oath as a Lego piece bit into the sole of his foot. He leaned over and pulled it off his sock. In the center of the living room, a fleece throw blanket covered the carpet. The blanket, in turn, was covered with the boys' sizable collection of Legos—more evidence of his brother's neatness. The boys could have their Legos out but the pieces had to remain on the blanket.

Matt wasn't surprised that Oliver responded to stress by doubling down on maintaining order in his life. Of the three Wolfe brothers, Oliver was wound the tightest. Sometimes Matt wondered how Serena put up with him.

He tossed the stray Lego onto the blanket, then sat down on the floor next to the pile. He began sorting through the plastic blocks and connectors. He pulled out a few rubber tires, then matched them with wheels. Piece by piece, a plane began to take shape. Wings, landing gear, propeller. He sorted through the master pile again to find a head and body to sit in the cockpit. Then he built a second, identical plane so each of the boys would have one.

He felt an overwhelming ache of love in his heart for his nephews. What they were going through and at such a young age ... he couldn't stand the thought of them hurting. He had always resented his mother's insistence that Jack not go into firefighting, had always chalked it up to her "coddling" him because he was so smart. Jack was too good to be in danger, but it was perfectly fine for him and Oliver ... that had been Matt's take on things.

He understood now why his mother never wanted her last child to follow her first two and her husband and twin brother. As hard as losing a sibling or a parent was, losing a child had to be worse. Matt couldn't imagine anything worse, for that matter.

And yet, Jack was now on staff at the St. Caroline fire department—and Matt worried about him. Jack was prone to over-thinking. He had a brilliant mind but it tended to get stuck for too long on things, considering too many possibilities, lingering on every shade and angle of a problem. On a call—in the heat of the moment, no pun intended—there just wasn't that kind of time. You had to make a decision in seconds—and it had to be the right one.

That's why I never worried about you joining the department.

He set the second plane down on the blanket. Did he just hear that? Ever since his mother died, he'd been hearing her voice in his head. One couldn't go twenty-six years listening to motherly advice without having echoes of it lodged in the recesses of one's brain. And Matt's brain had a lot of unexplored recesses. But sometimes—like just now—the voice sounded so real, so clear and so *there*, that it was hard to imagine he was just imagining it.

There's nothing wrong with your brain.

He heard his phone bleating from inside his jacket. He pushed himself up off the floor and retrieved his phone from the kitchen.

"Hey." Cassidy's voice on the other end was soft and concerned.

"Hi." He wanted her to speak again, just to hear the sound of her voice against his ear.

"How are the boys doing?"

"Okay, I guess. I mean, Cam was crying when I got here. They're upset Oliver didn't take them with him."

"So the boys know Serena's awake?"

"Oliver said he didn't tell them, but they suspect it."

"Are they okay now?"

"Yeah, they're both asleep. In Cam's bed." He lowered himself back down to the carpet, next to the Lego blanket.

"That's cute. Did you and Jack ever share a bed?"

He snorted. "Jack was six feet tall by the time he was twelve. We wouldn't have both fit in one bed."

"I guess you're right. I do remember him being pretty tall as a kid. Taller than everybody."

There was a long silence on the other end and Matt imagined he could hear her breathing. He couldn't really, but he *wanted* to hear it. He closed his eyes. With his free hand, he rubbed at the growing ache behind his temple. Cassidy was making him want all sorts of things … things he had never wanted before.

Dear lord.

And was it his imagination or was he hearing his mom's voice more often? Seemed like he was.

Makes up for all those years when you pretended to be deaf, eh?

Matt opened his eyes and he scanned the room, part of him totally expecting to see his mother leaning in the doorway of Oliver's kitchen. But he was alone.

"Hey." Cassidy's voice was even softer in his ear, soothing and arousing at the same time. "How are you holding up?"

He shouldn't be having these thoughts about her. "Fine. I guess. Yeah, fine." But they had kissed not even two hours earlier. She had kissed him back, too. He had joked about putting out her fire but … it was his fire that had needed extinguishing. His dad did him a solid by calling when he did, because if he had stayed … Matt shook his head, stopping his brain from jumping ahead to what might have happened next.

"I can't imagine what you guys are going through this year," she added.

Damn it. Had he missed anything she'd said?

You're good.

No, I'm not. I'm sitting here, talking to myself. He was starting to feel a little dizzy. It was getting late, he was tired, he was … emotionally strung out. Yeah, that was it. The boys, Serena, mom … it was more stress than he was used to. Plus, he still hadn't gotten laid since he sabotaged that opportunity in Annapolis with Maria or Maya or whatever her name was.

There is that, true.

He took a deep breath. "It's been hard. But we're managing." He felt a warm stinging in his eyes. He clenched his teeth until it went away.

"Becca says Jack is struggling. She went with him to take

flowers to the cemetery and she said she practically had to carry him back out to the car."

Matt tried to picture Cassidy's tiny sister hauling his six-foot-five brother over her shoulder. Surprisingly, he could. He knew Jack was struggling with their mother's death. They all were.

"We're taking turns putting flowers on the grave," he said.

"That must be hard."

He clenched his jaw harder, to the point where he seriously thought he might crack a tooth.

"It's supposed to be my turn this month. But I haven't done it yet."

"Why not?"

"I can't bring myself to go in there." He couldn't bring himself to even say the word, cemetery. "I haven't been since the funeral."

"I could go with you, for moral support."

"I would never ask you to do that."

"You're not asking. I'm offering. I'd be happy to go with you if you needed some help. That's what friends do, right?"

Funny how after all these years they were finally now friends.

"Thanks, Cass. I might take you up on that."

"Please do. Besides, I owe you after that kiss tonight. That was … something."

He didn't have the words to describe the kiss, either. But just the thought of it warmed his body. Her lips could light his fire and then blow it out with a soft whisper of air. Which made no sense at all. But very little in his life recently had made sense. His mother's death hadn't. Serena's accident didn't. Jack moving back home, joining the fire department, and falling in love with Cassidy's sister for sure didn't. So what was one more thing that defied any laws of reason? Especially a thing as small as a kiss.

"I'd be happy to do it again," he said.

CHAPTER 16

"Hi Jackie!" The Trevor family crowded around Becca's laptop. The remains of Thanksgiving dinner—the giant platter of turkey slices, balled up linen napkins, dessert plates practically licked clean of pumpkin pie and whipped cream—were pushed aside on the table. On the small screen was a collage of heads in Ohio—Jackie and her adoptive mother, Shari Weber; Shari's parents, Alice and Robert Weber—everyone smiling and talking all at once.

"How was your meal?"

"I burned the rolls again."

"Anyone planning to go out shopping later?"

More than one person groaned at the thought.

"What about tomorrow?"

Michelle Trevor had always kept Quilt Therapy closed on Black Friday, despite years of entreaties from Cassidy. The revenue they were forgoing nearly made her sick to her stomach. Cassidy had lobbied hard this year to be open—even if just with limited hours—but her mother held firm..

"People should spend the time with their families," had been her mother's verdict. At the end of the day, it was still her mother's shop. Not Cassidy's.

She slipped away from the videochat, and touched her mother's shoulder lightly. When Michelle turned her head, Cassidy mouthed, "I have to go. I said I'd be at Bay Acres by three."

Her mother nodded, then turned back to Becca's laptop and her first grandchild. Who'd have thought Becca would be the first one to have a child in the family? Although Cassidy couldn't imagine any of her sisters with children. Lauren? She and her boyfriend in California were apparently in no hurry to tie the knot. Natalie was too much of a social butterfly, while Charlotte had just finished college last spring and was job hunting in the big city.

And certainly not me. Cassidy grabbed her jacket from the front hall coat closet and headed out to her car. Bay Acres Nursing Home was a one-story brick building tucked in between a residential neighborhood and a strip mall shopping center on the north side of town. Cassidy was a regular volunteer there, spending a few hours once or twice a month, playing cards or board games with residents. She was a favorite with one particular group of five women.

"Cassidy! There you are!" The women, all in their seventies and eighties, were already gathered around a table in the wide open entertainment room. "We're playing poker today."

Cassidy pulled out the empty chair, draped her jacket over the back, and sat down. She enjoyed spending time with them. They were sassy and bawdy. As a result, Cassidy knew way too much about the male residents at Bay Acres. In fact, men were the current topic as cards were dealt.

"Francis Jeter wouldn't give me the time of day in high school, but now he's all over me like a cheap suit."

"Did you hear? Santana Cruz might be moving in next month." In unison, the women cocked their heads to one side, dreamy looks in their eyes. Someone sighed.

"Santana."

"Mmm."

"He always was a hot one."

"How about you, Cassidy? Got any hot prospects on the horizon?"

"Nope," Cassidy answered. "Not a one."

"We need to get that fixed."

"We can put together a committee to find Cassidy a husband."

Cassidy laughed. "You should start with a boyfriend first."

"You're not thinking big enough, sweetheart."

And so it went, round and round the table as they played their cards. Everyone had an opinion about how Cassidy could land herself a man. It was all in good fun but after an hour or so, Cassidy began to feel a familiar dispiritedness. As far as nursing homes went, Bay Acres wasn't bad. Still, the thought of ending up here someday with all the people she grew up with, went to middle school and high school with … it left Cassidy with the urge to jump into her car, start driving, and never look back.

Cards were being dealt for another round when the fire alarm began ringing, interspersed with the annoying computerized announcement voice, "A fire has been detected. Evacuate the building. A fire has been …"

MATT SPOTTED Cassidy's blonde head as he trudged back to the fire truck. She was standing by the officer's side door. What was she doing at the nursing home? He knew the Trevor family was gathered for Thanksgiving today, because Jack was there with Becca. His father and Oliver had taken the boys to Baltimore to visit with their mom, so Matt was the only member of the Wolfe family on duty at the station today.

It was four in the afternoon and he was bone-tired. Thanksgiving was always a busy day for the fire department. Between grease fires and smoke alarms set off by smoldering turkeys and marshmallow-topped sweet potatoes that burst into flames in ovens all over town, Matt spent all day on the go. His eyes left the brightness that was Cassidy's hair to glance up at the sky. In less than an hour, it would be dark and he still had one more thing to do today. A thing he should have done early in the morning before going into the station, if only he hadn't chickened out.

Now he would be carrying it out in the dark. What on earth had made him think waiting until he got off his shift was a good idea?

"Hey there." Cassidy's smile was as wide as it was bright.

"Wasn't expecting to see you here," he said. "Becca, maybe." He had barely enough energy to muster a laugh for his lame joke. Cassidy's sister had a bit of a reputation for always being around when buildings spontaneously burst into flame.

"I volunteer here."

"I didn't know that." He was impressed that she had time for it. "Good of you to come on Thanksgiving."

Cassidy shrugged. "Honestly, I needed to get out of the house."

"Are you going back in?" He shifted the fire extinguisher he was holding from one arm to the other. He couldn't wait to get out of his heavy turnout gear. Every muscle in his body was screaming for a hot shower.

"No," she answered. "They want everyone to rest. It was a more exciting Thanksgiving than planned. Headed back to the station?"

He nodded. "Yeah. Gotta clean up. Then I'm off." She was looking at him thoughtfully.

"I won't keep you then. You look exhausted."

"I am." *Ask her.*

She turned to go.

"Cass?"

She turned back around.

149

"I need to take flowers to ..." The rest of the sentence got stuck in his throat, and he prayed she remembered their phone conversation the night Serena woke up. That was ten days ago though, so maybe she didn't. He looked up again at the sky. "No, forget it. It's getting dark. I shouldn't—"

"Yes, I'll go with you." She reached out and pulled his sweaty, dirty, smelly hand into hers. "I'll pick you up at the station. How much time do you need?"

"An hour?" A little surge of energy awakened in his tired bones.

"An hour it is then." She gave his sweaty, dirty, smelly hand an encouraging squeeze.

MATT RESTED the bouquet of flowers on his lap as Cassidy pulled her car away from the fire station. The interior of her car was as neat and clean as one would expect of Cassidy. There were no candy wrappers or crumpled receipts littering the floor. No loose change rattling around in the cup holders. A green tree-shaped air freshener hung from the rearview mirror.

Cassidy had her life together. Not that Matt didn't. He certainly considered that he did—even if lately it felt as though his life had some loose threads dangling from it here and there. The loss of his mother was one thread. And he was bored at the station more often than he felt he should. That was another thread. But he lived in St. Caroline. A small town fire department responded to small town calls. There was never going to be a towering inferno here, which was a good thing. A five-alarm fire meant significant loss of property—or worse. He would never wish for that.

A day or two of boredom was normal for life. It was probably just his ADHD talking, anyway.

"So you had a busy day?" Cassidy asked.

He turned his head to look at her. "Yeah. Holidays usually are. How was your day?"

The nod of her head was measured and noncommittal. "It was good. A lot of talk about the wedding. Becca wants Lauren to be the pianist, but Lauren says she hasn't played in awhile."

"Yeah, I've been listening to Jack go on about the wedding a lot too."

'Not that I mind. I didn't mean to sound like I did. And I trust Becca not to put me into some hideous bridesmaid's dress."

"Do you still have those boots you wore in Texas at your friend's wedding?"

He saw a flash of white teeth behind her smile.

"I do. That was a pretty place to have a wedding. The Primrose Creek Ranch."

"I didn't get to see much of Texas when I was there," he said. "I was in class most of the time."

"You should definitely go back."

He tried to ignore the scenery they were passing—the familiar homes, even the cars he knew were always parked on a particular block—but it was difficult. Each block they put behind them put them one block closer to the cemetery.

"I want to be cremated," he blurted out. *Where the hell did that come from?* But as soon as the words escaped his lips, he knew they were true.

He caught Cassidy's quick glance over at him.

"Me too," she agreed.

"I can't stand the thought of being in a box under the ground. I mean, I know I won't be aware of it ..."

"I read an article a few months back where you can be cremated and your ashes get put into a planter with a tree sapling. Then they plant you in a forest somewhere and you become part of that tree. That's what I would like."

"Do you get to choose what kind of tree?"

"I believe you do," she said. "And we have just totally walked ourselves right into that conversation—'if you were a tree, what kind of tree would you want to be?'" Her laugh was like a whispered hush, a breeze winding its way through leaves high above a wooded floor. "And for the record, I have no idea. I haven't thought that far ahead."

Matt spent a few quiet moments contemplating what kind of tree he might want to be for all eternity. His musings were cut short, however, when the car rounded a bend in the road and passed the sign for the St. Caroline Golf Club. The St. Caroline Cemetery was just past the golf course. He took a deep breath and shifted the flowers on his lap. He could do this, right?

In another minute, they were pulling through the scrolled iron gates and onto the narrow road that wound its way around and between acres of marble headstones, ghostly pale in the dark.

"I've never been here at night," he said. He suppressed a tiny shudder. "I should have done this in the morning, before my shift started. Note to self."

"You'll be fine." Cassidy gently braked the car to a stop at a fork in the path. "Which way from here?" She squinted into the dark. "Left or right?"

"Left." So much information vanished from Matt's brain as quickly as it arrived, but the location of his mother's grave was burned indelibly into his memory even though he hadn't been back here since the day of the funeral. He and his brothers had agreed to take turns bringing flowers, and Matt felt shitty for weaseling his way out of it until now.

He had his justifications, of course. Oliver was so unemotional that he could handle anything. And Jack had Becca for support. Matt had no one, and he couldn't trust his brain either. Even now, with Cassidy sitting right next to him, he felt his thoughts spiraling into a dark tunnel.

A tunnel he was afraid he wouldn't be able to pull himself back out of.

Every day he looked at Oliver and saw a man who was coping

through sheer force of will, by directing his thoughts and feelings to places he could handle. Matt didn't have that kind of control. Matt's thoughts whipped him around as they pleased.

The car slowed to a crawl and he peered out into the dark at the marble ghosts lit only by the headlights. Overhead, clouds shadowed the moon.

"This is it," he said.

CASSIDY TURNED off the car and hurried around to the passenger side to open the door for Matt. Her gesture, which she considered entirely necessary—he had a large bouquet of flowers on his lap, after all—was reflected back at her in the surprise on his face.

"Here. Give me the flowers to hold while you get out." She cradled the blooms carefully in her arms. Matt had picked out a nice assortment of flowers—lilies, roses and carnations in orange and gold and burgundy. It was a lovely autumn arrangement in a brown wicker sleeve.

She watched as he swung his legs around and unfolded his body from her car. From the slowness of his movements, she could tell he was tired.

"Do you want me to do this for you?" she offered.

He looked at her, his forehead creased in confusion. "I can do it. But thanks." He took the flowers from her arms.

Fallen leaves were scattered across the grass. Matt's boots kicked them aside as he strode toward Angie Wolfe's grave. Cassidy followed behind at a discreet distance, in case he needed some moral support. The bright, obviously new headstone sat next to another that was identical in shape and size. The second headstone was clearly older, its marble dulled by time and weather. The words "Jack Alan Wegman, beloved son and brother," were carved into the stone. Angie Wolfe's twin brother and Matt's uncle. On the other side of her grave was an empty space, surely destined to be Tim Wolfe's eventual resting place.

Cassidy found it hard to imagine doing what Matt was doing right now. Her parents had purchased burial plots in the cemetery but she didn't even know where they were. Nor did she want to know yet. It was information she wouldn't need for years to come. And yet that was obviously not necessarily true. Her mother was the same age Angie Wolfe had been. Fifty-five years old.

She wanted to close the distance between herself and Matt so she could take his hand, offer him the support she would need in his shoes. But she held back, unwilling to imply that he wasn't strong enough to do this on his own. That said, if he broke down the way Becca said Jack did, she was going to be right there at his side. There was no way she'd make him do this alone if he needed help. That's what friends were for.

And they were friends, she and Matt. She knew there would be hell to pay if her family found out she was here with him right now, but she didn't care. Because who else would come here with Matt? She doubted he would have asked one of the guys at the station or a male friend. But he trusted her with his pain, with his weakness in the face of grief.

She held her breath as he stopped in front of his mother's grave, standing there for several long moments during which Cassidy's pulse beat loud in her ears. Then he kneeled down and carefully—reverently—placed the flowers against the marble stone. He took another moment to make sure the wicker sleeve was rooted securely in the dirt before standing up again.

Cassidy felt certain she knew what he was thinking—remembering the day of the funeral, the weight of the casket in his hands as he carried it from the hearse to the gravesite, the strain great on his broad shoulders. She watched those shoulders now, alert to any tiny movement beneath his jacket, any sign that he was losing control of his emotions. His back betrayed nothing though. The heavy canvas of his jacket rose and fell with the cadence of his breathing, nothing more.

She decided to give him a moment alone, and returned to the car. She sat in the driver's seat, her eyes trained on the curve of the steering wheel until she felt the passenger side door open. A rush of brisk night air grazed her cheek. He folded his body back into the seat next to her and pulled the door firmly shut. Then she felt the cool skin of his hand wrap around hers.

"Thank you, Cass," was all he said.

CHAPTER 17

The lobby of the Chesapeake Inn was the very definition of pandemonium. It was Sunday afternoon, the final day of the Winter Festival—and the final day to meet Santa and submit one's wish list. The children racing around the lobby were wired and their parents only slightly less so, thanks to the Inn's complimentary spiked eggnog. If pressed, Cassidy might admit to having a cup of it herself.

All in all, the festival had been a success. The Inn was fully booked and reservations at restaurants were a hot commodity. A few of the retail shops were even running low on inventory. As for Quilt Therapy, they'd had their best sales weekend since before the fire and nearly a hundred people had signed up to receive emails about the next weekend quilting retreat.

Cassidy turned her attention back to the line of people waiting to meet Santa. Douglas was as patient and ho-ho-ho jolly as he was yesterday even though he had confided to Cassidy that the suit and fake beard grew hotter and scratchier with every hour.

"When are we closing the line?" Ashley asked as she snapped a photo of a young brother and sister sitting on Santa's lap. "Perfect!" she called out to the waiting parents.

Cassidy pulled her phone from the pocket of her blazer. "It's five o'clock so we should close the line in half an hour. I'll let Danny know." Danny was a student at St. Caroline High and a soccer player. Matt had recruited him at the last minute to be an elf. He'd spent the weekend hamming it up in his green tights and waistcoat. If he didn't have a future in soccer, he might have one in acting. She sent him a quick text. *Close the line at five-thirty.*

She pocketed her phone and handed a sheet of paper to another set of parents whose children had just met Santa. "You can log into the 'Photography by Ashley Wardman' web site tomorrow morning to view a watermarked proof and order print copies. Instructions are on this sheet."

On Santa's lap, a toddler was having a panic attack. Ashley leaned back from her camera and tripod while she waited for the mother to talk the child back off the ledge. "Is that who I think it is?" she said.

Cassidy followed Ashley's line of sight to where an attractive woman in jeans and a green sweater stood. She wasn't wearing a coat, meaning she was probably a guest at the Inn. Her red hair was pulled back into a ponytail.

"That's Simone Adkins, isn't it?" Ashley added.

Cassidy adjusted her glasses. It sure looked like Simone Adkins, the Grammy Award-winning singer, but what would she be doing here? "I thought I saw her Friday night at the caroling on the square. She was just watching."

Simone Adkins had played a concert in St. Caroline the other summer. Cassidy hadn't heard anything about another since. Besides, when Natalie and Charlotte had gone to her concert in Baltimore last month—the evening Matt came over to her apartment and kissed her—the show had ended early. Simone lost her voice suddenly and mysteriously halfway through her set.

"I think it's really her," Ashley said before leaning in to her camera. The toddler's panic attack had been soothed to faint whimpering.

Cassidy thought so, too. She watched as Simone Adkins surveyed the scene—the Inn's decorated lobby, the line leading up to Santa's lap. As the population of kids in the lobby began to thin out, a few adults had gotten in line. Cassidy recognized most of them as locals, there probably to tease Douglas.

After a moment, Simone walked to the end of the line, ignoring the curious stares. When she got to the head of the line, she waved at Ashley as if to say "no photo, please." Ashley complied and stepped away from her camera. Cassidy watched as Simone gingerly sat on Douglas' lap, his hand on her back steadying her. There was a familiarity between them that surprised Cassidy. Simone's lips moved to speak, then she leaned in and whispered something in his ear. Whatever she wanted for Christmas was really top secret, apparently.

Then the tender moment was over and Douglas helped her up off his lap, just as he did with the kids. Simone disappeared through the front lobby doors of the Inn and into the early evening outside. Santa's visiting hours were over. Danny the Elf began gathering up signs. Ashley packed up her camera equipment while Douglas stretched his legs, stiff from sitting all afternoon. Cassidy walked over to him.

"Was that really Simone Adkins?" she asked.

Douglas nodded as he pulled off his fake white beard and rubbed his chin beneath.

"What did she want for Christmas?"

"She said she never wants to get her voice back."

Cassidy frowned. "Really? That's an odd request for a singer."

Douglas shrugged. "She seems to have her reasons."

Cassidy gave Ashley a warm hug. "Thanks for doing this."

"No problem."

She watched as Douglas helped Ashley carry her equipment out to the parking lot. Given that Ben was in hospice now,

Cassidy and Matt had both tried to persuade Ashley not to participate in the Winter Festival.

"We'll find another photographer. No worries," Cassidy had told her.

"I need to get out for a few hours here and there," had been Ashley's reply. "Ben's family is in town. They can stay with him while I'm out. Plus, the exposure will be good for my business. I'm going to need it when all is said and done."

Cassidy's phone buzzed and she pulled it from her blazer pocket. It was Matt. She held the phone up to her ear as she headed out to her car.

"Hi there."

"Santa winding down?" he asked.

"Yup. Santa has left the building."

Matt's laugh was loose and relaxed. Cassidy was glad to hear it. Ever since their visit to the cemetery on Thanksgiving, Matt was like a ball of tension and nothing Cassidy tried had been able to puncture it.

"We had a star sighting, too," she added.

"Oh yeah? The vice president stopped by to see Santa?"

"No, Simone Adkins. The singer."

"Ah. I remember her concert here. Not my kind of music, though."

"She seems to have lost her voice."

"I'm in luck then, eh?"

Cassidy rolled her eyes and opened her car door. "You're terrible. So where are you? "

"Just arrived at Elliott's to direct traffic for the lights. Did you make it out here last night?"

"No. I worked at the shop."

"Well, you should get out here tonight. Lights are on until nine. That gives you three hours."

She chuckled into the phone. "Yeah, I seem to recall seeing those hours on a spreadsheet somewhere."

"You're terrible, too. You know that?"

"We pulled this off, Matt."

"We did. Well, almost. Let's not count our chickens before they hatch. We still have a few more hours to get through without any major catastrophe."

Two and a half hours later, there'd been no major catastrophe —unless one counted the damage Cassidy had done to her checking account. She lifted her shopping bags filled with gifts for her parents and sisters into the trunk of her car. Stopping by the stores on Main Street served two purposes—getting some Christmas shopping done and checking in with the business owners to see how the Winter Festival had gone for them. The reviews were good—a few suggestions here and there—but mostly everyone was positive.

Her phone buzzed again, this time with a text from Matt. *Elliott said he'll keep the lights on for you if you want to come out.* She glanced at the time on her phone. Yikes. It was eight-thirty already.

Will you be there? She texted back. She didn't care all that much about seeing the Christmas lights. If she really wanted to, she could drive to Ocean City and see their display. But she wouldn't mind seeing Matt. They had spent so much time together while planning the festival but during the *actual* festival, they'd barely seen each other at all. He juggled a couple shifts at the station with directing traffic at the lights display and fixing the plastic wreaths that kept falling off their lampposts on Main Street. Cassidy worked most of her regular hours at Quilt Therapy in between helping Ashley. Not that Ashley had needed much help, but Cassidy had felt bad about Ashley doing the Santa photos at all.

It would be nice to have some free time again.

I'm here. Another text from Matt. *Park in Elliott's driveway.*

She was about to ask *why* but then tucked her phone back into her pocket. She could see the lights just by driving past. But that wasn't what she was most interested in seeing.

It took her nearly twenty minutes to make it out to Elliott's property. Even at this late hour, there was still a line of cars inching past his field, windows rolled down, phones and cameras clicking away. Finally, she reached the twin brick pillars that flanked the driveway. She flipped on her turn signal and pulled in. As she closed her car door, Matt startled her by stepping out of the shadows.

"Didn't mean to surprise you there," he said.

She took a deep breath to calm her racing heart, which—truth be told—had started racing even before she pulled into Elliott's driveway. The sight of Matt before her wasn't helping any either. He wasn't dressed in his usual attire, loose cargo pants and tee shirt. The jeans he wore were slimmer-fitting and his thin down jacket made his already broad shoulders look even broader. Peeking out of the collar of his jacket was a turtleneck sweater, the ribbed neck accentuating his strong, square jawline. A black knit hat was rolled down over his dark hair. Nearly every inch of his body was covered with clothing … and yet it only served to call attention to what was underneath.

"Come," he said. "Everyone else had to stay in their car to view the lights, but you're about to get a behind-the-scenes tour."

She followed Matt across the driveway. As soon as she stepped onto Elliott's lawn, the two-inch heel of her boot sunk into the soft ground and she stumbled. Matt spun around just in time to steady her.

"Thanks." She looked down at her dressier boots, then at Matt's work boots. "Guess I didn't dress for walking through a field."

Matt turned away from her and hunched his back. "Hop on."

"What?"

"Hop on. I'll give you a piggyback ride."

"I'm too heavy for that."

He looked back over his shoulder at her, a skeptical look on his face. "Don't be silly. I wear seventy-five pounds of gear on every call. I can carry you across a field."

She shrugged and grabbed onto his shoulders, giving a little squeak at the feel of his hands cupping her bottom as he pulled her up.

"Liked that, did you?" His voice was low and ... sexy.

She tried not to linger on that thought, even as her body was shouting its own opinion. *Linger! Linger!* But it was too easy to enjoy the way his hard muscles jostled beneath her hips and thighs as he strode across the uneven field. She tried to focus on the brightly colored Christmas lights ahead, but ... *damn.* Each step he took stoked in her a crazy need to be touched, to fuse her skin with his. That there were several layers of clothing separating their skin made no difference.

She tried again to focus on the lights. The closer they got, the more diffuse and out of focus the lights looked. They were meant to be seen from a distance, from the road, from the safety and comfort of a vehicle. The vehicle she was riding was beginning to feel very unsafe. In another ten feet, a whole Pandora's box of suppressed desires was going to crack open and make Cassidy want things she couldn't have.

Closeness in her life—she had plenty of that. She was close to her parents and sisters. Close to the shop's customers, many of whom had known her since she was knee-high to a grasshopper. But the flip side of that, oddly enough, was that she had no real social life to speak of outside her family. Most of her friends from high school and college had moved away for jobs and greener pastures.

She'd spent years telling herself that what she had was enough. It was more than enough to compensate for what she didn't have. Spending time with Matt, though, had spilled some sunshine into the closed-up cracks of her life and awakened a few of those suppressed needs.

The simple, human need to be touched.

To be *seen* by someone.

To have someone pick her up and carry her occasionally.

Beneath her hips, the jostling suddenly stopped.

"Here we are," Matt said. "The enchanted forest."

He loosened his grip on her thighs, allowing her to slide down off his back. Immediately a shiver convulsed her body.

"Where's your coat?" He frowned at her.

"Um, in the back seat of my car."

Her unzipped his light down jacket and handed it to her. "Here. Put this on."

She shook her head. "You'll get cold."

He tugged at the fabric of his turtleneck sweater. "I'm plenty warm in this. Go on." He thrust the jacket at her again.

"Thanks." She slipped the jacket on over her blazer. Just that simple motion unleashed the warmth and scent of his body around her. A moment of dizziness washed over her. When it passed, she followed Matt's path through a dozen Christmas trees set up in the field, each one strung with lights and topped with a large yellow star. In the middle was a clearing and a nativity scene.

After that came Santa's workshop. Nearly life-sized wooden cutout figures of elves held hammers and paintbrushes behind what Cassidy could see were oddly flat tables. From the road, the tables had looked more three-dimensional. It was a neat optical illusion.

"Sean and his students did a great job," she said.

"They did. Elliott was a big help, too."

She followed Matt into a maze of giant red and white striped candy canes and oversized presents wrapped in ribbons of lights. He stopped in front of a candy cane, his face glowing in the twinkling red light.

"This concludes our private, behind-the-scenes tour."

"Thank you," she said and impulsively reached up and pulled his head down to hers for a kiss.

He didn't kiss her back and immediately she regretted her impulsive move. What was she thinking? She wasn't thinking, that was the problem. The piggyback ride got her hormones all riled up and what should have been just a gesture of gratitude between friends—a playful sock in the arm, a brushing of finger-tips—had turned into a horribly awkward moment she now had to extricate herself from.

She released her grip on the back of his neck and was about to take a giant step backward when his hands squeezed her hips. He pulled her body against his and this time he kissed her back. Firmly. Definitively. No doubt about it.

She felt a warm pressure against the small of her back and then the press of his chest against hers. She felt something else pressing into her, as well. A hardness beneath the fly of his jeans. This was no take-pity-on-a-friend-and-end-her-dry-spell kiss, like the one in her apartment. Matt was turned on by this.

By her.

He pulled back from the kiss, his lips hovering just a breath from hers. "What does a guy gotta do to get you to stop thinking for a minute?"

She felt his fingers thread their way into her hair.

"Your brain might be telling you that this is overrated," he added "but your body is saying something different."

She suddenly became aware of the way her spine was arched forward, her breasts straining to push their way through the down jacket she was wearing. His down jacket.

"Sorry," she whispered.

He pulled his head back so he could look her in the eye. "You don't need to apologize for wanting to be kissed, Cass."

"We're just friends, though."

"So?"

"Friends don't kiss friends."

"Depends on the kind of friendship."

Cassidy knew where he was going with this. He'd broached the idea in her apartment that evening. *You need a friend with benefits.* It was an idea she hadn't taken seriously. After all, she grew up with the same message she imagined all girls grow up with—that sex goes with love. Her parents were living proof of that. Wildly in love for decades. Her childhood had been filled with those embarrassing moments, the sounds coming from her parents' bedroom that meant they were "having private time." She and her sisters still joked about it.

There was no question that her parents had a great sex life. But her experience of sex wasn't quite so "knock your socks off." She had boyfriends in college. She'd been in love with them—or at least infatuated. But the sex was never anything to write home about. Maybe her parents were right—you needed "true love" for sex to really fulfill its potential.

Or maybe great love had nothing to do with great sex. Who knew? Cassidy sure didn't.

"I like kissing you," he added. "Unfortunately, there are only five women in this entire world that I am absolutely not supposed to kiss. You are one of them. You and all of your sisters."

"Why not?"

"Our parents are friends. I'm not allowed to break your heart."

"What about Jack and Becca?"

"The rules are different for Jack. He's not going to break anyone's heart."

Cassidy snorted. "No, instead he just knocked up my sister. And no one knew about it for seven years."

Matt shrugged and gave a small, rueful small. "And for Jack, that ended up working out okay. Different rules."

"You're not going to break my heart." Her chin jutted out to emphasize her point. "We're just friends."

He considered her for a long moment without saying a word. Then he spoke. "What kind of friends?"

Should she and Matt do this? Friends with benefits? Maybe she was wrong about sex being overrated. *It depends on whether you've had a good lover or not.* The words he'd spoken in her apartment came back to her now. Maybe she really hadn't had a good lover before. It wasn't a stretch to believe that her college boyfriends had been just as inexperienced as she was. Matt had plenty of experience so, in theory, he should be at least competent in bed.

But what if it didn't work out? Dozens of thoughts flashed through her mind like an old-fashioned movie reel whirling out of control. She imagined herself naked before him. Imagined herself not knowing what to do in bed with him. Imagined him being disappointed. He might not hold the power to break her heart, but seeing him around town could be a recurring exercise in humiliation.

Matt gave up on waiting for her answer. He ran his calloused thumb over her cheekbone. "Just give it some thought, Cass," he whispered and leaned in to take her lips again.

She felt his tongue slip into her mouth, soft and warm, and instantly the nerves in her body lit up like the Christmas trees in Elliott's field. Her capacity for giving thought to anything, however, went immediately dark like someone had tripped over the power cord and yanked it out of the socket. She let her lips fall open and gave in to the light and the dark.

WHEN MATT BROKE THE KISS, his brain felt sharp and focused. Not even the hard pressure in his jeans was fogging up his mind. From the dazed look on Cassidy's face right now, her own mind was considerably less clear.

She needed to experience good sex. Everyone did. Matt had

very few core beliefs but that was definitely one of them. And if there was one thing he was good at, it was sex. He had no desire to break Cassidy's heart. Neither of them was in the market for a relationship anyway. But as a friend, he could give her this, an appreciation for how sex was supposed to be.

"Just give it some thought," he said again. Then he picked her up and tossed her over his shoulder to carry her back to her car. A little "eep" floated back to his ear, adorable and satisfying all at the same time.

CHAPTER 18

Cassidy counted twenty pallbearers carrying Ben Wardman's casket from the hearse to the gravesite, as many as could fit around the gleaming bronze-colored box. They were all students from St. Caroline High School. She glanced around at the crowd filling the cemetery. It looked like the entire town was here, to pay their respects to a popular teacher. There were more people in attendance at Ben's funeral than there had been at Angie Wolfe's. Cassidy was glad for that difference. Even a small difference might make the day easier for Matt and Jack.

She reached over and brushed Matt's hand with her fingers. Their families were standing together. Matt's fingers caught hers and held fast. She gave his hand a gentle squeeze, then tried to disentangle her fingers from his. He tightened his grip. This was living dangerously, the two of them holding hands right in the midst of their families. And for what? The winter festival was ten days ago, and she and Matt had seen each other only once since then. A run-in at Two Beans one morning. Now that the festival was done, they no longer had a reason to spend time together.

Mr. Wilson at the chamber of commerce was already making noises about the two of them co-chairing the festival next year but Cassidy had managed to be noncommittal about that so far. She had submitted her business school applications last week. With any luck, she wouldn't be living in St. Caroline next winter.

She did kind of miss Matt, though. He'd left open the whole friends with benefits thing in Elliott's field. *Just give it some thought.* But he hadn't mentioned it since then or gotten in touch with her or made any effort to see her. She couldn't exactly see herself calling him up and saying, "Hey, how about some no-strings-attached sex?"

In all likelihood, his enthusiasm had cooled over the past two weeks. Matt could have anybody he wanted. Maybe he had reconnected with the redhead from Annapolis. Plus, holding his hand right now wasn't sending her body into paroxysms of unbridled lust. It was just a kind gesture of support for a friend.

She did her best to ignore the heavy feeling of disappointment in her chest.

The reverend began to pray and Matt loosened his grip on her fingers. She clasped her hands in front of her and bowed her head. At "amen" the crowd began to disperse. Matt and his father headed toward the parking lot. Cassidy fell into step alongside her parents.

"We should stop by the reception at the high school for awhile," her mother said.

"We should," Casssidy agreed, though it was nearly the last thing she wanted to do. The reception after Angie Wolfe's funeral had been excruciating. Red-eyed people standing around, trying not to cry but not sure what to say to anyone either. What was there to say anyway? *Sorry for your loss.* Cassidy would be the first to admit that she had no idea what it was like to lose a parent or a friend or a sibling. Or someone you loved. Ashley Wardman had seemed so strong at the winter festival, snapping photographs of excited children on Santa's lap. But Cassidy also saw her in yoga class at Lucy's studio. If Ashley lost any more weight, she'd blow away in a faint breeze.

After forty-five minutes at the reception, she found her mother to let her know she was leaving.

"I'll swing by the shop to get the deposit for the bank," she offered.

"Oh, I'll do that, sweetheart. Don't worry about it." Michelle nodded toward Dan Trevor, who was talking to a group of parents on the other side of the large room. "As soon as I can peel your father away."

"Well, I'll stop by the shop anyway. I can work on Jackie's quilt for a little bit." She looked around for Jack and Becca. They'd already left, she guessed. "Christmas is right around the corner."

"I'm sure Becca would appreciate that. I'll see you there then."

NATALIE AND CHARLOTTE were closing up Quilt Therapy when Cassidy arrived.

"What are you doing here?" Charlotte asked, leaning in to kiss Cassidy on the cheek.

"I'm going to work on the quilt for a bit. I need to decompress after the day."

"I can imagine."

She sat down at the quilting frame. The shop was making a quilt as a Christmas gift for Jackie—an Ohio Star, in honor of her Ohio roots. The stars were pieced in a solid dark purple fabric—Jackie's favorite color—set against a lighter floral backdrop. She ran her hand across the top to find the tiny threaded needle left behind by the last person to work on it. She felt the sharp prick against her skin and tugged it free. She began quilting the center of one of the purple stars, rocking the needle back and forth through the fabric, loading several stitches before pulling the needle all the way through. Around her Charlotte and Natalie finished closing up the shop.

"How were sales today?" she asked.

Natalie gave a short bark of a laugh. "Um, everyone was at the funeral. That's all that really needs to be said."

"On the other hand, we got a lot done on Jackie's quilt," Charlotte added.

"I can see." Cassidy paused her hand for a moment to scan the quilt top. It was nearly half quilted. "Hope she likes this."

"We need to hope she likes a lot of things."

That was true. Jackie needed to like St. Caroline. And the Trevor and Wolfe families. Jack and Becca. Seafood. Hard to live on the Chesapeake Bay if you didn't like crabs and Old Bay seasoning, at the least.

The front door rattled as their mother let herself in. Cassidy turned her attention back to the quilt, focusing on making tiny, perfect stitches. If Jackie ended up not liking the quilt, it wouldn't be for lack of effort on Cassidy's part.

When Natalie and Charlotte left, Michelle sat down on the chair next to Cassidy, leaning over to peer at the stitches. "Nice."

"Thanks."

"You didn't go home and change first?" Her mother plucked at the sleeve of Cassidy's black silk blouse.

Cassidy shrugged. "I wanted to get here before Nat and Charlotte closed up."

"How was Matt today?"

"He was fine. Funerals are hard for him and Jack, you know."

"I know."

"Jackie is coming for Christmas."

"I am aware of that." Cassidy kept her focus on her stitches.

"This is a delicate situation for Jack and Becca. For our family and his. Please don't get in the middle of this."

"I'm not in the middle of anything. Matt and I just spent two and a half months working on a project for the town. My sister and his brother are getting married. It's hard for us to pretend that we just don't know each other."

The rules are different for Jack. Those had been Matt's words, in

171

between kisses in Elliott's field. *The rules are different for me too, aren't they?* And Cassidy wasn't even sure when that had happened. When Becca came home? Or had the rules always been different, but she'd just never noticed?

"I'm not going to ruin their relationship, mom. Or ruin Christmas or anything else."

She continued to quilt after her mother left. She had come here to decompress after the funeral. Now she needed to decompress after her mother's little chat. It rankled that her mother believed she would somehow heedlessly interfere with her sister's relationship, like she was some grand femme fatale. When in reality, she was the daughter without a social life, the grind, the worker bee, the daughter least likely to ever get married. She'd just spent several months juggling her job at Quilt Therapy and planning a large, town-wide business event —no easy feat—and now her life was back to its usual boring self.

She felt a pity party coming on, like a flash mob. Not that she'd ever seen a flash mob in person. In St. Caroline? *Heaven forfend.*

She stared sightlessly at the quilt as her hand worked the needle back and forth. She finished one block and started in on another. Normally, the peacefulness of quilting could center her in the middle of any storm but that zen felt just out of reach tonight.

Matt hadn't shown up at the reception that afternoon, and Cassidy was concerned. A picture of him in his cabin, alone, filled her mind. What was he thinking about? His mother? Or Ben, a man just a few years older than he was? It hit her suddenly that Ashley had fallen in love, gotten married, and lost her husband—and she was only three years older than Cassidy.

What am I waiting for?

She took another needleful of stitches, then secured the needle in the top. Someone else could pick this up tomorrow. A friend of hers had endured a rough day. She was going to do what a friend should do—go check on him.

MATT GROANED as he touched himself beneath the covers. It was too early to be in bed but he needed the stress relief. This was as good an outlet as any. When he was a kid, videogames were that outlet. Occasionally he played a round or two at the station with the guys when things were slow, but he felt foolish doing it. It just wasn't an adult activity and … *geez, focus.* He couldn't even pay attention to jerking off these days.

Go see Dr. Smythe.

He could add that to the list of things stressing him out. He was hearing his mother's voice practically every day now. And right now wasn't exactly an appropriate time.

I had three kids. There's nothing you can do that I don't know about.

He felt himself soften beneath his fist. "Thanks!" he shouted into the empty bedroom.

Sorry.

"Oh god," he moaned. *I'm losing it. I really am.*

He'd been doing fine until he went to the cemetery on Thanksgiving. Seeing his mother's grave, laying the flowers there … it had exactly the effect he'd feared it would. Made it impossible to keep pretending that it hadn't happened—her long illness, the agony of watching her health decline week by week, the dreaded phone call from the hospital … as long as he stayed away from the cemetery, he was fine. It was possible to keep his scattered brain from focusing on his loss, on the absence of his mother in his life. Now, though, it was all his brain wanted to focus on. Every time he tried to force his thoughts in a different direction, it was like his mind flipped him the bird and went skipping merrily right back to where he didn't want to go.

Of course, he would have to go back to the cemetery in

person. He and his brothers had agreed that they would keep flowers on her grave. It was cowardly of him to shirk his end of that agreement.

Christmas was coming up, too. One more thing on the list. The first Christmas without his mother. He wasn't sure how the family would weather it. They had neatly sidestepped the issue of holidays without her by spending Thanksgiving apart. Matt at the station. Jack at the Trevors' house. Dad, Oliver, and the boys at the hospital. But they couldn't spend every holiday that way.

On top of all that, he didn't even have Cassidy anymore. Not that he would ever burden her with this information, but she had been a grounding influence on him over the fall. At Ben's funeral today, he swore he was on the verge of passing out, and then she touched his hand. Instantly, he could feel his feet solidly on the ground again. It was weird how calming her presence was for him. But now that the festival was over, they didn't really have a reason to see each other.

A knock sounded on the door. He closed his eyes. *Just keep still and they'll go away.* Like the bogeyman. That's what his father used to tell him when he was a kid and afraid of thunderstorms. It was a phase, what could he say?

Damn long phase.

I got over it. What the hell—he was answering back now?

The second round of knocking was louder. It couldn't be either of his brothers. They never bothered to knock. Nor did any of his friends, come to think of it. They all just barged right in.

"Matt? Are you home?"

It was Cassidy's voice. He threw off the covers, straightened the waistband of his pants, and … more or less fell out of bed, whacking his leg against the steel bed frame in the process.

"Ouch. Coming!"

He hopped out to the living room, his shin smarting from the impact.

"Just a minute!" he shouted. He didn't want her to leave. After all, he'd just been thinking about her. Even though the prospect of Cassidy-inspired stress relief was gone, if he could get her to hold his hand that would still be a big help. A distraction, at the least.

He yanked open the front door. "Hey."

She was still dressed all in black—black wool coat over a black silky blouse, black skirt, black suede boots with a small heel. He had changed into nylon soccer pants and a tee shirt at some point, though he was hard pressed to remember exactly when. He stood aside to let her in, then pulled the door firmly shut behind them.

"How are you feeling?" she asked and laid her hand on his bare forearm. Her touch was cold from standing on his porch while he was hiding in bed, but the charge it sent down his spine was decidedly hot. He covered the hand with his own, then wrapped his fingers entirely around hers. He wanted the same calm she had given him in the cemetery that afternoon. He *craved* it.

"I'm good," he replied.

The twist of her lips looked skeptical.

"All things considered," he added. He let go of her hand and brushed the shoulder of her coat. "Can I hang this up for you?" She allowed him to take the coat.

"I was worried about you. I didn't see you at the school."

He hung up her coat in the narrow coat closet tucked away in the corner of the room, then turned back to her. "I went to the station to help sort deliveries for the giving tree. Figured there'd be so many people at the school that no one would miss me."

The look on her face was so tender, so concerned, that even Matt was able to read its intent. She had missed him.

It's okay to miss people.

Damn. Was that his thought or ... well, it had to be his

thought. He only had one brain, right? But lately it felt as though his brain was split into two parts.

"You didn't have to drive all the way out here," he went on. You could have called."

"On the phone, you would have just said you were fine." Then she laughed in a way that said she was laughing at herself. "Besides, I'm having a rebellious moment."

She laughed again, this time more of an amused snort. Which was so ridiculously adorable. Why was everything Cassidy did so ridiculously adorable? If he was going to spend time with her, he needed to come up with a synonym for "adorable."

"How so?"

"My mom gave me the whole 'don't ruin Christmas for Jack and Becca' spiel again."

"Ah. So you're flipping off your parents by coming here in person?"

"Real mature of me, I know."

He extended his arm to gesture at the room. "Maturity is a stranger here." He wanted to hear her laugh again. "I'm glad you're here, Cass. When you held my hand this afternoon ... that really helped."

She held out her hand and he took it, then pulled her into his arms. He sank into the immediate calm that washed over him. She was like a drug, and every time he touched her it only increased his need for another hit of it.

"Let's do this, Cass."

"Do ..."

Her words trailed off but she was smart enough to know what he was referring to. And he was smart enough to know that she wouldn't have come over here tonight if she hadn't been giving the idea at least some consideration.

"Neither of us is seeing anyone else," he added. "It makes perfect sense."

"For me, it makes sense. My love life is non-existent." She

wriggled out of his embrace. "But you have other options besides me."

"So? I don't have to choose every option that's available."

"But why me?"

"I like you. And I want to prove to you that sex isn't overrated."

"You want to indoctrinate me into the pleasures of the flesh?"

"Uh, I don't know what kind of books you've been reading but … yeah. Something like that."

She considered the idea, focusing her gaze on a spot over his right shoulder. Then her eyes returned to his face. "How would it work? Do I just come over and we hook up? Once a month? Once a week?"

He went into the kitchen and retrieved a yellow legal pad and a pen from the junk drawer. He leaned on the countertop and began to write. "Matthew Dean Wolfe and Cassidy Ann Trevor hereby do consent to a friends with benefits situation for a term of no less than one night and no more than—how long do you want this to last?"

She shook her head at him, a disbelieving look on her face. "You're making a contract?"

"Sure. Why not?"

Her body began to shake as she tried to hold in her laughter.

"That's sounds so … legal. How many of these have you written?" She wrapped her arms around her waist as her efforts to rein in her laughter failed.

"I haven't written any before. So what maximum term do you want?"

She took off her glasses and wiped her eyes with the back of her hand. "Until I leave for business school?"

"Did you get in?" He looked up from the legal pad.

"I submitted the applications. Won't know for a few more months."

"I'm sure you'll get accepted everywhere you applied." He put pen to paper again. "So for a term of no less than one night and no more than—" He counted off the months with his fingers. "—eight months. That puts us at August, roughly."

"You'll be bored with me long before then."

He looked at the tear-streaked skin on her flawless cheeks and the way her warm brown eyes were adorably—there was that word again!—unfocused without her glasses. He didn't foresee boredom being an issue in the near term.

He leaned over the notepad on the counter, writing as he spoke. "Either party can terminate this agreement at any time with thirty days' notice. How's that?" He held up the notepad for her to see. "Hey, this *is* a legal pad. That makes it legally binding."

She squinted at his neat, dark handwriting. "How about thirty minutes' notice? That way, when you're on a date, you only have to stall for half an hour before you can take her home."

She looked away from the notepad a beat too quickly. He set it down and scratched out another sentence.

"This is an exclusive agreement between said parties. Relations with any other party invalidates this contract immediately."

"No sleeping with anyone else?"

He cocked his head at her. "Is that going to be a problem for you? Thought you said you haven't had sex in a million years."

"I was thinking more for you." Her voice was quiet.

"I'm actually a one-woman-at-a-time kind of man." He drew two long, straight lines at the bottom of the contract. "Here. Sign so we can get started."

CASSIDY WATCHED as Matt switched on the bedside lamp, bathing the room in a soft glow. That helped the ambience. Some. Still, his bedroom wasn't exactly the most romantic setting for what they were about to do. Then again, romance had nothing to do with it.

They looked at each from across a divide of three feet. Three feet, physically. Mentally, the divide felt a lot greater than that to Cassidy.

"So how do we do this?" she asked. "Normally, one thing leads to another or someone gets seduced."

The slow smile that spread across Matt's face was maybe the sexiest thing she'd ever seen.

"Have you ever been seduced?" he asked.

She only had to think for a split second. "No."

"Do you want to be?"

"Some day, sure."

"We'll save that for a more advanced lesson."

They continued to stare each other down across the three-foot divide.

"I'm getting nervous."

"I don't bite." He mock-leered at her.

Her tiny laugh was nervous, anyway. She shot a glance toward his nightstand. "I know what's in there."

"I think we should save those for a more advanced lesson, as well."

"So we're back to how do we do this?"

"We can do it anyway we want. If you could start anywhere, where would it be? What would make you comfortable?"

"Are you like this with all women? This nice?"

"I'm a gentleman, Cassidy. I wasn't raised by wolves."

Why was she surprised by his good manners? Over the past several months, nothing he had done indicated he had anything but impeccable manners. Well, except for ditching a date in Annapolis. But that had ended well for Cassidy—with him in her hotel room.

Where he had been the perfect gentleman.

"Would you take your clothes off? So I can look at you?" she asked.

"Of course."

In one smooth movement, he stripped off his tee shirt. In a second, equally smooth movement, he pushed down his soccer pants. She caught a glimpse of black boxer briefs before he kicked the pile of fabric off to the side. Her first instinct was not to look *there*, but then her eyes dropped to his crotch. He was still soft. This was going to be really awkward if they couldn't get turned on by each other, she thought.

She let her eyes drift up to his flat abdomen, then to his chest. Dark hair covered the well-defined muscles she found there.

"So far so good?" he asked.

She nodded mutely. She'd never considered herself to be particularly picky when it came to men's bodies, but it was entirely possible that Matt's body was going to spoil her for anyone else. He slowly turned around and her breath caught in her throat at the sight of his broad back and his … ass.

"Oh my god." Her voice was barely above a whisper but he caught her words anyway.

"You've never seen a man's ass before?"

"Not one like that." She thought for a moment. "Normally, by the time the man undresses, things are so far along that I don't get to see his body very well."

Matt turned to face her, then gestured toward the bed. He sat down on the end of the mattress.

"You looked nice in your suit today," she said.

"Off topic." He patted his hard thighs. "Sit on my lap."

She took a step toward him, then reconsidered. She leaned over to pull off her suede boots and knee socks. She straightened and reached behind her back to unzip her skirt. The moment of truth. Or, well, one of what would probably be many moments of truth tonight. If they didn't abort this crazy mission within the next few minutes. She let the wool fabric drop to the floor.

"You have beautiful legs, Cass."

She walked toward him and straddled her beautiful legs across his. It was impossible to notice that he wasn't quite so soft anymore. When his hands slid over her thighs and edged beneath the hem of her silk blouse, she closed her eyes and swallowed a moan. Her breathing was already on the verge of being out of control as his fingers spread around the curve of her hips.

"That feels so good," she said quietly.

"It's supposed to feel good." He gave her hips a gentle squeeze. "If it stops feeling good, say so and we'll stop. Or I'll try something different."

"Just touch me."

His fingers left her hips and reappeared at the buttons of her blouse. One by one, he worked each button through and pushed the soft material off her shoulders. It landed in a hushed heap on the floor behind her. Then she remembered her underwear. A utilitarian tee shirt bra in a nude color designed to be invisible under clothing. Her bottoms were the same shade of medium beige. At least they matched.

"Sorry," she said and opened her eyes.

Her apology seemed to fall on deaf ears. Matt's dark eyes were nearly black as he drank in the sight of her breasts rising and falling with each ragged breath. He ran his thumbs over the edges of her bra and Cassidy felt perilously close to passing out. He was barely touching her skin and yet it felt so damn good. Amazing, in fact.

He leaned in and kissed the swell of her cleavage. His hands slipped around to the back of her bra, and tugged at the band. "May I?" he asked.

"Please."

She felt her bra release, the straps dropping down her arms, and then his palms grazing her nipples. Her hips squirmed involuntarily on his lap. In one swift action, she felt herself lifted up and flipped around, then deposited gently on the bed. Matt's naked body was now over hers. And though he most definitely was hard as a rock now, he spent the next half hour touching her everywhere—with his fingers, his lips, his tongue.

It felt so over-the-top good, her body both completely relaxed and exquisitely alert all at the same time. But as the minutes passed and her body stayed resolutely on that knife's edge of arousal, seemingly nothing he did was able to push her off into the free fall of release. Her thoughts began to stray away from her body. It must be getting late. Natalie would wonder where she was. Matt was probably getting tired and wondering when he'd get his turn. So Cassidy did what she'd done every other time she had found herself in bed with a man.

She faked it.

CHAPTER 19

*M*att turned off the gas burner on the stove and fixed two plates of scrambled eggs, bacon, and toast. He poured two mugs of coffee and set out the half pint container of cream. He cocked his head and considered the small breakfast bar, with its rustic wood base and scratched and scorched formica countertop. He folded the paper napkins in half so they formed triangles and added the glass salt and pepper shakers Becca had dug out and filled for him a few months back. Back when Jack was still crashing at Matt's cabin and Becca was spending time here. She had insisted she couldn't use salt straight from the supermarket canister, that it poured out too fast. Matt imagined that her sister, who was in his shower at the moment, might have the same issue.

Lordy me. Was beginning to think I'd never see this.

"Not raised by wolves." Matt stopped, realizing he'd just said that out loud. He really did need to make an appointment with Dr. Smythe to discuss his ADHD medication.

He heard the shower turn off down the hall. He took a sip of coffee to calm his brain. *I know how to entertain a woman, Just because I generally don't doesn't mean I don't know how to.*

The bathroom door opened and thirty seconds later, Cassidy appeared—dressed in her funeral outfit from yesterday, her long hair dark and damp around her shoulders. Her face was clean and slightly shiny without makeup. It made her look younger. It made him want to see her dressed in more casual clothes.

Like one of his shirts. And nothing else.

"Good morning," he said as she pulled out a barstool and climbed up.

"You didn't have to fix me breakfast." She poured a healthy dash of cream into her coffee.

"Didn't want to send you home on an empty stomach." He didn't want to send her home at all. He pushed that thought aside. They were friends with benefits, which reminded him … he slid the legal pad across the counter toward her. "I made an addendum to the contract."

"Oh yeah?" She leaned in to read it.

"Yeah. No faking orgasms allowed."

He watched as her cheeks flamed.

"Sorry. It was taking so long and I didn't want you to have to wait."

"The waiting is half the fun." He shoveled a forkful of eggs into his mouth and swallowed. "No, make that ninety percent of the fun."

"So is this your thirty minutes' notice?" she asked, not looking at him.

He put his fork down and frowned at her. "Hell no. It's just me putting you on notice that no faking is allowed."

She still wasn't looking at him, so he reached out his hand and tipped her face up.

"Have you ever had an orgasm?" he asked.

"Of course I have." But she couldn't maintain eye contact, a dead giveaway that she was lying. "Little ones, anyway."

He released her chin. "There's no such thing as a little orgasm,

Cass." He took another sip of coffee. "You're not leaving here until you have one."

Over on the coffee table, his pager buzzed.

Cassidy chuckled. "Apparently, I am."

"Shoot," Cassidy muttered as she pulled into the parking lot of her apartment building. Natalie's car was parked in the usual spot. She swung around to the back of the building and found an out-of-the-way spot there. How was she going to explain another overnight at Matt's? She didn't go over there intending to spend the night.

Upstairs, she turned the key in the door as slowly as she could and held her breath as she pushed it open. She took one step inside, quietly closing the door behind her. The coffee maker in the kitchen was sputtering brew into the glass carafe. Otherwise, the apartment was quiet. She let out her breath and tiptoed down the short hall to her room. Five seconds, that was all she needed. Five seconds of total silence and maybe Natalie wouldn't notice that she was just arriving home. At the end of the hall, the door to her bedroom was closed—with any luck, Natalie thought she was still asleep.

But no such luck. Cassidy was one step past Nat's room when the door swung open.

"Hey! You're home."

She turned back to face her sister. "Yeah. Um …" She wracked her brain for a quick explanation. *I just ran out to the store. I left something in my car. I went for a walk … in the cold.* She could see Natalie's eyes registering her outfit though. The black coat and boots, in contrast to Natalie's jeans and turtleneck sweater.

"Just for the record," Natalie began. "I don't care what you and Matt do."

"We're just friends." *Friends with benefits. Contractually bound.*

Nat shrugged. "Like I said, it doesn't matter one way or the other to me."

"Don't tell mom and Becca, though. Please."

"I won't."

"Promise? We're just friends but ..."

Natalie crossed her heart. "I know how mom feels about it. Also for the record, I don't agree with her. And Becca is so lost in love at the moment, I don't think she believes anything could ever come between her and Jack."

"Wow. That's cynical."

Her sister shrugged again, apologetically this time. "Jack's a great guy and all, but he did get her pregnant seven years ago." Natalie put on her leather jacket. "I gotta go. I'm opening up the shop today."

"Are you okay?" It wasn't like Natalie to be quite this cynical. "I feel like we haven't seen much of each other lately."

"You've been busy. No worries. I'm fine. Gotta go."

In the shower, Cassidy turned the water on as hot as she could stand it. She dunked her head beneath the spray, then spun around to let the tiny needles of water hit her shoulders and back. Her body felt different this morning, and it was no mystery why.

I had sex last night!

Matt had ended her dry spell. Well, technically speaking. She was surprised when he called her on the whole faking-an-orgasm thing. No one had ever noticed before. Or, if they had, no one had ever said anything. Even without the Big O, though, the night with Matt was easily the best she'd ever spent with a man. He had some mad skills in bed, no two ways around that. Skills so mad her body was still buzzing, skimming along on the edge of arousal.

She shampooed her hair, rinsed, and turned off the water. Just as she pulled the shower curtain aside, she heard the bleating of her phone from her bedroom. She grabbed a towel and ran across the hall dripping wet. By the time she got there, the ringing had stopped. She snatched the phone from her bed and checked the call log. Lauren.

Hmmm.

She called her back while simultaneously trying to squeeze the water out of her hair with the towel.

"Hey!" Her sister picked up.

"I was in the shower." Cassidy sat her wet body down on the bed, toweling off her legs. "What's up?"

"I've decided to come home for Christmas, after all."

"That's awesome. When?"

"Today. I'm at the airport now."

"Today?" The towel paused in her hand. "What's going on?"

"I need to get away, that's all."

"Did you and Cole break up?"

"No." A long pause. "Not yet."

"Oh Lauren." Cassidy's heart stung for her twin sister. "When does your flight get in? Which airport?"

"I'm flying into Dulles. I land around eight."

"Do mom and dad know?"

"Not yet. I called you first."

"You need a ride." Cassidy didn't bother to phrase it as a question.

"Yes. If you're not working today."

"I am, but you know mom will let me leave early if it's to pick you up."

"Can I ask a favor?"

"Always."

"Can you pick me up by yourself? I know mom will probably want to come along but ... I need to talk to you."

≈

Cassidy stared sightlessly at the giant metal baggage claim carousel, her thoughts bouncing back and forth between Matt (wondering what he was doing) and Lauren (wondering what was going on in her life). Well, what was going on immediately was that her sister was on a plane taxiing to a gate here at Dulles International Airport.

Outside, a light snow was falling. Normally, the first snow of the season never failed to lift her spirits, filling her with a sense of impending holiday cheer. Tonight, it was doing nothing for her mood. Whatever was going on in her sister's life made her pathetic problems seem, well … pathetic.

I have a great job.

A great family.

I'm not homeless.

I'm waiting to hear back from business schools.

She cataloged all the things that were right about her life.

I don't have a boyfriend but I am having sex with a hot firefighter. No pun intended.

Of course, that might not actually happen again—contract or not. Matt clearly hadn't been amused by her fakery. She sighed. That had happened this morning, a time that now seemed like eons ago.

The baggage carousel chugged and stuttered to life. She watched as a lone suitcase circled round and round. This was the most depressing part of an airport, she thought. Waiting for your luggage so you could leave and go home. Most people liked coming home. Even if a trip had been wonderful, they still found it comforting to come back home. Cassidy didn't. She preferred the leaving, the immediate future rife with the possibility and serendipity of new experiences, new places, new people.

She turned back toward the escalator, sensing that Lauren was on it. Seconds later, Lauren stepped off the bottom riser and Cassidy was shocked by her sister's appearance. She was heavier through the waist and thighs, her face rounder, her hair bleached from the southern California sun. Maybe the differences weren't enough for someone else to notice, but they couldn't have been more noticeable to Cassidy if they were outlined in neon.

She ran to her sister, engulfing Lauren in her arms.

"Easy there, Cass," Lauren mumbled into Cassidy's shoulder.

"What is going on?" she demanded.

Behind them, the baggage carousel picked up speed and luggage was clunking out onto it nonstop.

"Let's get my bag. I'll tell you in the car."

But in the car, Lauren was no more forthcoming than she'd been inside the airport. Cassidy steered the car onto the airport toll road for the drive east toward Washington and then beyond, to the Eastern Shore. The night sky outside glowed with the ambient light of the suburbs—office parks, the neverending miles of traffic, neighborhoods getting denser and tighter the closer they got to the city.

Cassidy glanced at her twin from the side of her eye. "You got new glasses."

"Oh. Yeah. I've had these awhile, actually. I don't like to wear my contacts on the plane. The air dries my eyes out."

"They look good."

"Thanks."

"So Becca wants us to go shopping for the wedding next week. Did she mention that?"

In her peripheral vision, she saw Lauren's head nod. "Natalie said something about it."

"And Jackie's coming in for a week."

"How are things going with Jack and Becca?"

"Good. Things are going good." How could having a simple conversation be so awkward with her sister? With her *twin* sister, for pete's sake. "You haven't spoken to Becca lately?"

"Spoke to her three days ago. Just asking for a second opinion, that's all. Did you send your business school applications in?"

"I did." She felt Lauren's hand on her forearm.

"Good. I know you'll get in."

"I haven't told anyone yet though." *Except for Matt.*

"No worries. Mum's the word." She laughed softly at her double entendre. "So how'd that winter festival thing turn out? Mom said it helped make up for last summer, sales-wise."

"It did. It turned out nicely, I have to say. I don't plan to be around next winter to spearhead it again, but it was a good idea on the town's part."

"You and Matt Wolfe didn't kill each other?"

"Apparently not."

She shot a neutral smile at her sister. She and Lauren used to share every detail of their lives with each other, until Lauren dropped out of college and moved away. She missed the days when she and Lauren were closer. Nonetheless, she had no intention of bringing up her beneficial friendship with Matt Wolfe. It was bad enough that Natalie knew. Even that was one person too many.

Traffic thinned out on the other side of the city, but the snow was falling heavier.

"Are you hungry?" she asked.

"Famished. All they fed us was those cracker and grapes snack boxes. On a cross-country flight!"

"Tell me about it. I can't remember the last time I got something even halfway resembling a real meal on a plane."

"I'd settle for something halfway resembling a sandwich."

The bright lights of a fast food restaurant beckoned ahead and Cassidy pulled into the drive-through lane to order burgers and fries. As she turned to hand a bag of food to Lauren, she noticed her sister's rounded stomach again. *Oh no.*

"You're not pregnant, are you?" she asked quietly.

Lauren looked at her like she was crazy, then burst into what could only be called maniacal laughter. "Dear lord, no." She managed to get out three words before she was overcome by a fresh bout of giggles. "I'm just fat."

"You're not—"

Lauren waved off Cassidy's words. "I've been stress eating. It's okay to acknowledge the obvious." She unwrapped her burger and took a bite. Chewed. Swallowed. Contemplated the burger for another moment. "Once upon a time, I did think I'd have children with Cole. But that idea turned out to be just laughably ridiculous."

"Why do you say that?"

"Cole is gay."

"What?" There was no way Cole could be gay. "You two have been together for almost seven years now."

"I know."

"Is he bisexual?"

"He says not."

"Well then … how did you two …?"

"Not well, that's for sure."

Silence expanded to fill the interior of the car as Cassidy struggled to process this new information. She had always liked Cole. Well, as much as she knew him. Which wasn't all that well, even after seven years, come to think of it. She knew him mostly through Lauren talking about him. He rarely came with her on trips to St. Caroline.

"Why did you stay with him then?" Cassidy lifted her soda from the cup holder and took a long, cold draw to prevent herself from saying something she might regret later.

Lauren was quiet for several minutes, but Cassidy waited her out.

"I was afraid."

"Of what? Him?" If Cole had ever hurt her sister, she was so turning this car around right now and driving back to the airport. She'd fly all night to California to chew his ass to shreds.

"Of being alone. All the way out there."

"You could have come home."

Lauren coughed on the last bite of her burger. "Come back

with my tail between my legs? And have mom and dad say 'I told you the acting thing wasn't going to work out?'"

"Damn it. Who cares what they think?" But she knew Lauren was right. That's exactly what their mother would say. Hell, Cassidy had heard her dance around the subject of Lauren's career more than a few times over the years. They were disappointed Lauren never finished college. And while she made a living doing commercials, it wasn't the grand artistic life Lauren had envisioned.

Impulsively, Cass flung a french fry at the windshield. The grease kept it stuck to the glass.

"Are you going to eat that?" Lauren said, after a long comedic beat.

They burst into laughter together and the comforting familiarity of having her twin next to her washed over Cassidy. Even their laughs were identical.

Lauren peeled the french fry off the windshield, rolled down her window, and tossed it out into the night. She took a napkin and rubbed at the grease mark on the glass.

"Well, that didn't really help," she said.

"I'll clean it tomorrow."

Cass's phone buzzed inside her purse. Somebody had texted her.

"Want me to get that?" Lauren asked.

"No, I'll check it later."

"Are you sure?"

"It's probably just mom."

The Chesapeake Bay Bridge was blessedly uncongested at this hour. They sailed across the eastbound span in no time, Lauren staring off at the lights of Annapolis to her right.

Cole gay? Cassidy turned that idea around and around in her head.

"I would never have guessed," she said quietly.

Her sister sighed. "I had my suspicions."

CHAPTER 20

"*A*re you even thinking about me, sweetheart?"

Cassidy's attention snapped back to the man hovering above her. The naked man hovering above her. The naked man that was Matt Wolfe.

"Yes. Of course I am."

"You are the worst liar."

"Sorry."

He rolled off her hip and stretched his finely-muscled body alongside hers. "So care to share what you were thinking about when you were supposed to be thinking about ..." He traced his finger across the outline of her ribcage. "... me?"

"I was wondering whether everyone believed my story about having to go home because I had menstrual cramps." Before coming to Matt's cabin, she'd been at her parents' house where her sisters had gathered for a welcome home dinner for Lauren. After dessert, Lauren pleaded jet lag and went upstairs to rest.

"Well, you didn't have to come over. You can always say 'no' when I ask."

A ticklish shiver convulsed her body and disturbed the pool of desire that was deep in her hips.

"Do you want to leave and go back?" he added.

Did she want that?

"No. I'd rather be here."

"I don't want to keep you from Lauren. I know you don't get to see her that often." He trailed his fingers right down the center line of her abdomen.

"I wasn't getting to spend much time with her, anyway. Mom was monopolizing her company."

"Imagine that. A mother wanting to see her daughter."

She swatted at his hand. "I'm Lauren's twin. I outrank my mother."

He snorted. "If you say so."

His fingers were getting perilously close to the pool of desire. She took a deep breath to keep her hips from pressing up into his hand. In response, he brushed his thumb over the point of her hip bone.

"Your body wants to be here. But your mind keeps slamming on the brakes."

Her field of vision filled with his dark hair as he bent his head to her breast. His lips closed softly around her nipple, a sensation she'd nominate as one of the wonders of the world. She shut her eyes and tried to give herself over to it, to the exquisite flicks of his tongue against her skin, to the way his warm breath seeped into even the tiniest of her veins, to the pool of desire that was pulling her under. He slipped a hand beneath her bottom and rolled her over. She felt his weight press onto her back, his knee pushing her thighs apart, a kiss planted onto her shoulder.

She was safe beneath him. She felt that all the way to the very marrow of her bones. It was an odd feeling, this mix of comfort and desire, relaxation and blinding need. If she could just hold herself balanced at that unlikely intersection, she knew an orgasm would meet her there.

If only.

Matt shifted his weight to lift her right hip an inch, entering her and cupping his hand between her legs. Her cheek sunk into the pillow, her eyes rolled back into her head as he simultaneously rocked himself inside her—gently, rhythmically—and stroked her. If this didn't send her spiraling into pleasure, nothing would.

But it didn't.

It came close. Oh so close. Tantalizingly, torturously close.

But no cigar.

HE COULD TELL the exact moment she gave up. He felt her muscles go slack beneath him. Not slack in that post-orgasmic my-bones-are-now-officially-jello sort of way. But slack as in the white-flag-of-surrender way. He touched his forehead to her smooth shoulder. She'd been close. He knew it. The rhythm of her hips had made the switch from shallow, desperate chasing to the deep, measured climb to the top.

It should have been unstoppable, past the point of no return. But something had happened, and he wasn't sure what. Had his angle veered off ever so slightly? Did his finger slip and press too hard? Matt held a near scholarly interest in the female orgasm. He was fascinated by it, and not just because it had to happen before he could take his own. Every woman had an entire repertoire of orgasms, as endlessly variable as his own fascination in them. And yet, they were as fragile as a butterfly's wings.

"Don't wait for me," she whispered into his pillow.

The words made his soul ache.

ith its pale grey walls and glossy black floor, the Pearls & Lace Wedding Atelier looked more like a chic art gallery than a bridal boutique. Instead of canvases and sculptures, the hushed, spacious rooms were populated with headless mannequins wearing all manner of silks and satins, organza and tulle, seed pearls and lace. The color palette ranged from pure white to soft ivory, with the exception of one display of dresses arrayed along the side wall, away from the front window. Black dresses.

"What about this one?" Lauren circled one of the black gowns, a big-ass grin on her face. The dress consisted of a tight strapless bodice and a voluminous tulle skirt adorned with shiny silver studs along the hem. "I mean seriously, with black Chuck Taylors?" She bit her lip to keep some semblance of a straight expression on her face.

Cassidy piled on. "Or what about combat boots?"

Becca, who was dressed for shopping in a perfectly sedate pair of black pants and a green sweater, rolled her eyes. "Not my style anymore."

"That's a pity," Charlotte said.

"Can you imagine Jack's face if you came down the aisle wearing that?" Natalie chimed in.

Cassidy pulled out her phone and snapped a photo of the black gown. "I'll get mom's opinion," she said, texting the photo back to St. Caroline.

The response from their mother was immediate. *"NO!!!"* Cassidy flipped the phone around for her sisters to see.

"Is that really a wedding dress?" The five Trevor sisters all turned toward the source of the sixth voice—Jackie, standing there in purple jeans and winter boots, her long blonde hair bright against a black turtleneck.

"Has Becca ever showed you any pictures of herself from when she was younger?" Natalie asked.

Jackie shook her head.

"We'll have to remedy that," Lauren laughed.

"Guys, I admit to being the fashion-challenged one in the Trevor family." Becca scanned the mannequin-filled showroom. "How about we fan out and see what's here? Serious possibilities only, please."

Cassidy squinted through her glasses at the sea of white and ivory fabric. She couldn't imagine herself ever going through this process—choosing a dress, planning a glorified party. None of it held any appeal to Cassidy. *Elope, that's what I would do.* She circled a few mannequins, then stopped behind one. She glanced around to make sure her sisters were all focusing their attention elsewhere, then texted the photo of the black wedding gown to Matt.

What about this one?

When no response was immediately forthcoming, she shoved the phone back into the pocket of her jeans and perused more mannequins. There were several dresses she thought Becca would look lovely in—especially the one covered in sheer tulle blooms. With Becca's long hair and slender figure, she would look like a fairytale forest princess. Becca was probably one of the few people who could pull off that sort of look.

She pulled out her phone to snap a photo of the forest princess gown when the device buzzed with a text. It was Matt, weighing in on the black dress.

YES!! I'll even chip in. Anything to see the look on Jack's face.

Cassidy looked up, guiltily, to see if anyone was watching her. No one was, but she noticed that Jackie had wandered away from Becca and was standing amongst the flower girl dresses. The seven-year-old was taller than the shop's childlike mannequins. She had inherited Jack's height and his blonde hair. His quiet, thoughtful demeanor too, as far as Cassidy could tell. In fact, as far as Cassidy could tell, her niece had inherited practically nothing from Becca.

What a complicated situation. Becca and Jack had hooked up only once at a high school graduation party. Becca ended up pregnant, ran off to Ohio, and gave the baby up for adoption. But now the adoptive mother was terminally ill and had asked Becca to adopt Jackie back. It all seemed fated by the universe. How else to explain both Becca and Jack moving back to St. Caroline last summer and falling in love?

She walked over to the flower girl section of the shop. "So what do you think?" she asked Jackie. "See any you like?"

Jackie looked up at her. "You're aunt Cassidy, right?" Then doubt shadowed her face. "Or are you Lauren?"

"You were right the first time. I'm Cassidy."

"Sorry. It's hard to keep everyone straight."

"No need to apologize. You'll figure us out eventually," Cassidy assured her.

Jackie stopped in front of a dress made of pale pink cotton eyelet. "This one is pretty," she said. "Do you know whether Becca has chosen colors for her wedding yet?" she asked. "My mom says the bride usually chooses a set of colors."

Cassidy wondered whether Jackie would ever feel comfortable calling Becca "mom."

"I think Becca is probably open to suggestions," Cassidy answered. " Now that we've ruled out black as an option."

Jackie cocked her head to study the pink dress further. Off to the side, a saleswoman had materialized, waiting to see if she could offer any help. "There are girls at school who wear black all the time," Jackie mused. "They think it makes them cool. Or different or … something."

Cassidy gave a little laugh. "Yes, I believe that's why Becca wore it. To be … something."

Jackie looked up at her, a thoughtful smile on her lips. "You're lucky to have sisters." She nodded, as if affirming to herself the rightness of her pronouncement.

"Well, aunts are like sisters. Only cooler and more … something." Cassidy kneeled down so both her niece and the pink dress were in her field of vision, trying to visualize one on the other. "And you have lots of aunts now."

"Cam thinks I'm going to be his sister." Jackie's attention strayed to another dress, two childlike mannequins over.

"You could certainly be *like* his sister. To Mason, too. The Wolfe family is mostly boys. They could use a woman's influence, I think."

Jackie turned back from a sleek white sheath of a flower girl dress—a dress that struck Cassidy as way too chic for a wedding in St. Caroline—to give her new favorite aunt a knowing look of agreement.

"How is Cam and Mason's mom doing?"

Cassidy struggled to keep a neutral expression on her face, surprised that Jackie knew about Serena. *Who thought it a good idea to tell her about that?* Jackie seemed to read her thoughts.

"Mason told me she's been in the hospital."

Mason. Of course. Cassidy nodded. "She's doing better now."

Jackie nodded back. "That's good."

Cassidy wondered what was going through the little girl's head. According to Becca, Shari had been in and out of the hospital since summer. And Serena? Cassidy wasn't entirely clear on how well she was or wasn't doing. Every time she asked, Becca clammed up. As did Matt. Serena was awake but beyond that, no one wanted to say.

Little Jackie had a lot in common with the Wolfe family, Cassidy reflected. They were all dealing with the absence of a mother in their lives. Cassidy's mom had come right out and said that the addition of Jackie to the family was helping Matt's dad— it was a distraction from his grief.

Suddenly, Cassidy's breath froze in her chest. Becca and Jack's relationship was so much bigger than just the two of them. Why hadn't she seen that before now? She watched as Jackie finished looking at the flower girl dresses, circling back around to stand next to the pink eyelet one. Clearly her favorite.

What would happen to Jackie if Becca and Jack's relationship didn't work out? They seemed solid, sure—Cassidy's presence in the middle of a forest of wedding gowns was proof of that. And Becca was committed to adopting back Jackie, with or without Jack. But anything could happen. Over the past year, a lot of "anythings" had happened in the Wolfe family.

Jackie was already going through more than a seven-year-old should have to cope with. She was about to lose her adoptive mother. She was slated to move from Ohio to St. Caroline before the next school year. She was clearly a little overwhelmed by going from a small family—her mother and grandparents—to the much larger Trevor and Wolfe clans. To have her "new" parents— her biological mother and father—split up on top of that ... Cassidy closed her eyes and took a long, deep breath.

"Cass? Are you okay?"

When she opened her eyes, Lauren stood before her.

"Becs has some dresses she's trying on. Do you want to weigh in?" Lauren added.

"Sure." She looked around the shop. "Where'd Jackie go?"

"She's in the dressing room, too. She picked out this adorable pink number."

How long did I have my eyes closed? I didn't black out, did I? No, she knew she hadn't, she thought as she followed Lauren to the back of the shop where the dressing room suite was. It was just that a lot could happen in thirty seconds when you weren't paying attention.

MATT WAS by the giving tree, sorting and organizing present deliveries according to volunteer driver, when the door to the station opened and a blast of cold air rushed in. He leaned around the tree to get a clear view of the door. Becca was supposed to bring Jackie by after dress shopping to say "hi" to Jack, who was on duty this afternoon and tonight. Matt hoped Cassidy would be with them. Only two days had passed since their evening together, but he longed to see her again. Not that he had asked. He knew she was busy, with Lauren in town for the holidays—and now Jackie, too. On the other hand, he knew that Quilt Therapy was closed until after Christmas, which was a mere three days away.

Being in bed with her felt so good, even if he hadn't yet mastered the mysterious art of giving her an orgasm. That was only a matter of time, though. He would figure it out sooner or later. Preferably sooner, of course.

He watched as Becca and Jackie walked into the main bay, the little girl clutching Becca's hand, a hesitant look on her face. Kids came into the fire station in one of two ways. Either they rushed headlong into the bay and practically launched themselves at the trucks or they were a little more cowed by the size of the room and the scale of the trucks, which even Matt had to admit looked bigger up close.

"Hey there sweetpea!" His father's voice was loud and wrapped in a generous helping of affection. His dad lit up like a Christmas tree every time Jackie came to St. Caroline for a visit.

Matt looked back toward the front door—and there she was. Cassidy. Her bright hair, those tortoise-shell glasses. It was maybe Matt's deepest, darkest secret—the utter lust in his heart (and elsewhere) that was inspired by the sexy librarian look. A look Cassidy had volumes of. He was overcome by the urge to pull her behind one of the trucks and kiss her speechless.

Unfortunately, half the population of St. Caroline seemed to be in the fire station at the moment. In addition to his dad and Jack there were the department crew members on shift (with no one out on a call), two of Cassidy's sisters, and assorted gift delivery volunteers. Even Doug Preston, who was reprising his role as Santa—complete with fake beard and red suit—was on hand to help deliver gifts. And then there was Simone Adkins, a famous singer who had apparently lost her voice and was, for some reason, in St. Caroline …? Matt still hadn't figured that one out, nor met anyone who had.

Slow down, sweetie.

And why hadn't it occurred to him to ask Cassidy to help deliver gifts? Afterward, they could go back to his place and he could give her the gift of an org—

Mattie. Take a deep breath. Breathe.

There was that voice again. Mattie. *I don't refer to myself as "Mattie." Just FYI.* Great, he thought. I've gone from talking back to myself to reprimanding myself over the use of a nickname.

Dr. Smythe?

He rolled his eyes at himself.

Time out for the eyeroll.

Just super. Some men turn into their fathers. *I'm turning into my mother.*

There are worse things, you know.

He forced himself to take a deep breath. Not that it helped much.

A slightly heavier version of Cassidy was headed his way. Her twin, Lauren. He didn't remember her being heavier but—

"Hi Matt," Lauren held out her hand in greeting.

He shook it. People used to say that Cassidy and Lauren were nearly impossible to tell apart, but Matt had never understood that. Sure, from a distance. But up close, there were a ton of differences. Cassidy's eyes were a little wider set, her lips just a shade fuller. And while all the Trevor sisters—save for Becca—tended toward blonde and tan, Lauren's time in southern California had made her the most tanned of all.

Not to mention, he had never once been attracted to Lauren.

Conversational skills?

Oh right.

"How was dress shopping? Any luck?"

Lauren nodded. "Becca wants to look around a bit more, but there were definitely some strong contenders."

"Good. That's … good." The words had dried up again. He had no idea what to say to Lauren, a problem he generally did not have with Cassidy. "How's L.A.?"

"The same."

He knew that wasn't entirely true, not as far as Lauren was concerned. Cassidy had told him about her sister's relationship woes.

"You need any help over here?" Lauren asked.

Matt looked around at the piles of wrapped gifts sitting in a sea of empty wrapping paper rolls and snippets of sparkly ribbon. "I think we've got everything under control."

"Well, if you change your mind … Cass and I have time. We're leaving Becca and Jackie here." She glanced toward her sister and niece, who was enjoying an impromptu moment with Santa.

As Lauren drifted away, he wondered why Lauren came over to speak to him, and not Cassidy. It couldn't be just to say "hi." He replayed their conversation in his head, looking for a clue.

Overthinking, Mattie.

True. He *was* overthinking. Overthinking all things Cassidy, for that matter. It was hard not to, though. She was on his mind all the time. For a brain that couldn't focus on tying his own damn shoes half the time, it was remarkably persistent when it came to Cassidy. He forced his attention back to the list of names, addresses, and gifts to be delivered. He needed to get this done and get out on the road. They were up against a hard and fast deadline—Christmas Day.

He sorted out the rest of the presents, then picked up as many as his arms could hold. He headed for the station's side door, the one that lead out to the small parking lot. He was stacking the presents on the passenger seat of his pickup, too lost in thought to notice someone approaching from behind.

"Hey there."

He yelped and one of the smaller boxes flipped from his grasp, bobbling next to the dashboard for a moment before it landed back in his hands. He set it down and backed his head and shoulders out of the truck. Cassidy stood there, her hands clutching the unzipped edges of her winter coat together. Her body language was closed, defensive. He'd learned that in the fire investigation class he had taken at the fire academy in Texas.

"Can we talk?" she added.

Even Matt's addled brain recognized that this was shaping up to be a conversation he wasn't going to like. The signs were all there. Her body language. The measured, even tone of her voice. The fact that she had followed him out to the parking lot. *Give me another chance,* he pleaded silently.

"Come with me to help deliver these gifts," he said.

She glanced nervously back at the station. "I need to drop Lauren off at the house."

"Give her the keys to your car. She can drive herself and I'll drop you off." Her expression remained skeptical. "You don't have to come with me for the entire route. Just … we can talk and then I'll take you home."

Ten minutes later, he had her in his truck, boxes piled on her lap and on the floor around her feet. He couldn't help himself. He pulled out his phone and snapped a picture of her. She looked too adorable for words.

"All you need is an elf costume," he said.

She smiled—a small smile but, hey, he'd take it. "Maybe I should be helping Santa instead."

Right. Over Matt's dead body.

"I think Santa already has a helper," he pointed out.

"I noticed. What's going on there?"

He shrugged and turned the key in the ignition. "No clue. I'm not plugged into the St. Caroline grapevine."

Her smile widened, just a bit. "I thought about asking Lucy after yoga, but I couldn't figure out a graceful way to bring it up. Apparently, Simone Adkins is still staying at the Inn."

"How did dress shopping go?" Yeah, he was recycling a conversational gambit.

"Good. Becca didn't go for the black dress."

He chuffed out a laugh. "That so would have been her ten years ago, though."

"Yeah. It would have."

He navigated the pickup through the streets of St. Caroline. A light snow was falling, like ash floating down from a fire. A white Christmas, wouldn't that be nice? His mom had always hoped for a white Christmas.

"So what did you want to talk to me about?" he asked. Not that he needed her to spell it out letter by letter for him. She was having second thoughts.

"We need to terminate our contract."

Yup.

"*We* need to?" he said.

"I need to. No, *we* need to."

"Why? I mean, if it's because ..." Damn, why was he having trouble talking about sex all of a sudden? *It's just sex.* "Give it a little time. It will happen, I promise. Unless it's just really distasteful to be with me." He took a quick glance at her before returning his attention to the road.

"No. It's not ... that. It's Jackie."

"Jackie? I hope she doesn't know about our contract." *Stall. Try for a lighter tone.* He couldn't tell whether the little noise Cassidy made was one of amusement or irritation.

"She's losing her mother, Matt. And moving to an all new place, starting at a new school in the fall, going from a really small family to ... us. And I admit, we Trevors can be a bit much to take all at once."

"Us too," he agreed.

"I know Becca and Jack seem solid at the moment. But things can change. Becca is going through with the adoption no matter what, but what about Jack? Is he going to stay in St. Caroline if he and Becca break up?"

"I think ... I ..." Would his brother stay? "I don't know. He seems happy working at the station. He says being a firefighter is what he wants to do with his life." Matt sensed he was arguing a losing battle here. "You know, they might break up independently of us."

She was quiet for a minute, watching the snowflakes fall outside. "For her to think she's getting a new mom and dad and then for that to fall through ... I couldn't live with myself."

He reached over and covered her left hand with his. "I get it, Cass. I'm disappointed, but I respect your decision."

"Are we still friends?"

"Of course we are. Just ... without the benefits."

She laughed quietly, then her voice grew serious again. "It would be one thing if we were really a couple, you know. In love and all that. Then it might be worth the risk, worth fighting our families over. But … we're not." She took a deep breath. "It's too much to risk just for sex." She looked over at him and gave a rueful smile. "Even for good sex."

He gave her hand a squeeze, then put his back on the steering wheel. "Do you want me to drop you off at your parents' house?"

"Can you take me to the shop? Lauren was going there from the station."

Matt backtracked through town to Azalea Street and Quilt Therapy. He pulled up to an empty spot at the curb. They looked at each other for a long moment, then he leaned over the center console toward her. She leaned away.

"Please don't," was all she said before getting out of the truck.

He sat there, watching her walk toward her family's quilt shop, watched her disappear inside. *I should have kissed her anyway.* He had the feeling he was going to regret it for the rest of his life.

CHAPTER 22

*I*t snowed on Christmas. Of course. The one thing that had always made his mother as giddy as a child was a white Christmas—and she wasn't here to see this one. He tried to think back to last Christmas, trying to recall whether it had snowed, but his mind came up blank. So many Christmas Days … so hard to remember them all. This was definitely one they were all going to wish they could forget.

He climbed the front steps to the porch of his parents' yellow Colonial, his arms laden with wrapped gifts. He set the packages down on a dry spot on the white floorboards of the porch and then returned to his truck to retrieve the rest. He might have gone a little overboard on gifts for Mason and Cam. But that was an uncle's prerogative, right? Spoiling his nephews—and now niece?

Besides, he might not ever have kids himself. He'd never been able to picture it, or been able to imagine settling down with just one woman. Variety was the spice of life, wasn't it? He'd tried tying himself to just one woman for a friends-with-benefits deal and even that didn't stick.

Inside the house, he arranged his presents around the already impressively large pile of gifts surrounding the twinkling Christmas tree. He pulled aside one of the boxes he'd wrapped and stuck it behind the tree. It was flat and wrapped in silver paper, a wide red ribbon finishing it off. Of all the presents he had wrapped, Matt had taken the most care with this one. He had the paper cuts to prove it.

"Ho ho ho! Santa's here!" he shouted. The pleasant aroma of bacon cooking drew him toward the kitchen, where he found his dad and Jack making breakfast. "Where is everyone?"

Tim Wolfe flipped another large waffle onto a red and white platter. One of his mother's Christmas dishes, Matt noted.

"The girls are upstairs. Becca's braiding Jackie's hair, I believe," his dad replied. "Ollie and the boys are on the way."

"What can I do to help?"

Jack was turning strips of bacon in the skillet. Matt scanned the rest of the scene. A ceramic pitcher shaped like the head of Santa Claus sat on the table, filled with maple syrup. Someone had poured orange juice into the nice glass carafe that only got used on holidays. The Mr. and Mrs. Claus salt and pepper shakers were out, if unnecessary for waffles. The stack of green cloth napkins looked ironed, even. He'd bet his last dollar that was Becca's doing.

So many little things that were the same this year, and yet they couldn't hide the big glaring difference. Angie Wolfe wasn't here.

"There's a cantaloupe in the fridge, if you want to slice that up," his father said. "You know how Cam loves his fruit."

That was another difference—his father was here. Normally, in years past, he spent most of Christmas day at the station so other crew members could be home with their families. Matt got the melon from the refrigerator and sliced it. He was stacking the slices in a large serving bowl when there came a commotion and a swish of cold air from the front of the house. Oliver and the boys had arrived.

Matt deposited the bowl of fruit on the dining room table en route to the living room, where Oliver and his sons were shedding their snow-dusted winter coats. Matt kneeled down to help Cam, whose zipper was stuck at the bottom. He could tell Cam was unusually frustrated, even for a five-year-old.

"Hey buddy." He gently peeled his nephew's fingers off the zipper. "Let me do it." Matt quickly detached the two sides of the coat and pushed the sleeves off Cam's sturdy little body. He held the coat up for Oliver to take. That was when he noticed Cam's red-rimmed eyes.

"Merry Christmas, dude," he said softly, giving Cam a tight hug. "Did Santa make it to your house?"

Cam nodded.

"Well, looks like he might have left a few here for you, too."

Cam looked over his shoulder at the Christmas tree and its moat of presents. "Those are from Paps."

"You never know. I'm hoping Santa left some for me here because you know what?"

"What?"

"I forgot to put up a tree in my cabin so there was nowhere for Santa to leave my gifts."

Cam regarded him with an expression that was halfway between sympathy and "well, you're an idiot then."

"Hey guys." Tim Wolfe poked his head into the living room. "Waffles and bacon will be on the table in ten seconds."

That cheered up Cam considerably and he practically exploded away from Matt in his haste to get to the dining room. Matt stood to face Oliver.

"What's going on with Cam?"

"He doesn't want to go to Baltimore today. He doesn't want to 'miss Christmas.'"

"He can stay here. I'm going into the station later today to do some paperwork for dad. He can tag along with me there." Cam and Mason were as familiar with the St. Caroline fire department as Matt had been as a child. From the dining room came the sound of chairs being pulled back from the table. "Still no improvement?"

Oliver shook his head. "Her memory only goes up to a point early in our marriage. She's pretending to remember the boys, but even that ends up just confusing them. They're trying to talk to her about school and friends and stuff like that. And she just doesn't remember any of it." Oliver took a deep breath.

Matt put his arm around his brother's shoulder as they slowly walked toward the dining room. "So leave Cam here today. And Mason, if he wants. She maybe needs a break, too."

"I think Mason gets what is going on," Oliver said, very quietly. "But Cam wants to just launch himself into her arms every time we go, and I can see in her eyes that ...," Oliver stopped and bit his lip hard to force back the shine in his eyes. "... her memory isn't the only thing that's gone. Where the boys are concerned." Oliver slipped out from beneath Matt's arm and headed for the tiny powder room tucked behind the coat closet. He waved his arm above his head as he went. "Go on. I'll be there in a minute. Tell them not to wait."

Matt joined the rest of the family in the dining room. "Ollie said not to wait."

"We'll wait," his dad said.

When Oliver slid into his chair between his sons, Tim Wolfe began grace. A tiny sniffle from Cam caught his attention. Then the light, powdery scent of Becca's perfume. It reminded him of his mother, who in years past was the one to say grace at breakfast on Christmas. She would have loved to shop for a granddaughter. His heart ached with longing for his mother, but it also ached from the knowledge that she would miss so much that was yet to come. More grandchildren. More holidays. More weddings.

His own problems were trivial, in comparison. Cassidy broke up with him. His pride was wounded, that's all. *You weren't even dating her to begin with.* She was right, anyway. Both their families had enough complications to deal with at the moment—the last thing they needed was one more. Better that Cassidy had ended their little agreement now instead of in six months when they had gotten used to it. He waited for the snarky voice in his head to kick in. But there was only silence.

She's already under your skin.

There, he said it for the snarky voice. He hadn't heard the voice all day. Come to think of it, not yesterday either. The realization was a relief. Maybe he didn't need to go see Dr. Smythe, after all.

He tried to hold his attention on his father's voice, but only snippets here and there took hold. Your blessings … loved ones … as we celebrate … he could sense Mason and Cam fidgeting in their seats. Matt was getting fidgety too.

"Amen."

From around the table came the echoes of everyone else's "amens." Including the snarky voice, only without its usual note of snark. His fidgeting stilled. It was unmistakably his mother's voice.

He opened his eyes and glanced around the table. Instead of the usual post-grace scene—everyone reaching for their glasses of juice or mugs of coffee, someone starting the waffle platter on its journey around the table, the clank of the butter knife as one of the boys fumbled it—there was a long moment of quiet. In the eyes of his brothers and father, Matt saw the same distant look he knew was mirrored in his own gaze.

Maybe he wasn't the only person hearing voices.

CASSIDY SAT on the sofa next to Lauren, waiting patiently while Jackie and Cam played elf and handed out presents. She stifled a yawn. She was stuffed to the gills from the huge Christmas dinner her mother had served, and dessert was still on deck. Lauren gave her a gentle jab in the ribs to wake her up.

Becca and Jack had brought the kids over after spending the morning at the Wolfe household. Apparently, Cam hadn't wanted to go to the hospital with his dad and brother afterward. Cassidy couldn't blame him. According to Becca, Serena was awake but suffering from long-term memory loss—as in she couldn't even remember that she had children. She was trying to pretend, for their sake, but Jack said she was just as confused as they were. Oliver was at his wit's end. His wife was awake, but she had come out of the coma a somewhat different person.

"Here, Cassi—Aunt Cassidy." Jackie handed her a flat box wrapped in heavy silver paper. The wide red ribbon was tied off in a perky bow on top.

"Thank you." She turned the gift over, looking for a tag or card. "Is this from Santa?"

Jackie leaned in and whispered, "It's from Uncle Matt."

"Oh." Cassidy felt everyone's eyes on her, most of all her mother's. Maybe this was a gift she shouldn't open in front of everyone. She gave the box a tiny shake, then glanced over at Becca for guidance. Her sister gave a tiny shrug. *Great.* Becca had no idea either.

She took a deep breath and slid her thumb beneath the red ribbon to slide it off. She separated the wrapping paper at the seam and pulled out the box. *Please let this be something that's fit for public consumption.* No lingerie, no lingerie, no lingerie, she silently chanted in her mind. Carefully lifting the top of the box, she peeked inside. Whatever was in there swaddled in layers of green tissue paper. Who knew Matt was such a meticulous gift wrapper? She pushed her fingers beneath the tissue paper. It was fabric, soft. A silk-cashmere blend, if she had to guess.

"Cass," her mother said. "The suspense is killing us."

"It's a scarf!" The words rushed out of Cam's mouth as though he'd been trying with all his might to hold them in. "Uncle Mattie told me," he added.

Cassidy realized she was holding her breath as she opened the box completely and spread aside the tissue paper. It was, indeed, a scarf. She lifted up the length of fabric and shook it open. It was a gorgeous, rich crimson color and large—more of a shawl than a scarf.

"That's beautiful, Cass," her mother said. "Hold it up to your hair."

Cassidy did as her mother asked, but she knew already that the color would set off her blonde hair perfectly. She looked in the box for a card from Matt. But the only item she found was a business card from the shop where he had purchased the shawl. Eileen Drysdale Designs, a small shop on one of the side streets near the marina. Cassidy had been in there once or twice. It was expensive, as in a scarf was probably the only thing she could afford. Or that Matt could afford.

She carefully refolded the shawl and placed it back in the box, feeling terrible that she hadn't bought him a gift. She wasn't even sure why he had given her one.

"Jackie, why don't you open that one over there?" Her mother was pointing to a large present.

Cassidy was relieved to have everyone's attention diverted elsewhere. Matt giving her a Christmas present wasn't exactly helpful in terms of reassuring her mother that nothing was going on between them. And nothing was anymore! Cassidy had done the prudent thing and ended their friends-with-benefits experiment. As experiments go, it had been mostly an embarrassing failure anyway.

"That's an Ohio Star pattern."

Her mother's words brought Cassidy back into the moment. The purple quilt they'd all made was spread open across Jackie's lap.

"Thank you," Jackie said quietly, the expression on her face that of stunned uncertainty. "Do I get to take this home with me?"

"Oh honey, of course you do," Michelle answered.

Jackie carefully folded the quilt back up and placed it on her growing pile of gifts. The Jackie sitting on the carpet in front of the Christmas tree was a different girl than the one Cassidy saw in the dress shop. Today's Jackie was quieter, more self conscious, clearly less at ease.

When all the gifts were opened and Jackie was playing with Cam, Cassidy and Becca gathered up the discarded wrapping paper and bows. In the kitchen, Cassidy shook out a trash bag and held it open as Becca stuffed the paper inside.

"Have you told Jackie yet that she'll have to learn to quilt?" she joked.

Becca shot her a smile. "She seems a little intrigued by the shop."

"Is she okay today? She seems quieter."

Becca nodded. "Just a little overwhelmed by all the family. I think Shari might have gone overboard on the whole 'be on your best behavior' advice. I think Jackie feels like she's auditioning for a role she might not get."

"Oh." Cassidy's eyes widened at the thought. "I guess we are a little much to take all at once."

Her sister shrugged. "We wanted to ease her into things, but Shari's condition is getting worse pretty quickly. We never had much time to pull this off in the first place and we have even less now."

"Well, anything I can do to help …"

Becca smiled. "I know. Jack and I realize how lucky we are to have so much help here. I shudder to think what would have happened if I were still living in Ohio when Shari tracked me down. I wouldn't have been in the right place to do this there."

From the front of the house came the chime of the doorbell, followed by Cam's excited "Uncle Mattie's here!"

"That was a gorgeous scarf." Becca took the trash bag from Cassidy and tied it off.

"Yeah." Cassidy really wished Matt hadn't given it to her, though. Or given it to her in private. She could see the questions in her sister's eyes, and she had no good answers to offer.

"So Cam's going to the station for the rest of the day?" she said instead.

"Yup. I'd better go get his coat out of the closet."

She heard Matt's voice from the living room, answering the polite questions her parents were posing to him.

"How's your father?"

"Is he at the station today?"

"Tell him we'd like to have him over for dinner some evening."

She needed to thank Matt for the scarf, and the soles of her feet tingled with the urge to move. But she used every ounce of willpower to keep them rooted to the kitchen floor. Jackie's welfare was paramount—and Cassidy's heart ached with the thought that the little girl thought she was auditioning for a spot in their family when everyone had taken her into their hearts immediately. Going out there would call her family's attention to the gift again. Best not to remind them of her and Matt's friendship. Because that's all it was. All it would ever be.

She would text her thanks to him later.

CHAPTER 23

"*I* should have bought control-top pantyhose to go with this." Lauren smoothed the fabric of her black lace cocktail dress. She slipped her feet into black heels and spun around for Cassidy's inspection.

"You look great."

Lauren twisted around to look at the back of her dress in the hotel's full-length mirror. "It's hard being around skinny mini Becca for two weeks. She eats like a horse and doesn't gain an ounce. Just the smell of chocolate goes straight to my hips these days."

"Well, if it's any consolation, Becca will probably be pregnant within the year." Cassidy squeezed into the mirror's reflection to check out her own outfit, a dark green dress with a twisted halter neckline and a too-short hem. "I'll have to be careful sitting down in this thing."

"Who's going to be sitting down? We're going to dance in the new year."

Cassidy and Lauren were in Ocean City, Maryland, for a New Year's Eve party at a hotel bar called the Blue Sky Lounge. The hotel had opened last spring and was about as hip as Ocean City got. Which wasn't saying much, but they had judged the odds of running into anyone they knew here to be much smaller than going to a party in Annapolis.

Lauren was heading back to California in two days. Cassidy wanted her twin to herself for a spell. That was the downside of a large family—too much competition sometimes. But Cassidy and Lauren were a separate unit within the family, as far as Cassidy was concerned. She was entitled to some time alone with her other half.

She looked at the alarm clock on the nightstand separating the two queen beds. "Yikes, it's almost nine. I still need to dry my hair."

She and Lauren shared the bathroom's double vanity, Cassidy blow-drying her hair while Lauren applied her makeup. Lauren was applying liner to her left eyelid when her phone rang. Cassidy clicked off the hair dryer to get rid of the background noise. Three minutes later, Lauren returned to the bathroom.

"Who was that?" Cassidy asked.

"Cole, wishing me a happy new year."

"Oh. That was nice of him." Cassidy managed to keep most of the sarcasm out of her voice. She was the only person in the Trevor family who knew about Cole coming out of the closet. To everyone else, Lauren had said simply that the relationship was on the rocks.

Lauren rolled her eyes, then set to work on lining her right eye. "He's also a little bent out of shape that I'm not out there to make the rounds of parties with him tonight. He doesn't understand why I'd rather be here."

"Because I'm more fun. Duh."

The sight of her sister's laughing face in the mirror made Cassidy happy. It had been years since she'd had a date with a man on New Year's Eve, but tonight there was no one she'd rather be with than Lauren.

"And because this is Operation Get Lauren Laid Before She

219

Goes Home to Break Up With Gay Boyfriend," Cassidy added, removing her glasses so she could rub blush into her cheeks. "Because you *are* breaking up with him, Lauren. I don't care if he wants you to stay with him through one more season of his TV show. That's not your problem."

"I don't want to upset his career right now. His character on the show isn't gay."

"Repeat after me. Not. Your. Problem."

"I know. I'll do it."

"Promise?"

"I promise."

"Because I'm going to call you every damn day until you do."

Lauren sucked in a deep breath, held it, and then let it go. "Please do," she said quietly.

MATT STRUGGLED to pay attention to the cute woman in front of him. And she *was* cute—short dark hair, busty, full lips, tight dress. But his ADHD was under assault from a perfect storm this week. When he walked into the Blue Sky Lounge, he was already stressed and tired. Add two beers to the mix and … he was only catching every fourth word Cute Woman was saying. She was older, too. Not that he was in the habit of discriminating against older women but … *damn it.* What was that train of thought? It came and went so fast, Matt barely had time to register it.

Oh yeah right. Cute Woman was older. Late thirties, he guessed. He forced his eyes to track her lips in an attempt to maintain focus. Hawaii, she was talking about a trip to Hawaii. Ollie and Serena had honeymooned there. He couldn't remember which island, though. Maybe Ollie should take her back to see if that might jog her memory. *Jack and I could watch the boys.*

He started to lift his beer to his lips, then thought better of it. Matt rarely drank to the point of getting drunk. That's why he and Sean were spending New Year's Eve at this fancy bar—*excuse me, "lounge."* They had wanted to avoid the party hardy scene in Dewey Beach where twenty-somethings from DC and Baltimore got blitzed on cheap drinks and woke up next to people they had no memory of ever meeting.

Part of him, though, did want to get blitzed and forget the entire past week. For starters, the weather all along the eastern seaboard had gotten bitter cold, which meant more people using fireplaces and woodstoves, which meant more house fires, which meant more calls for Matt and the crew. This was the first night he'd had off since Christmas.

And then there'd been the call two nights ago. Matt wouldn't mind forgetting that. Just after midnight, they received a call about a fire in a barn that had been converted to stables. The owner had placed a space heater in the loft area to keep the pipes from freezing. Matt had only been on one call before that involved rescuing horses from a fire. The word "chaos" didn't begin to do justice to what it was like trying to get large, panicking animals out of a smoke-filled building.

Matt had climbed into the loft to try and fight the fire at the source with his fire extinguisher, which was the wrong thing to do. The totally absolutely no-bones-about-it wrong thing to do. His father had chewed him out royally afterward at the station, in front of everyone.

"You *know* what we do in these situations." His dad was barely containing the urge to yell. "Get the horses out, then put out the fire from the exterior so it doesn't spread to other property. The barn is always going to be a total loss."

His father was right—Matt did know what to do in that situation. He had trained for it. He had responded to enough barn fires to know that they burned quickly.

"Why did you *do* that?" Tim Wolfe had, finally, yelled.

Why *had* he done it? Normally, on a call he could focus like nobody's business but that call was too much stimuli even for his wicked fast brain. He couldn't process everything that was happening—nor could he ignore it. So he'd gone up into the loft to escape it, to get above it all. That's when the loft floor partially collapsed.

"You could have been killed!" His father was still yelling at that point. "Other people could have been killed!"

Matt glanced down at the palms of his hands, still red and tender from where he had grabbed onto hot timber to catch himself.

"Are you even paying attention to me?" the cute busty woman in front of him whined. She waved a manicured hand before his face. "Hello?" She turned and strode away before Matt could answer, grabbing her friend, who was talking to Sean, as she went.

"Sorry, man," he apologized.

Sean shrugged. "No worries. More fish in the sea, right?"

Never a truer statement, Matt thought, but still he felt bad. The only reason they were here in Ocean City on New Year's Eve was for Sean to get laid. "Ring in the New Year with a bang," was how he put it. Matt wasn't sure what he wanted tonight. No, that wasn't true. He knew exactly what he wanted, wanted it so hard that he was practically hallucinating it right now.

"Hey," Sean said. "Is that Cassidy Trevor and … someone who … looks a lot like her?"

Matt had forgotten that Sean was not a St. Caroline lifer. His parents had bought the Blue Crab Bistro awhile back, then Sean followed a few years ago to take a teaching job at the high school.

"That would be Lauren. They're twins."

"Really?"

Sean turned to look at Matt and the glint in his eye was just short of diabolical.

"No," Matt said. "That ain't happening."

"Oh come on, man. Twins! I thought you had the hots for Cassidy."

"No." Where did Sean get that idea? It was true, of course, but it wasn't supposed to be common knowledge. "We just worked together on the winter festival. We're friends. Sort of."

In truth, he wasn't sure whether they still were friends. When he'd gone to the Trevor house to collect Cam on Christmas, Cassidy hadn't even come out to the living room to say "hi." She thanked him for the scarf by text. But just seeing her now brought on an intense sense of calm. He was suddenly grounded again after a week of turmoil.

Lauren's eyes came to rest on him. She nudged Cassidy. Matt smiled. The expression on her face remained neutral, but she and Lauren were heading their way. His evening just got a whole lot better.

CASSIDY WATCHED as the woman talking to Matt waved her hand irritatedly in his face, then stalked off, taking her friend with her. *You don't deserve a man like Matt.* She followed the woman with her eyes until Lauren nudged her in the side.

"Let's go say 'hi' to Matt and his friend," her sister proposed. "Who is …?"

"Sean Crane. He's a teacher at the high school. Soccer coach too, now that Ben Wardman is … well, you heard about that."

"Upbeat, Cass. We're here to have fun tonight, remember?"

"Sorry."

"No need to apologize. Just plaster a big, beautiful smile on that face of yours."

"Who's the wingman here?" Cassidy tottered after her sister toward the tall bar table Matt and Sean were standing around. *Damn these heels.* She could feel the hem of her dress riding up her thighs already. That might explain the big grin on Matt's face. He was going to make merciless fun of her for this dress.

That's not important, she reminded herself. She was here to have fun with her sister.

Lauren strode right up to Sean and stuck out her hand. "I don't believe we've met. I'm Lauren Trevor."

"You two are twins, I'm told." Sean looked between Lauren and Cassidy.

"I'm the voluptuous twin," Lauren joked.

Her sister was a woman on a mission. Sean Crane wasn't a bad looking guy. Tallish, with sandy blonde hair. A little older than she and Lauren. She couldn't think of anyone in town he had dated. On the other hand, she also hadn't heard any alarming stories about him. Her impression of him from the winter festival was that he was down to earth, a man who could build things. The opposite of Cole in more than a few ways.

Lauren could do worse for a one-night stand.

"Voluptuous is good." Sean was definitely meeting her half-way. "Can I get you a drink?"

Cassidy felt a warm hand on her bare shoulder and turned to face Matt. "I think we may have just both lost our dates for the evening." She smiled.

"Are you okay with this?" Matt inclined his head toward Lauren and Sean, then lowered his voice. "He wants to hook up tonight."

"So does she."

"Thought she had a boyfriend in California."

"They're breaking up."

"Ah. Sorry to hear that."

She eyed Lauren and Sean, who were now deep into flirty conversation. Matt edged away from the bar table and swung her around so they were facing the opposite direction.

"That dress is very pretty on you," he said.

"Thanks. You look nice, too."

"I clean up okay when I have to."

He was more than "cleaned up" tonight. He was wearing dark

slacks and a deep pink button-down shirt, which Cassidy would not have said was Matt's style but looked good on him none-theless. The top button at the collar was undone and his grey knit tie was loosened. She noticed him frowning at her.

"What?" she said, her hands going immediately to the halter strap around her neck, checking to make sure it was still in place.

"I was trying to figure out what was different about you tonight."

"Besides this dress?"

"Well, that too. But you have on different glasses."

She touched a finger to the bottom of her frames. "These are my dressier ones." She had swapped out her usual tortoise-colored frames for silver wire frames.

"I like them."

"Thanks. I'm a little surprised to see you here." More than a little, actually.

"I did almost bail on Sean, but I needed to get away for a weekend. It's been a rough week."

"I heard. Are you okay?"

He held up his hands so she could see the still tender skin on his palms, but nodded. "How was your Christmas?"

"Good. It was good. Thank you again for the scarf."

"I saw it in the shop and thought it would look nice on you. Besides you saved me from looking like an idiot on the winter festival."

"That's not true," she said. None of that was true. There was no way Matt just happened to be browsing in Eileen Drysdale's shop. Not on a firefighter's salary. "You did just as much as I did." She glanced over her shoulder. "Sean, too."

She had just turned back to Matt when she felt a tap on her shoulder. It was Lauren, holding out her drink.

"Finish this for me? We're going to dance."

Cassidy took the pink cosmopolitan from her sister's outstretched hand and then watched Lauren and Sean disappear into the crowd on the dance floor. She laughed. "I guess I wasn't expecting to get ditched this quickly." Then another thought occurred to her. "Um, you don't have to hang out with me, you know. I don't want to screw up your evening … if you're here to, you know."

Matt's smile seemed a little sad. "I'm not here to … you know. Are you?"

She shook her head. "It was my idea to go out tonight, but I just wanted some one-on-one time with Lauren. And the breakup has her feeling down on herself. I want her to see that other men will find her attractive."

"I'm sure plenty of men will. Although it looks like they'll have to get in line behind Sean tonight. He's a good guy, though."

"That was my impression of him." Why was their conversation so stilted? A month ago, she would have said that she and Matt were good friends. But now it felt like they were … two people who had just met in a bar.

A minute later, Matt excused himself to use the men's room. She craned her neck to scan the dance floor, but Lauren and Sean were out of sight somewhere in the middle of the gyrating mass of people. She stared vacantly at the couples dancing, wondering how many of them had arrived together and how many had just met. Was it terrible that she didn't want to see Matt pair off with someone tonight?

Yes, it was terrible, she decided. Or half-decided. Because she shouldn't care. In fact, as his friend, she should want good things for him, right?

Except she wasn't feeling the friendship tonight.

Maybe you can't be friends with someone after you've been friends with benefits.

AT TEN SECONDS TO MIDNIGHT, Matt was leaning against the bar, holding the third beer he was pretending to drink that night. The crowd began to count down to the new year.

"Ten! Nine! Eight!"

A few pieces of paper confetti leaked from the ceiling.

"Seven! Six!"

The deejay played a drumroll sound.

"Five! Four!"

Matt tried to remember where he was last New Year's Eve.

"Three!"

Spent it at the station, he recalled.

"Two!"

The dancing had stilled. Cassidy was standing next to the guy she'd been talking to and dancing with for the past hour. He would kiss her at midnight—which was exactly one second from now—and Matt would stand right here and torture himself by watching. What else could he do? He couldn't march out there and shove the other guy aside. Cassidy had ended their arrangement.

"One!"

Confetti rained down. Noisemakers shrieked. Auld Lang Syne broke out. Another man's lips were on Cassidy's lips.

Welcome to the new year. Same as the old year.

THE KISS WAS NOT GOOD. Cassidy knew that the instant the kiss began. The guy was mashing her lips. If she parted her lips—which she had no intention of doing—she might chip a tooth. His breath tasted of beer and peanuts. *I'd rather be kissing Matt.* She had studiously avoided watching him as the evening wore on. She didn't want to see him chatting up a woman, maybe clasping her hand as they walked toward the dance floor. Didn't want to see her body pressed against his whenever a slow, romantic song came on.

At the same time, she knew she had forfeited her right to care when she ended their short-lived friends-with-benefits arrangement. The only reason the memory of going to bed with Matt lingered so freshly in her mind was that he was the only man she'd had sex with in the past two years. She knew that was it. As soon as she slept with someone else, the attraction her body felt to his would dissipate. At the moment though, the thought of going to bed with someone else was thoroughly unappealing.

The crowd around them began belting out Auld Lang Syne and Cassidy broke the kiss so she could join in. Loudly—so there was no chance of a second kiss.

assidy leaned in toward the hotel's bathroom mirror to get a closer look at her chin. Was she breaking out? She washed her face a second time and brushed her teeth. After the singing faded away in the lounge, she'd found Lauren, Sean, and Matt back at the bar. Cake and champagne at midnight were included in the ticket price for the evening, and the three of them were going to indulge. Cassidy decided to call it a night.

She put on her plaid flannel pajamas and was pulling back the covers on one of the queen beds when she heard a knock on the door. Lauren must have lost her key card. Without looking through the security hole, she opened the door.

It wasn't Lauren.

It was Matt.

"I've been sexiled by Sean and your sister," he said.

"Seriously?"

"Yup. Note to self: next year, don't share a room."

She took a step backward and held open the door. "Well, I guess you can crash here then."

"Sorry. I'm making a habit of crashing in your hotel rooms."

"I don't mind."

She sat down on her bed and propped the pillows up behind her. Matt sat on the edge of the other bed.

"Do you want to watch television?" she asked, looking at the remote control on the nightstand.

"Sure."

She flipped through channels, scanning for something interesting. When she came up empty, she leaned over the floor between the beds to hand him the remote. "Here. Maybe you can find something worth watching."

He clicked off the television. He pointed the remote at her open suitcase on the hotel's dark dresser. "You brought the scarf."

"I did. I really like it. I feel bad that I didn't get you anything. I'm sorry."

He set the remote back down on the nightstand. "You know what I really wanted that Santa didn't bring me?"

"A new fire truck?"

"A kiss from Cassidy Trevor."

"You don't ask for much. Easy to see how Santa might have overlooked it."

There was no overlooking the sexy half smile that was gracing Matt's face at the moment. It was an invitation if Cassidy had ever seen one. Of course it was. *This is Matt Wolfe we're talking about here. Mr. I Only Do Casual Sex.* He'd just been sexiled from his hotel room so no wonder he had sex on the brain.

"When I knocked on your door, I wasn't sure you'd be alone," he said.

She rolled her eyes.

"Yeah, that kiss at midnight was pretty uninspiring," he added.

"You were watching me?"

"Just making sure he didn't try and cop a feel."

"What would you have done if he did? Defend my honor?"

"Rip his head off."

"You're pretty territorial for a former friend with benefits." She attempted a weak laugh.

"You know, you never gave me your termination in writing."

"Didn't know it had to be in writing."

"The original agreement was in writing. Stands to reason that the termination should be too."

She glanced at the hotel's small notepad on the nightstand, sitting right next to her dressy glasses. He followed her gaze.

"It has to be on a legal pad to be binding."

Cassidy half-snorted, half-laughed.

"I love when you do that."

"I know. It's so sexy, right?" She tweaked the collar of her flannel pajamas. "Along with these."

"You certainly came prepared for a hot evening." He leaned over his legs, untied his shoes, and tossed them onto the floor. "Do you own any sexy lingerie?"

Cassidy made no answer. He had her there. She didn't.

"No further questions, your honor," he went on. "I rest my case. This woman needs a friend with benefits more than anyone I've ever met."

She watched as he peeled off his dark socks, then wiggled his toes.

"You look like you're settling in over there." She was overly conscious of her own bare feet sticking out from the legs of her pajamas. She resisted the impulse to wiggle her own pink-painted toes.

"This is starting to look like a long court case."

"Did I tell you that you look nice in that shirt? It's a good color on you." Cassidy needed to gather her thoughts about her, not to mention her wits. She was committed to not going to bed with Matt again—her reasons were still valid and in place—but the commitment was wavering a bit with him lying on an actual bed.

"Nice redirect there, but thanks." He made a show of unbuttoning the top few buttons. "Are you really going to start the new year off with that other guy's kiss? Not the greatest beginning, if you ask me." He rolled onto his side, propped his head up with his hand, and smiled. "Could mean bad luck for the rest of the year."

"So what are you proposing?"

"Just a kiss. Nothing more, if you don't want it."

"You could go back downstairs. I think the bar's open until three."

"I could. But I came here instead."

"Why?"

"I like a good challenge?" He rolled his eyes at her.

"So just a kiss?"

"Just a kiss. What happens in Ocean City stays in Ocean City." He glanced toward her suitcase. "Get your scarf."

"Why?"

"Please? You're worse than Cam with all the 'whys.'"

"I just want to know what you're going to do with it." But she slid off the foot of the bed and grabbed the scarf. When she turned around, Matt was standing right next to her.

"I'll show you what I'm going to do with it." He took the red scarf from her hands. "Scoot back up on the bed."

She did as he asked, her heart beginning to race already. There were really only two things she could think of to do with a scarf in the current situation. Tie it around her eyes or tie it around her wrists.

He climbed up on the bed, too, and adjusted the fluffy hotel pillows behind her. "Comfortable?"

She had only a moment to nod before he draped the folded scarf across her eyes and tied it behind her head. He gave it a gentle tug.

"Too tight? Too loose?"

"It's fine." A little nervous thrill awakened near the base of her spine. "So what's the point of this?"

"The point is to get you to stop thinking so much."

"I'm feeling self conscious now because I can't see the look on your face."

"Don't analyze what's happening, Cass. Just relax and let it happen."

"I don't think I—" His finger pressed firmly on her lower lip. "Shhh."

His finger drifted from her lips to her chin, then traced the curve of her neck down to the base of her throat. The little nervous thrill was more like a clanging alarm clock now. If only she weren't wearing these silly plaid pajamas. Why hadn't she bought something a little more feminine? *Because you're not supposed to be doing this. Not with Matt.* She hushed up the voice. *It's just kissing.*

"Cassidy." Both of Matt's hands were cupping her face now. "I can tell you're thinking. And when you're thinking, you're not present in the moment."

"Sorry—"

And then his lips were on hers—not lightly, but not hard either. She felt the mattress shift beneath her and she realized that he had just straddled her legs. For some reason, the image of that in her head was ... very arousing. And she couldn't even see it, in actuality. His hands gently pulled her head toward his and his lips explored hers, navigating the softness, the curves. She reminded herself to breathe. Then he deepened the kiss, sucking her lower lip into his for a moment before brushing his tongue over hers. The urge—*the need*—to just give into this was overwhelming, to let herself disappear into the swirl of pleasurable sensations taking over her body.

She understood the point of the blindfold now.

When he broke the kiss, she nearly whimpered with disappointment—at both the end of the kiss and the knowledge that she couldn't have this exquisite pleasure on a regular basis. Not with the man straddling her thighs right now and tenderly caressing her cheeks. And so far in her life, this man right here was the only source of it.

"Are you okay, Cass?"

She nodded.

"Do you want me to take the scarf off?"

She hesitated before answering. Twin impulses warred within her. They should stop. She should untie the scarf and they should find something on TV to watch, like the platonic friends they were supposed to be. On the other hand, her body was charged with arousal right now.

"No," she whispered.

He reached around her to tighten it just a hair. "What happens in Ocean City stays in Ocean City."

His voice was throaty with something she'd rather not contemplate. She wasn't supposed to be thinking right now, anyway.

"You promise?" she said.

"I promise. What we do is between us."

That wasn't really true. But maybe just for tonight—for one night—it could be.

"What do you want to do?" she asked, suddenly mindful again of her plaid pajamas.

"Let me show you. You tell me if you want me to stop at any point."

His fingers touched the top button of her pajama shirt. One by one, she felt them release until the shirt was entirely undone. He slid the flannel fabric aside.

"You're beautiful, Cassidy." He ran a finger down the center-line of her sternum, between her breasts and down her stomach. "I mean that." His hand toyed with the elastic waistband of her pajama pants. "Lift up your hips."

She did and he slid the pants down her legs. She heard them hit the other bed with a soft whoosh of fabric against fabric. With her sense of sight blocked off, even the slight change of temperature from pajamas to bare skin was arousing. When she felt his palms rest for a moment on her ankles before skimming up her calves, she was sure she was about to pass out.

Over the next hour, she lost complete track of time as he touched her legs, her arms, her stomach. He lavished copious amounts of time on parts of her body she was fairly certain no one had ever touched before. Or even noticed. Like that spot at the back of her knee. The skin over her collarbone. The curving underside of her breast. Most guys just went straight for the obvious places, in her experience. Matt took his time and explored.

He knew his way around a woman's body. That was for sure. And every time the matter of where he had gained that knowledge—the question of how many women that must have taken—began to worm its way into her pleasure-fogged brain, he would touch her someplace new and the thought would instantly evaporate.

Oh. My.

When Cassidy opened her eyes in the morning, those were the first two words that bubbled up from her sleepy unconscious. Not *what time is it?* Or *where am I?* Or *whose body is that in bed with me?* (She already knew the answer to that question.) In fact, her brain doubled down on the thought and resurfaced the words again, just for good measure.

Oh my.

She'd had an orgasm last night. And all he had done was touch her with his hands and fingers, patiently guiding her to the very edge of pleasure. Not letting her fall back at the last minute, but instead slowly pulling her away from terra firma and then catching her as she fell.

It was heavenly. Glorious. And some other adjectives she was still too pleasure-addled to come up with. *So that was sex.* Except, well, it wasn't. Not really, she supposed. They didn't do "the deed." All they did was touch each other. But ... *my oh my.*

She turned her head to look at Matt sleeping next to her. The hotel's comforter had slipped off his broad shoulders. It took all her willpower not to trace her finger over the outline of his muscles, to snuggle up against him and drape an arm over his ribcage. That would be cuddling—and cuddling probably wasn't allowed between friends with benefits. Their contract hadn't been that specific. It wasn't even supposed to still be in effect, for that matter.

What happens in Ocean City stays in Ocean City.

She wished they could just stay in Ocean City.

SHE WAS ALREADY AWAKE behind him. He could tell by her breathing. It no longer had the almost perfect cadence of sleep. And he'd spent a good portion of the night wide awake, listening to her beautifully rhythmic breathing. Normally, an orgasm put him to sleep afterward like someone flipped a switch. Not last night. He had lain awake, just enjoying the utter sense of peace and calm that enveloped his body like a warm bath. The last thing he had wanted to do was fall asleep and lose it.

Right now, however, he was torn between two actions. On the one hand, he wanted to leap from the bed, fist punch the air, and strut around the hotel room like a peacock. He had given Cassidy an orgasm last night. Not just any orgasm, either. He'd seen enough women have one to be able to judge the quality. Cassidy had been so lost in hers he'd thought he might have to do CPR on her afterward.

On the other hand, he also wanted to roll over and kiss the ever-loving hell out of her. If only he knew what her thoughts were this morning. She might be lying there, entertaining second thoughts. She might not be receptive to a round two.

Last night was for her. All he had wanted was to make her feel good. No reciprocation needed from her, so after she came down from her orgasm he had begun touching himself. She tugged the scarf from her eyes and watched for a few minutes, then asked, "What do you think about when you do that?"

"I'm thinking how much softer your hand would feel than mine."

He closed his eyes as the memory took shape in his mind. She had reached over and stilled his fist. Pried his fingers off and replaced them with her own—which were even softer than his feeble brain could imagine.

He knew he should open his eyes to the harsh morning sunlight leaking through the hotel's drapes. Remembering her touch—the impossible softness, the hesitation, her uncertainty— none of that was doing anything to alleviate his morning wood. He had to have set a new world record for quickest orgasm last night.

As much as he wanted to just lie there and luxuriate in the memory, he couldn't pretend to be asleep all morning. Fish or cut bait, as his dad liked to say. He could get up, or he could roll over and begin kissing the ever-loving hell out of her.

He rolled over.

CHAPTER 25

*I*t didn't take long for Cassidy to learn the name and location of every cheap motel within a twenty-mile radius of St. Caroline. "What happens in Ocean City stays in Ocean City" became "As long as it doesn't happen in St. Caroline …" The Roadside Inn. Bay Hamlets. King Crab Motel. She and Matt snuck away once or twice a week—schedules permitting—to add the benefits to their friendship.

Cassidy decided that January was the best month of her entire life so far.

It was the third week of the month and Cassidy was sitting in Kellie Brownington's office in Annapolis to discuss the retail and tourism panel she had agreed to participate in. The Northeast Retail Show in Boston was only three weeks away. *Time flies when you're having fun.* And Cassidy was having fun—she just couldn't admit it to anyone. Or even appear to be unusually happy, which was proving harder than expected. Even Natalie—who was usually pretty self-absorbed, in Cassidy's opinion—had noticed her mood change.

Good sex'll do that to you.

No, make that *great* sex.

Right that minute, Matt was waiting for her in a hotel in downtown Annapolis. A nice hotel, not some cinder block motel that would fit right into a cheesy horror movie. As soon as this meeting wrapped up, that's where she was headed.

Cassidy watched as Kellie gathered up a stack of materials on the show, bios on the other panelists, and some articles she felt would be helpful for Cassidy to read ahead of time.

"You made your hotel reservation, right?"

For a split second, Cassidy thought she was referring to the hotel Matt was in.

Cassidy nodded. "Did that back before the holidays."

"Good. Whew. Sorry. I've got pregnancy brain these days. I can barely remember what I did yesterday, let alone two months ago."

"Congratulations, by the way."

"Thank you. Here you go. Call me or email me if you have any questions." Kellie slid the stack of materials across her glass-topped desk. "Otherwise I'll see you in Boston."

In the parking garage, Cassidy located her car and set the materials on the back seat. Then she texted Matt. *Leaving office now.*

He responded with a happy face emoji and *Room 325. Left off the elevator.*

He had booked a room in the same hotel they'd spent the night together in back in October. This time nobody would be sleeping in a chair.

When she got to room 325, the door was ajar just enough to keep the lock from catching. She knocked lightly, then pushed it open, locking it behind her. She dropped her overnight bag on the floor and walked past the bathroom, the closet, the mirror. The lighting in the room was dim and the air smelled faintly of cinnamon, which she quickly saw was coming from a lit jar candle on the desk.

Matt was leaning back into the pillows on the bed, a sexy

smile on his face. Even though the sheets and duvet were pulled up past his waist, she was pretty certain that smile was the only thing he was wearing at the moment.

She unwrapped the red scarf from around her neck. It was just a length of fabric—and heaven knew, she worked around miles of fabric every day—but wearing the scarf gave her an extra boost of confidence so she wore it as often as she could. It reminded her of something new she had learned about herself recently: she could be sexy. She wasn't just nose-to-the-grind-stone Cassidy Trevor.

"Are we using this tonight?" She gave the scarf a little mata-dor-like wave.

He shook his head and reached beneath the covers, pulling out ... a set of handcuffs. The purple velvet-lined ones from his nightstand at home. She had completely forgotten about those.

"I want you to see what we're doing tonight." He picked up a tiny key from the nightstand and unlocked the cuffs. "Do you trust me?"

"As long as we don't lose that key."

He chuckled. "I've responded to a few calls where people lost the key."

"In St. Caroline?"

"Yup, even in sleepy old St. Caroline."

He made a show of carefully placing the key back on the nightstand. Then to her surprise, he proceeded to drape the metal cuffs over his own wrists.

"Here. Close these for me."

"We're putting them on you?" She wasn't expecting that, but she clicked them shut for him. "Now what?"

"Now whatever. You decide." He lifted his restrained wrists and tucked them behind his head.

"You're not really all that restrained," she observed as she leaned over to unzip her short boots and pull them off.

"It's symbolic."

She laughed as she straightened back up and unzipped her wool dress pants. She and Matt might not be in love, might not be a true couple, but sex with him was fun. More fun than she had expected it to be. In the past, she was always too worried about impressing a boyfriend so they'd fall in love with her or not break up with her. With Matt, the sex was just sex. If she pulled her sweater over her head and her hair went wild with static electricity—or someone accidentally elbowed the other in the ribs—they just laughed it off.

She draped her pants over the back of a chair. When she turned back to the bed, Matt had kicked off the covers. She was right about what he was wearing. Her eyes took in his nude body. He was dark everywhere she was light. Hard with muscle everywhere she was soft. Their bodies fit together like two pieces of a puzzle.

"Are you going to just stand there and gawk? I'm getting a little chilly here."

She grabbed the hem of her sweater and pulled it over her head. Static electricity crackled through her hair, but no one laughed this time. Instead, Matt's eyes darkened and his erection lengthened right before her eyes.

"That's new," he said.

She looked down at the lacy bra and panties she was wearing, her first set of truly sexy lingerie—barely there lace in a deep navy blue.

"I like it," he added.

"I hoped you would."

She straddled his body on the bed, ran her palms over the smattering of dark hair on his chest, then leaned in to kiss him. Normally, his hands would cup her head or jaw as they kissed. She missed that at first, missed being kissed. Then it hit her. She needed to kiss him, and the thought sucked the breath from her lungs for an instant. By cuffing himself, he had put her in charge. An intense heat rushed her body.

She drew her lips away from his. "Have you ever done this before? Put handcuffs on yourself?"

"No. Usually the shoe's on the other foot. So to speak."

Unspoken words hung between them. He trusted her. Sure, lots of people trusted her. Trusted her to keep Quilt Therapy profitable, trusted her with boosting holiday sales at every business in town, trusted her to speak knowledgeably on an industry panel. She was so trusted in those areas that she almost took that trust for granted. And yet, her mother didn't trust her not to screw up her sister's relationship and new family. Hell, Cassidy didn't trust *herself* with that responsibility.

Matt trusted her with all of that. He knew that she would be discreet about the "benefits" they engaged in. He trusted her enough to try new things. He trusted her with his desires.

"So when do you leave for Boston?" Matt handed her a warm washcloth and a dry towel, then slipped into bed next to her.

"I fly up February eleventh. Return on the fifteenth."

He rubbed his wrists where the metal cuffs had bit into his skin.

"Hope that doesn't leave marks," she said.

"I might have to wear gloves for a few days." He winked at her and enjoyed the sleepy, satisfied smile he got in return.

"Yeah, that won't look suspicious. A few times there, I thought you were going to break those things apart."

He had thought so, too. He was unprepared for just how intense the pleasure would get.

He snuggled his body up against hers. "I've wanted to try that on myself for years."

"So why now?"

"I knew you wouldn't laugh at me."

"I think I was laughing *with* you a couple times."

He pressed a kiss into her bare shoulder, then lifted the washcloth and towel from her hands. He tossed them onto the floor at the foot of the bed. "Laughing *with* me is okay."

And then, because he needed to keep reminding himself of what exactly he and Cassidy were doing, he asked "the question."

"Have you heard back from any of the schools yet?"

She shook her head. "I should hear in March."

"I'm sure you'll get in everywhere." Don't lose sight of that, he told himself. *She's leaving.*

"All I need is one. Texas is my first choice, though."

"That's a bit of a hike." Not driving distance—which was good. When she left for school, this would all be over. That was a good thing, because she didn't want their relationship to become public knowledge and he didn't want a relationship period. Not a serious, long-term one. He didn't "do" relationships.

She shrugged. "I'll come back to visit."

Would they hook up on her visits home? *Probably not.* She'd meet a nice guy out there, someone educated, someone who "did" relationships. And he'd thank Matt someday for helping Cassidy feel comfortable with her body and with sex. Well, not really. *But he should!* Matt was getting her ready for the next stage in her life. Because they were friends. Because he liked her. Because he wanted her to be happy.

Although she seemed pretty happy right now.

He waited for what he had nicknamed the "voice of reason" to weigh in, but it was quiet tonight. It had been quiet for awhile, come to think of it. Maybe he didn't need to make an appointment with Dr. Smythe, after all. Maybe all the sex he was having with Cassidy had relieved his stress levels. She was pretty good medicine for any number of things ailing him.

"So how are things at the station?" she asked. "Is that state rep still coming to visit?"

"Yeah. The first week in February. Two weeks from now. I'm almost done with the report."

Tension between summer residents and the town of St. Caroline was a perennial issue. Last summer, the Secretary of State's home had caught fire. Even with mutual aid help from other fire departments in the area, the house was almost a total loss. Matt's dad had gotten an earful from the governor over that.

"I'm enjoying it, though," he added.

"Enjoying what? Writing the report?"

She rolled her body around to face him more fully. Her lovely breasts grazed his chest. He traced his thumb around her nipple, enjoying the way it made her chest vibrate with her effort to control her breathing.

"Yeah, that and coming up with our recommendations. It's a nice change of pace, looking at the big picture of things and all." It was also helping to redeem him in his father's eyes—hell, in everyone's eyes—after the debacle with the barn fire. He used to be good at two things: being a firefighter and sex. Now the first one was in question. Fortunately, the second still held. He wrapped his arms around Cassidy's warm body and pulled her close.

CHAPTER 26

*R*epresentative Hartwell cut an imposing figure as he chatted with some of the crew in the station—tall and broad shouldered, with dark hair that was beginning to grey at the temples. It wasn't hard to picture him as the Naval Academy quarterback he was twenty-five years ago. But Matt felt good about the politician's visit so far.

Matt and his father had pulled every relevant number they could come up with. Fire department budgets, town growth, tax revenues, cost of personnel and equipment, the cost of training a new firefighter. Matt had taken the representative on a driving tour of St. Caroline so he could see firsthand the growth the town had experienced over the past ten years. St. Caroline was no stranger to wealthy part-time residents, but there were more of them now than there used to be. They were buying up land and pushing the boundaries of the fire department's service range further and further out into the countryside. The homes seemed to get bigger and more lavish with each passing year, too.

And the taxes they paid didn't always cover the extra costs the town incurred as a result.

Hartwell was also surprised to learn the cost of a new fire

engine—roughly half a million dollars, and that was before equipment. Not that St. Caroline was asking for a handout. On the contrary, as Matt pointed out, the department was embarking on a fundraising campaign soon.

"We do 'fill the boot' campaigns every year to raise money for the community. This year, we're asking the community to help us back." Hint hint, he thought.

Three days later, Matt learned that Rep. Hartwell did indeed take the hint. Jack stopped by Matt's cabin after work, and Matt was glad for the company. Cass was in Boston and, well … he missed her. Not just the "benefits"—although, of course, those too. But he had gotten used to their near nightly chats on the phone and the silly texts she sent throughout the day, which sometimes veered into flirty territory. He was liking the "friends" part of their arrangement almost as much as the "benefits."

There were things he couldn't talk about with male friends, like his worry that he was losing his edge as a firefighter. He had always been able to focus on a call, but now he wondered whether that had been more luck than focus … and whether his luck was starting to run out. In an emergency situation, there wasn't much margin for error—and he had fallen into that margin in the barn. That frightened him. He couldn't admit that to most people, but he could tell Cass. Who was she going to tell? Officially, they weren't supposed to be talking to each other that much.

Hint hint.

When Jack rapped on the cabin door, Matt was looking at a photo Cass had texted earlier in the day—a selfie she'd taken outside Faneuil Hall, the red scarf wrapped around the collar of her winter coat, her cheeks pink from the cold. He sighed without even realizing he was doing it. His body yearned for hers. It was like suffering withdrawal from a drug.

Hint hint.

The voice was back again, too. He needed to schedule an appointment with Dr. Smythe, after all.

"It's unlocked!" he shouted out as he clicked to close the photo on his phone. His brother—all six foot five of him—burst through the cabin's front door and strode straight over to Matt. He lifted his hand in a high five. Matt slapped it.

"What's that for?"

"We just got an anonymous donation."

"By we, you mean ...?"

"The fire department, idiot. Looks like you sweet-talked that representative pretty effectively."

Matt shrugged and shoved his phone into the pocket of his pants. "How big a donation?"

"BIG. One point five million."

Matt's eyes bugged out of his head. "No way."

"Yes way. What did you say to the guy?"

"I told him we were launching a fundraising campaign this spring. And when I took him on a driving tour of the town, I pointed out that most of the new construction is happening on the other side and that if we had a second station over that way, we could reduce response times. And that the town owns property over there that's more or less earmarked for the fire department, but we don't have the money to build on it."

"Damn. I'd donate money after that spiel. If I had any. Got anything to eat?"

"You're not eating with Becca tonight?"

She's out of town for a couple of days, meeting with the woman she's doing that quilt commission for."

"Oh. Okay. I've got leftover pizza. That's what I was planning for dinner."

"You have enough to share?"

"Sure." Matt headed into his small kitchen. He yanked open the refrigerator door and pulled out the pizza box. "Pepperoni okay?" He set the box on the breakfast bar, nudging aside some mail and a legal pad.

"Sure. Whatever."

"I don't have any beer. Soda?"

"No beer?" Jack made a face of mock horror. "Soda's fine."

"I'm trying to cut back on beer and sugar. Improve my diet." He handed Jack a can. Matt was trying whatever he could think of in an attempt to be less "scattered." Meditation, even, though he didn't mention that to Jack.

Jack popped open the can of soda and Matt saw the next seconds unfold as if in slow motion. He tried to get to the legal pad quickly but without looking suspicious. Failure on both counts.

"What's this?" Jack asked.

Matt tried to snatch the pad of paper from his brother's hands, but Jack spun away from the breakfast bar with it in his hands. Matt ran through a litany of swear words in his head.

"Matthew Dean Wolfe and Cassidy Ann Trevor hereby do consent to a friends with benefits situation for a term of no less than one night and no more than eight months," Jack read from the legal pad. "Either party can terminate this agreement at any time with thirty minutes' notice. This is an exclusive agreement between said parties. Relations with any other party invalidates this contract immediately."

Jack slowly turned back around and dropped the pad onto the countertop with a dramatic flourish.

"Seriously." Jack set down the can of soda, never taking his eyes off Matt. "Becca's sister?"

Matt said nothing, which seemed the most prudent course of action at the moment.

"Aren't there enough other women in the world for you? You have to play around with Cassidy?"

"It's not like that, man—" Matt's explanation was cut short by his brother's fist, neatly applied to Matt's jaw. Matt stumbled backward and then hit the floor with his ass. His brother had quite the arm on him these days—and that thought was cut short by the sight of Jack's long body lunging toward him on the floor. Should he fight his brother? He didn't want that. Maybe he should just sit here and let his brother pummel him for a few moments. He was fairly certain Jack would get it out of his system quickly.

He scrabbled to get up to his feet but Jack shoved him hard and he skidded backward across the vinyl flooring.

"I cannot effing believe you," Jack growled. "Becca's sister!"

Matt rubbed his jaw. "I seem to recall a party last year where you tried to foist me off on Cassidy."

"That was before Becca and I—"

Boys! Boys!

They both stopped and cocked their heads, listening.

"Did you hear that?" Matt asked, even as he knew it made no sense whatsoever that Jack would be hearing the voices in his head.

"Yeah. I'm always hearing in my mind what mom would say in any given circumstance."

"Me too."

Jack sat back heavily on the floor. "So like right now, she'd be sending us to our rooms to think long and hard about our behavior."

"And we can't come out until we're both ready to apologize."

"Even though it was your fault." Jack glared at him.

"What? You're the one who hit *me*."

Oh good grief. They both said the words, even as they also heard it in her voice.

"Well, glad I'm not the only one losing my mind," Jack said.

They stared at each other for a long moment across the kitchen floor. Finally, Matt spoke. "Cassidy said she doesn't think Becca would mind."

"She probably wouldn't. I'm minding on her behalf."

"I'm not sure Cass needs someone defending her honor." *That would be my job, anyway.*

"You know, I really came over here to ask you to be my best man."

"Oh." Matt pushed himself up off the floor. "Guess I screwed that up."

"Nah. Who else am I going to ask? Oliver's still a wreck. Not hopeful that'll change before May."

"Ian?" Matt held out his arm to help his brother to his feet.

"Please." Jack rolled his eyes. "I'm stuck with you."

Apologize. The voice was stern, then softened. *Or hug it out.*

Matt looked at his brother and opened his arms wide. Then he dropped them to his side.

Or dance off.

They both looked up at the ceiling, though Matt wasn't sure that's where she was. "She's haunting us."

"Huh. They say people become ghosts when they have unfinished business here on earth."

Raising kids is always unfinished business. Obviously.

Matt tried his best to hold it back—he didn't want to laugh at his mother—but at the sight of his brother trying to do the same, the laughter rolled forth uncontrolled. When they finally got a grip on themselves, they gave each other a brusque man-hug and Jack asked, "When's your shift tomorrow?"

"Three to midnight. Since I don't need Valentine's Day off." He looked his brother pointedly in the eye.

Easy.

CHAPTER 27

*I*t's Valentine's Day, Cassidy thought, as she inserted the hotel key card into the door. She'd been so busy all week that she hadn't even thought of it. Not that it mattered. Like it didn't matter last year. Or the year before. Or probably next year, either.

It was four-thirty and the last afternoon session at the retail show had just concluded. The tiny green light flashed and she pushed the door open. She was going to drop her heavy tote bag of notes and swag before heading back downstairs to have drinks at the hotel bar with some people she'd met. Tomorrow, she would catch her flight home.

She was ready to go home, oddly enough. The retail show had taught her a lot—and she'd had some fun, too. Her fingers were itching to quilt, though. And she missed … she pushed that thought away. She needed to begin weaning herself off of Matt. As soon as she heard back from schools and knew where she'd be going—that would be a good time to break things off.

She dropped the tote bag onto the bed, freshly made up since she left that morning. A foil-wrapped square of chocolate lay on one of the pillows. She touched up her makeup in the bathroom mirror and was about to leave when she remembered the scarf. The hotel had been chilly all week. She grabbed her red scarf from the back of the desk chair, draped it around her shoulders like a shawl, and headed for the elevators.

CHAPTER 28

*M*att sat at the back of the fire station's day room, balancing his open laptop on his knees. At the front of the room, the big screen television was tuned to a hockey game that several of the guys were watching with avid interest. Matt tried to ignore their periodic outbursts as shots were made or pucks went wide. He was perusing the web site of the fire academy in Texas, reading course descriptions and schedules.

Emergency resource deployment planning. Financial management for fire departments. Fire training design. *Hmmm.* He might be good at that one, designing simulations and training exercises. When he was at the fire academy in September, he had taken the lead on a simulation project. It turned out well and he had enjoyed it, to his surprise.

Or what about fire investigation? His dad often tapped him to help with that. St. Caroline didn't really need a full time fire investigator but ... *you could always move somewhere else.* Matt stared blankly into space, then squinted his eyes to try and get a better grip on that thought. Was that his brain speaking? Or his mother? *What do you think of that idea,* he silently asked her. *Would I make a good fire investigator?* No answer came back. Maybe she was off harassing—*haunting, I mean!*—Oliver. Given Jack's absorption in the hockey game, she didn't seem to be bothering him at the moment.

A loud cheer erupted from the front of the day room. Matt looked up. Then the cheers turned to groans as the game cut away to a newscast. There'd been a shooting. The room fell silent as they watched the screen, transfixed. It took a minute or two before the details became clear. Boston. A hotel lobby. Matt slowly lifted his laptop from his knees and set it on the floor next to him. He took long, but deliberate, steps to join Jack and the others in front of the television.

What are the odds?

"Which hotel?" he asked quietly.

"The Seaport Plaza," someone in front answered.

That was the hotel Cassidy was staying at. His lungs froze in his chest. Jack's phone buzzed and he knew who it would be. Becca. He listened as his brother took the call.

"Yeah," Jack said. "We're watching now." A long moment of silence. "Okay. Keep us posted."

Matt continued to watch the screen as the camera tried to zoom in on the scene, only to be pushed back by police. It wasn't real. It wasn't actually happening. He was watching something on television. Television happened to other people. Not him. Not someone he knew.

He felt Jack move in right next to him.

"They're trying to get in touch with her."

"But they can't?"

"No news is good news."

Matt had never understood that saying. It was patently false. He took another step closer to the television as the camera suddenly got a clear shot of the hotel lobby, which was empty now, save for the many police officers on the scene. She was probably fine. In all likelihood, she had been up in her room. The camera slowly panned the scene and it was then that he spotted it. A flash of red lying on the floor as the camera moved past. The red scarf he had given her.

It can't be. You only saw it for a split second. But he knew. He just did.

"Cassidy's been shot."

CHAPTER 29

*T*here was a deep ache in her left shin. And her skin was uncomfortably hot. Voices. There were voices, too. Lots of them. Where was she? She tried to open her eyes, but couldn't. Couldn't move her limbs, either.

I'm dreaming. That had to be it. Because she was at the retail show ... in the hotel ... she'd gone up to her room ... then back down to the lobby to meet some people at the bar ... and then ... there was a lot of noise and people screaming ... chaos ... Cassidy felt a sharp pain in her leg and fell ... she tried to get up but her leg wouldn't hold her ...

Panic welled in her chest. She might not be dreaming. She tried to move again. Anything. An arm, a finger. Open her eyes. Open her mouth to speak. But it was like her brain and her body weren't connected anymore.

She tried to latch onto the voices, onto words, onto anything. But she was tired. So tired.

Am I paralyzed? The thought hit her like a freight train. *I was shot.* An image of ambulance doors closing flashed through her mind. *Am I okay?* She remembered the bright lights of a corridor. *Am I alive, even?*

She heard a new sound, like the wheezing of a door as it opened and then drifted shut.

"Oh Cassidy." It was Lauren's voice. Lauren!

She felt a hand on hers. She tried to flip her own hand over and grab her sister, but again nothing. She screamed silently in her head.

"How was your flight?" Her mother's voice.

A phone pinged.

"Who's that? Daddy?" Her mother again.

"It's Jack," Becca responded. "Matt's on his way."

Cassidy strained to hear more, but there was nothing. Was no one speaking or were her ears not working either?

"You have to let go of this, mom." Lauren again. *But let go of what?*

"Jack says he loves her." Becca.

"He told Jack that?" That was Natalie's voice. Was the whole family here?

"Not in so many words, but Jack knows his brother. He can tell."

There was a long silence and Cass began to think again that she might be dreaming. Because … Matt loved her?

Then she heard her mother's voice again. "All parents fail their children in some ways. But I think daddy and I failed Cassidy the most."

Mom and dad failed me?

"How so?" That was Lauren's voice. Cassidy focused on identifying each person speaking—if she could keep her brain zoomed in on that, she could resist the overpowering urge to go back to sleep.

"We were new parents and there were two of you. And Lauren, you were the fussy baby. Colic. You didn't like to nurse. You took forever to sleep through the night. You teethed with a vengeance."

"Gee sorry, mom."

"Then Becca came along, and then Nat and Charlotte. Daddy's practice was growing. Cassidy was such a low maintenance kid." Long silence. When her mother spoke again, her voice was quieter, subdued. "But not asking for attention isn't the same as not needing it."

Was she the low maintenance kid? Cassidy pondered the idea. *Well, yeah.* When you're part of a big family, it helped if at least one person was low maintenance. And her mother was right. Lauren hadn't been it. Nor Becca. Nor Nat. Cassidy remembered the struggle of trying to get five young kids into the car without someone having to go back inside and use the bathroom one more time. Or getting five teenagers in and out of two bathrooms before school.

Cassidy had always wanted to slow things down as a kid, get things under control. Even now, she wanted to go back to the idea of Matt being in love with her but her family had already moved on to something else. She loved them but they were exhausting sometimes. *A lot of the time.*

The phrase "herding cats" came to mind. Cassidy laughed.

YOU COULD LOSE everything in a heartbeat. Matt sat in a hard vinyl chair in a crowded hospital waiting room in Boston, surrounded by people thinking that exact same thing. Everything could change in an instant.

He knew that. *He knew that.* He had organized his life around that knowledge. That was why he didn't do serious relationships. That way when they ended—which they always would—it wouldn't hurt. Likewise with firefighting. He joined the department because that's what the men in his family did. It was expected of him. Out of all the people in St. Caroline who could join the fire department, it made the most sense for a Wolfe to do it. Matt and his brothers had grown up in the station. By the time he graduated from high school, he already knew what other people would take years to learn.

But it had never really been a conscious choice. Nor was it a recent revelation that if his dad fired him tomorrow, he wouldn't necessarily be that sad. Being a firefighter had always been something to focus all his attention on. Having it meant he didn't need to have anything else in his life. Didn't need to think about what else he wanted in his life.

My life is full! Jam-packed! I'm on call a lot—it makes relationships difficult!

Because wanting things meant you cared about things. And caring about things meant you were going to get hurt when you lost them.

Things! Things! She's not a thing! Yeah, that was definitely his own voice. When he needed a voice of reason, of course it was nowhere to be found. And hadn't everything been just fine in his life before his mom died? He'd been content to be on at the St. Caroline fire department, content to be a doting uncle, to be a cantankerous brother, content to have the reputation of a dating expert—or man-whore, depending on whom you asked.

That was then. The death of his mom had cracked his shell of contentedness—he wasn't content with having her gone for the rest of his life. *Not content with that at all!* Now he wasn't content with anything, it seemed.

He lifted his head from where he'd been staring a hole into the scuffed linoleum flooring and looked around for a familiar face. The Trevors were already at the hospital, but he had yet to see any of them. Just as well. Already he felt like an interloper here. He wasn't supposed to care about Cassidy enough to spend a small fortune on a last-minute plane ticket from Baltimore to Boston.

Maybe it was just selfishness on his part, his desire to be here. The only time he did feel content anymore was when he was with her. And she'd been away five days already. He glanced at the clock on the wall, loudly ticking away the minutes. It was after midnight. Maybe they wouldn't even let him see her. But he had to try, so that at least she would know he cared enough to come.

He dropped his head back into his hands to resume staring at the scuff marks on the floor. He was so tired that the marks were beginning to form actual shapes in his head. Someone sat down in the empty chair next to him. An older man, based on the shoes that now covered some of the scuff marks.

"Son," the person said.

Matt looked over at Dr. Trevor. Cassidy's father. A man who had stuck a needle in Matt's arm more than a few times when Matt was a kid. He imagined Dr. Trevor might want to do something similar right now.

"She's awake," Dr. Trevor said. "The gang is on their way out here right now."

"Is she okay?"

"She's going to be fine. I spoke to the surgeon earlier. She got hit in the lower leg and it fractured her tibia. They had to put a plate and screws to hold the bone, but she's going to be fine."

"She was lucky."

"She was. Very."

The thought that Cassidy had been very lucky wasn't much comfort to him. Just the opposite, in fact. Luck was a fickle guardian angel. How many times had he been on a call that could have turned out badly were it not for luck?

"Daddy!"

He looked up to see the rest of the Trevor family walking toward them. Mrs. Trevor did not look surprised to see him. Not particularly pleased, either.

"You can go in for a few minutes. The nurse said it was okay," she said to her husband.

Matt felt the older man's hand heavy on his shoulder. "Come on, Mattie."

~

Cassidy had just closed her eyes when the door to the room opened again. She felt a kiss planted on her forehead. From the smell of the aftershave, she knew it was her father.

"I know you're probably tired, sweetheart," he said. "I just wanted to see you."

She opened her eyes. "Thanks," she said weakly. "Can you tell me what happened?" In all the excitement that her laughing and opening her eyes had created, no one had bothered to tell her exactly what was going on. She'd gotten shot in the leg, obviously. She remembered being put on a stretcher and brought to the hospital. She remembered the bright lights of a corridor but after that, things got fuzzy. There were so many ambulances coming from the hotel, so many people brought in. Because hers weren't the most serious injuries no one had really explained what had happened to her.

"You have a fractured tibia," he answered. "You were in surgery for a bit. They had to put in some hardware to repair it."

"Oh." She wiggled the toes on her left foot.

"Are you in any pain?"

She thought for a moment. Was she in any pain? "No," she answered. "It's manageable."

"Well then, I'm heading back out to the waiting room. I need to try and calm your mother down."

Cassidy gave him a wan smile. "She *is* a little agitated."

He leaned in and dropped another kiss on her forehead before leaving. She had just closed her eyes again to rest when she heard someone say her name.

"Cass?"

It sounded like Matt, but he couldn't be here already. Could he?

She heard what sounded like a chair being moved next to the

bed. She opened her eyes and there he was, his hair looking like he'd combed it with a rake.

"You look like hell," she said, managing a smile for him.

"You don't look much better."

Her smile widened.

"How do you feel?"

"I've had better days, I think." She watched him carefully for a moment. "You didn't have to come all this way." Becca's words came back to her. *Jack says he loves her.* But Matt couldn't love her. That wasn't in their contract. She was leaving St. Caroline to go back to school. And because Matt didn't do serious relationships.

"Someone had to come up here and chew out your ass for this." The smile on his face was soft, but Matt always cocked his head to one side when he was joking. His head was perfectly upright now.

"Umm, not my fault?"

Only that wasn't what she had read in her mother's eyes. *This would never have happened if you had stayed home.* Lauren had gotten the same message over the holidays, too. *If you had stayed home and married a nice boy from St. Caroline ...* Cassidy loved her mother—everyone did, which of course was part of the problem. But was it terrible that she thought her mother was a coward sometimes? That she was afraid of the world?

"This could have happened anywhere. I'm not going to live my life in fear."

I'M LIVING my life in fear these days.

Matt didn't say those words out loud, but that's what he felt. Every morning, he woke up and hoped that there wouldn't be a serious call in to the fire department that day. He was sucking at his job lately, and he had a job one couldn't afford to suck at—it put too many other people in danger.

And right now, he was sitting in a hospital in Boston with a heart that hurt more than a heart should be able to hurt … and that scared him more than anything.

She wasn't wearing her glasses. A few months ago, she would have looked completely strange to him this way. He was used to it now because she insisted on taking them off when they had sex. He liked to think he was a pretty good read of her eyes. He wasn't seeing fear in them at the moment. He was seeing exhaustion. A certain toughness he had always associated with her, even from afar when they were kids. Her makeup was smeared below her eyes, and he knew she'd be upset if she found out later that no one told her. He wet a paper towel at the small sink in the room and then carefully wiped away the black smudges.

"Now I don't look like hell anymore?" she said.

He leaned in and kissed her, then kissed her more deeply. She turned her head to the side.

"I have morning breath."

She did, that was true. He didn't care.

"It's not morning," he assured her.

"What time is it?"

"After midnight by now, I think."

"So technically morning."

"So technically, I don't care about your morning breath."

"You can't do this, Matt."

"Do what?"

"Becca said you … she said you love me."

"And?"

"And you can't do that."

Unfortunately, it seems that I can.

"You never officially terminated our contract."

"Matt. Be serious. Please."

He collapsed back into the hard hospital chair. Why were hospital chairs always so hard? So you wouldn't let yourself get comfortable in one? What were the odds of that?

"I'm touched that you came all the way up here to see me. I am."

She held out her hand and he took it in his. The warmth of her skin shot up his arm and stabbed him in the heart. Felt that way, at any rate.

"But …" she went on.

"But you're leaving to go back to school. I know that."

"So why?"

He shook his head. He knew the "why" but he wouldn't burden her with it. He'd had plenty of time to think about it on the drive to the airport, in the terminal, on the plane, in the cab. And even though his heart hurt like a bitch, as soon as he walked into this room there was that peacefulness. He was content just to be here with her.

Yet at the same time he wasn't content—he wasn't content to just see her secretly, whenever the two of them could steal away without being noticed. He wasn't content to just eat cold pizza in bed with her. He wanted to hold open the door to a restaurant for her. Wanted to hold her hand in a movie theater. Wanted to prevent other men from kissing her badly. But those were his own selfish reasons, solutions to problems that were his. Not hers.

"I think you're confusing sex with love," she said.

He squeezed her hand, then released it and stood. "You're probably right." But the look in her tired brown eyes said she didn't believe he was capable of mistaking one for the other any more than he did.

CHAPTER 30

*C*assidy loaded tiny stitches onto the needle and pulled it through the pristine white cotton. It was Becca's wedding quilt, a whole cloth quilt—no piecing, just thousands upon thousands of stitches creating an intricate design in thread. She glanced over at the box of band-aids and pile of leather thimbles on the nightstand. No bleeding allowed on this one!

She was in the guest room in her parents' house—aka her old bedroom. Her mother had been making this quilt in secret, but realized she was running out of time. Becca and Jack were getting married at the end of April and it was already the second week of March. Cassidy went to physical therapy every morning and came here in the afternoons to quilt, in lieu of working at Quilt Therapy. Until her leg healed, she couldn't spend hours on her feet.

She took another needleful of stitches, then sat back to look at the big picture. The quilt was only half finished. *It's going to take a miracle to get this done in time.* She adjusted her glasses and squinted hard at the stitches she just took. She sighed, pulled the needle off the thread, and tugged the stitches back out. Of all the Trevor girls, she was the worst one for the task at hand. Becca was far and away the best hand quilter in the family—better than their mom, even. Even Natalie and Charlotte were better than Cassidy. Given her injury, though, it made sense from a time perspective that she be the one to do this.

There was a knock on the door, then a jiggle of the doorknob. "It's me, Cass."

Cassidy got up to unlock the door and let her mom in. "Sorry. Didn't want Becca barging in on me."

"She's at a dress fitting today."

"Oh." She wasn't sure whether she should be disappointed or relieved that she was missing out on all the pre-wedding activities.

Cassidy's old bed was pushed up against the side wall, to make room for the quilting frame. Her mother sat down on the edge of it.

"How are things going?" she asked.

Cassidy rethreaded the needle. "It's getting there." She rocked the needle in and out of the fabric. "I like the idea for this." She nodded at the quilt. Double Wedding Ring was a traditional quilt pattern. Normally it was pieced, but her mother had decided instead to quilt the pattern onto a whole cloth top. "Becca will appreciate it."

She felt her mother's eyes on her as she quilted. Their relationship had been strained since Boston, even though she and Matt weren't seeing each other anymore. He had mailed her a written termination notice, the sting of it softened by two dozen pink roses. Cassidy had gone back to being the "low maintenance" kid. Except for one thing.

"Mom. There's something I need to tell you." She said it without looking up from the quilt.

"You're pregnant."

"Ouch!" Cassidy jerked her hand out from under the quilting frame. "Damn it, mom! Get the bleach pen!" The shock of her mother's words had caused her to prick herself with the needle.

Her mother crawled beneath the quilting frame to zap the blood spot with bleach. After a minute, she crawled back out.

"It'll be fine."

Cassidy tore open a band-aid and covered her finger. "No, I'm not pregnant."

"An STD?"

Cassidy shot her mother a look. "Not that either. It has nothing to do with sex at all, as a matter of fact." Obviously her mother was spending way too much time contemplating her sex life. "I've applied to business school. To get my MBA."

"Okay ... does Talbot College have a program for that?"

"No." She waited a beat, to give her mother time to process the implications of that single word. "I've applied to programs in other parts of the country." She held her breath.

"I take it you don't know where you're going yet."

"I'm waiting to hear back on my applications. Should be this month."

"You're moving away." Her mother recapped the bleach pen and tossed it back into the nightstand drawer. She flopped back onto the bed.

Cassidy anchored the quilting needle in the fabric, then joined her mother.

"When?" Michelle asked. "Fall?"

"Maybe summer. The programs all start officially in the fall, but I've looked into taking a few summer classes. Plus, I'd need to find an apartment and everything."

"And you have the money for this?"

"Most of it. I've been squirreling away." She exhaled a short laugh. "Not having a social life makes it easy to be frugal."

"So you've been planning this for awhile." Michelle rolled onto her side to look at her daughter.

"I wouldn't call it planning. More like thinking about it."

"Am I the last to know?"

"No. Only Lauren knows I've applied. And ..."

"And Matt?"

Cassidy nodded.

Her mother reached over and tucked a lock of Cassidy's hair back behind her ear. "I was worried about him breaking your heart. It never occurred to me that it would work the other way around."

"I don't think I've broken his heart, mom. Not for long, anyway."

CHAPTER 31

The menswear shop in Annapolis was dark and hushed with thick carpet underfoot and rich wood paneling on the walls. In the tailor's workshop in the back, Jack stood on a square platform as the tailor checked the length of his tuxedo pants. Even though Oliver was present, Matt kept an eye on Mason and Cam. It was habit by now. The boys were goofing off in front of a full-length mirror, gyrating their bodies and making silly noises to imitate the funhouse mirrors on the Ocean City boardwalk.

"Guys, shhh," Oliver warned them.

"Looks perfect to me," the tailor pronounced his verdict on Jack's pants. "What do you think?"

Jack took another look in the mirrors surrounding the platform. "Looks good. What do you guys think?"

Matt and Oliver nodded their agreement.

"Okay, next!" the tailor said.

Matt looked over at Oliver. "Why don't you go? Then you can get the boys out of here."

As soon as Oliver stepped onto the platform the tailor began tugging and straightening the jacket. Matt could see his brother's shoulders stiffen beneath the black fabric.

"Is Serena going to the bachelorette party?" Jack asked.

"I don't think so. Not with her parents still in town." Oliver's left shoulder twitched.

"Oh," Matt and Jack said simultaneously. There had never been any love lost between Ollie and his in-laws.

Matt and Jack glanced over at the boys, but they were still preoccupied with their fine selves in the mirror.

"How's that going?" Jack asked, his voice low. He and Matt moved closer to Oliver.

"About as well as can be expected," Oliver replied in an equally quiet voice. "Which is to say not that well."

"Where are the girls doing the party?" Matt changed the subject.

"At the Inn. Spa day and then lunch. They're combining the bachelorette party with a going away party for Cassidy."

Matt's stomach muscles clenched as though he'd just been punched. *A going away party.* Not that it was a surprise. He knew Cassidy was planning to go back to school. She had told him that acceptances or rejections would arrive in March. It was now March. But a Going Away Party—he imagined a banner with the words in capital letters—was so ... *official.* He couldn't keep pretending it might not happen.

"Where'd she get in?" he asked.

"Just about every place she applied to. University of Texas at Austin is where she's going, though. You didn't know that?"

"I've been out of town." Which was true. But that wasn't really the reason he didn't know where Cassidy had decided to go to school. They had eased out of each other's lives after her trip to Boston. The Trevors had closed ranks around her. Well, supposedly it was to help her out while she was recovering. But to Matt it felt like he'd been forced out of the inner circle of her life.

Still, it hurt that she hadn't told him directly.

"Yeah, how was Texas?" Oliver chimed in.

"It was good." Matt had spent the first two weeks of the month at the fire academy in Texas, taking a course.

"So you think fire investigation is what you want to do?" Oliver added.

"I think so, yeah. Maybe."

"I think you'd be good at it," his older brother twisted around to take one last look at his pants hem in the mirror.

"I guess they won't be having a male stripper at Evangeline's, at least." Matt couldn't get his brain away from the going away party, much as he wanted to.

"They're having that artist, you know, the one you did the lights with—"

"Elliott? What for? As a stripper?"

"Guys." Oliver stepped down from the platform and cocked his head toward Mason and Cam. "Last thing I need is for them to go home and talk about ... *that* ... in front of their grandparents."

"Sorry."

"Your turn."

Ollie clapped Matt between the shoulder blades as Matt stepped onto the platform to let the tailor fuss and mumble over how the tuxedo "hung" on him.

"Elliott is going to do a group portrait of them all as a going away gift to Cassidy. Nothing fancy, just a pencil drawing."

"Who's paying for that?" Oliver shrugged out of his tuxedo jacket and returned it to the hanger.

"Becca sweet-talked Elliott into doing it for practically nothing. They all chipped in to help pay for it. Michelle and Dan, too." Jack laughed. "They sure can't afford his normal rates. His stuff is pretty popular with the tech crowd in California."

"A portrait? Huh." Matt recognized the dull ache in his chest as jealousy. Maybe Cassidy and Elliott had been seeing each other. He shoved that thought out of his mind so hard, his fists clenched.

"Relax," the tailor said as he tugged on Matt's jacket sleeves.

Elliott could afford to do a long-distance relationship with Cassidy. He could fly out to Texas every weekend. Hell, he could probably just paint out there. What difference did it make if he was painting in Texas versus Maryland?

A thousand jealous thoughts were pounding their tiny little fists on the inside of Matt's skull.

"What time is it?" he asked.

"Two o'clock. Why?" Jack answered.

"Do you know who's working at the Trevors' shop this afternoon?"

"Natalie and Becca, I assume. Cassidy's been working at home lately, because of her leg."

Matt ignored Jack's pointed look.

IN HER APARTMENT, Cassidy sat at the big wooden table that she and Natalie used for quilt projects. She sliced a rotary cutter through a stack of fabric, making long narrow strips to be used at the summer quilting retreat. She kept screwing it up though, the cutter going off track halfway down and creating wavy strips of fabric. She tossed the ruined pieces onto a growing pile of rejects and started over. Since her trip to Boston—everyone avoided saying "since the day she got shot"—her mother and sisters had been giving her projects that were ill-suited to her natural abilities. She was not the best person to finish Becca's wedding quilt or cut fabric when it had to be done accurately.

She loved quilting but she was better at the business side of things. She wasn't going to miss cutting fabric or bundling fat quarters. She set down the rotary cutter and stretched the fingers of her right hand. She tried to think of when she had last worked on a quilt of her own making. Before Christmas? Thanksgiving, even? Actually, she hadn't spent much time on her own quilts over the past year at all. She had spent more time working on other people's quilts—the community quilts her mom kept on the quilting frame at the shop, Jackie's Christmas quilt, Becca's white wedding quilt. The last top she had pieced just for herself was still just that—a top. She hadn't even added batting and a back to it yet.

She rubbed the achiness in her knuckles. She was going to miss working with her mom and sisters, but running a quilt shop had definitely sapped some of the pleasure of quilting for her. It would be nice to just quilt for fun again.

She had just picked up the cutter again when someone rapped sharply on the door to the apartment. She looked over at the crutches lying on the sofa. "Who is it?" she called out.

"Me."

Matt.

"Cassidy's not here," she called back. She didn't want to see Matt. Well, she did want to see him—and that was the problem. She missed him with a fierceness that took her breath away, with an intensity that had her questioning her decision to move. She could always apply to schools closer to home and be able to spend weekends in St. Caroline.

No. She knew it was best for her if she moved farther away than Baltimore or DC. It wasn't just that she wanted to leave St. Caroline. She wanted to see more of the world. Texas was just a start. And yes, she knew where her mother stood on the matter. *I went to Boston and look what happened.*

"Well, I know it's not Lauren in there because she's probably a better actor than that."

"The door's unlocked." She gave in.

Besides, she'd kick herself from here to the moon if she stayed on the east coast and then she and Matt broke up in a year. Or six months. Because he didn't really love her. Maybe he wasn't confusing sex with love, as she had accused him of back at the hospital. But he definitely mistook worry for love. A dog doesn't change its spots. Matt wasn't the sort to settle down for long.

She watched from across the room as the door slowly opened. Matt stepped into the apartment, his arms full with flowers, a bottle of champagne, a wrapped gift, and a stuffed animal. He plucked the latter from the crook of his elbow and tossed it at her. She nearly caught it, too, but it bounced from her hands and landed on the floor behind her. She twisted around in the chair to stare back at it.

"I'll get it. Stay where you are."

He set the champagne and bouquet of flowers on the kitchen counter. At least they weren't roses this time. These were your basic supermarket flowers—lilies, carnations, mums. Pretty, though. Lots of colors. He dropped the wrapped gift onto the table in front of her on his way to pick up the stuffed animal.

"Here." He held it out to her.

It was a stuffed steer.

"Go longhorns," he added.

She bit back the real smile that was fighting to break through and instead plastered a forced smile on her face. "Thanks."

"So when do you leave?"

"The week after the wedding. I'm taking summer classes. But I need to get out there before the summer term begins so I can find an apartment."

He looked over at the crutches. "Will you be off those by then?"

She shrugged. "Maybe. Lauren's driving me out there and then spending the summer."

"What's she going to do there all summer?"

"Take some painting classes at the community college."

"Ahh. Sounds like fun."

Cassidy laughed at him and this time it was genuine, not forced.

"Okay, so it doesn't sound like fun to me." He backtracked to the kitchen and lifted up the champagne. "But this calls for a toast. Someone escapes St. Caroline at last." He popped open the champagne. "Glasses?"

"Nat and I don't have champagne flutes."

"Seriously?" He gave her a disbelieving look.

She shook her head. "Sorry."

He laughed. "Neither do I. Or I would have brought them along." He held up the bottle. "To bigger and better things." He handed it to her.

She lifted it to her lips and took a sip, the bubbles fizzing and dancing on her tongue. She took another quick sip, then handed the bottle back to Matt. He took a swig, too.

"Are you on call tonight?" she asked.

"Nope. So I can have champagne." He took another drink and handed the bottle to her again. "That present is for you, too." He leaned his elbows on the tabletop.

She looked down at the wrapped box. It was wide and flat, covered in polka-dotted paper and finished off with a blue satin ribbon. Carefully she slid the ribbon off the box and removed the paper. When she opened the box, she found a red scarf—identical to the one he had given her for Christmas and that she had lost in Boston.

"Oh. You have to take this back," she said.

"Why? It's to replace the other one."

"I know but … I know how expensive these scarves are."

"The shop gave me a discount since it was for you."

"A big discount?"

He sighed an exasperated sigh. "It was sizable, yes. That's all I'm going to say about it."

She rubbed the fabric between her fingers. It was a beautiful scarf and she had been sad to lose the first one. She looked up at him. "Thank you."

His eyes were soft with … well, it was definitely not worry. "This isn't how this was supposed to turn out."

"I know. It was supposed to be easy. A few months of fun and nothing more, because you were leaving."

"And because you don't do serious relationships. This isn't entirely my fault."

"It's not your fault at all. You're holding up your end of the bargain. You're leaving town. It's me who screwed everything up."

The regretful look in his eyes made her heart ache.

"I love you, Mattie. I really do. But I can't stay here. I'd always wonder, 'what if?'"

"I would never ask you to stay. Which is why I'm not going to kiss you right now, even though I'd run naked through a burning building for another kiss from you." He held her gaze for a long time before lifting his elbows off the table and standing up. "I would never ask you to change your dreams for me."

MATT STOOD before the iron gates of the cemetery, taking a minute to look at the bright green of new spring grass and the budding canopy of leaves overhead. Winters weren't particularly harsh in St. Caroline, but the shift from winter to spring felt quicker than usual this year. Or maybe he was just more attuned to change since he was undergoing whiplash levels of it lately.

He passed through the iron gates, a large bouquet of flowers in his arms. It wasn't his month to do this, but he was here none-theless. His mother didn't seem to spend much time here, anyway. He quieted the normal storm of thoughts in his head, listening for a response.

Silence.

Maybe she was off tormenting Jack and Oliver today.

Go easy on Ollie though, okay? Serena coming home was

supposed to make everything go back to normal. But that wasn't happening. His brother's life wasn't even close to normal.

Chatting with his mom this way was comforting, even if she didn't answer all the time—a fact that still made him wonder whether he was just hearing voices in his head. Jack said he heard her, too. But it could be that craziness ran in the Wolfe family. After all, Jack dropped out of law school to become a firefighter. Hard to call that anything but certifiably nuts.

He strolled through the winding rows of gravestones, listening to the gravel crunch beneath his boots. It was kind of a pleasant sound, actually. He should be thoroughly depressed after seeing Cassidy, but his mood was weirdly buoyant.

I have a plan, mom.

He listened for a moment. Nothing but the sound of gravel crunching.

It might not work.

It was entirely possible that Cassidy had been trying to save his feelings when she said, "I love you, Mattie. I really do."

All my life I've always just wanted the things that everyone else wanted for me. And you and dad were great! Don't get me wrong—you wanted good things for me. But it absolved me of responsibility for deciding what I want for myself. Dr. Smythe said that, and I think I agree.

The gravel walking path took a gentle curve just before Angela Wolfe's grave. He paused for a moment and took a deep breath. The air was cool and fresh. On this side of town, the air's scent was a mix of saltwater and farmland. Even in the winter, Matt rolled down his car windows as soon as he hit the Bay Bridge. This was what home smelled like, what it would always smell like.

So I know she's the daughter of your friend, Michelle. Maybe you could put in a good word for me there? And Jack already defiled one of the Trevor girls. He did it first!

If she was around, that would get a response from her. But still nothing.

I mean, I never got anyone pregnant. All those lectures on "protection?" I'm the one who was paying attention!

He carried the flowers over to the marble stone that was engraved with her name. He carefully laid them on the ground in front, then folded his legs and sat down.

I want what you and Dad had. I want what Jack and Becca have, what Ollie and Serena have. And I want it with Cassidy Trevor because I'm crazy in love with her. I have a plan, as I was saying. I'll let her decide whether she wants me.

There was still no response from his mom. He wasn't sure whether that was good or bad. Not that it mattered anymore. He knew what he wanted, and he had a plan to get it.

reathe. Breathe. Cassidy tried to focus on the cool spring air, on the pale green of her mother's dress, the sharp black tuxedos the groomsmen on the opposite side of the aisle wore, on the lovely music Lauren was playing on the white baby grand piano … on anything but the increasingly intense ache coming from her left leg. The doctor had allowed her to take off the brace, but she still needed crutches when she was standing or walking for long periods of time.

But today was Becca's wedding. She couldn't very well stand up here in her lovely pale blue bridesmaid's dress with an ugly metal crutch under one arm. From the front row of white guest chairs, her mother caught her eye and Cassidy returned a tight smile.

"Breathe," her mom mouthed.

Matt was standing on the other side of the aisle, between Oliver and Mason. Mason was adorable in his child-sized tuxedo and blue cummerbund. She could feel Matt's eyes on her but she refused to meet his gaze. They had said their goodbyes and had mostly avoided each other at the rehearsal dinner last night. She and Lauren were set to drive to Texas next week.

The pain in her leg was making her lightheaded. The only thing worse than fainting at her sister's wedding would be bursting into tears at the prospect of having to say goodbye to Matt again.

Breathe.

A delighted murmur rippled through the assembled guests as Jackie and Cam began making their way down the aisle. Jackie was wearing the pink eyelet dress she and Cassidy had looked at in the dress shop. Cam wore his own miniature tuxedo with a pink cummerbund that matched his cousin's dress. He looked equal parts proud and terrified.

Cassidy lifted her sights to the Chesapeake Inn, where Becca was waiting for her cue. After a week of on-and-off rain, the weather today was perfect. The sky was blue and marred by not a single cloud. The Inn's expansive back lawn was green and dry. In her peripheral vision, Cassidy could see the bay sparkling in the sunshine. Moving discreetly in the back was Ashley, taking pictures.

Becca and Jack couldn't have asked for a more beautiful day for their wedding.

Jackie and Cam split apart and took their respective places with the groomsmen and bridesmaids. Cassidy wobbled as a sharp pain shot through her leg. Natalie, standing next to her, steadied her with a firm hand on her back.

Breathe.

IT TOOK all of Matt's willpower not to rush across the ten feet separating him from Cassidy. She was so clearly in pain. He had seen her crutches leaning against a wall in the Inn—he hoped Jack and Becca hadn't told her she had to leave them inside but more likely it was just Cassidy's stubbornness. Just like she was stubbornly refusing to look at him right now. Just like she had stubbornly refused to socialize with him last night at the rehearsal dinner.

But Matt had a plan, and he could be stubborn too.

Stubborn doesn't even begin to cover it.

He bit back a smile. *Glad you could make it today.*

Wouldn't miss it for the world.

The music slowed and the guests turned around in their chairs as Becca emerged from the double French doors of the Inn. They all watched as she made her way across the green lawn, her father holding her arm. Matt heard Jack's inhale when she reached the top of the aisle. He glanced at his brother, whose face shone with happiness and joy.

Two down, one to go.

He looked over at Cassidy again and resisted the urge to roll his eyes. *Just look at me already.* Ah, no matter. He had a plan. He didn't know whether it would work or not. Cassidy had a mind of her own. That was one of the things he loved about her, of course, and his plan took that into account.

He was so focused on his favorite bridesmaid that the sudden appearance of the bride in his line of vision took him by surprise. The fabric of her dress swished as she joined his brother beneath the white latticed arch. Dr. Trevor let go of her arm and sat down next to his wife. The minister from the Episcopal Church made a lifting motion with his arms, and the guests rose for the prayer.

Matt bowed his head and closed his eyes. He had never been able to pay attention through an entire prayer, no matter how short. His brother's wedding was going to be no different. And in any case, in his head the minister's voice was drowned out by the sound of someone quietly weeping.

CHAPTER 33

*J*uly

Cassidy was lying on her stomach on a chaise longue by the pool, a textbook splayed open between her hands, when a sheet of paper parachuted onto the paragraph she was reading. She flipped it over, then rolled onto her side to look up at her sister.

"What's this?" she asked.

Lauren was grinning like the Cheshire Cat. "Matt Wolfe's new address."

Cassidy looked at the piece of paper again, then frowned. "This is an address here in Austin."

"Yup. Sure is."

Cassidy sat all the way up now. "And you know this ... how?"

"I saw him on campus today after my figure drawing class." While Cassidy was taking classes at the University of Texas, Lauren had enrolled in an art class at the community college.

"And he just gave you his address?"

"No, I called Becca for that afterward." She laughed. "Like thirty seconds afterward."

"Did he see you?"

"I waved to him. He waved back."

"Did you talk to him?"

"Nope. He kept on walking."

Cassidy stared at the address. "This isn't a hotel?"

Lauren shook her head. "He's taking fire investigation classes at the community college. And working at some fire training facility out here."

"Huh. Wonder why he didn't tell me he was out here?"

"Maybe because you barely spoke to him at the wedding."

Cassidy lay back on the chaise and closed her eyes, the paper with his address still in her hand. Matt had left St. Caroline. He was out here in Texas.

"Wait—you said he has a job here?"

"That's what Becs said. Some sort of project manager type position."

"Is there toner in the printer?"

Lauren half laughed, half snorted. "Odd thing for you to be concerned with at the moment. But yes, I replaced the toner two days ago."

"Thanks. I've got something to print out."

MATT HAD JUST FINISHED SETTING the table in his tiny apartment when his phone buzzed with a text from Becca.

She's on her way.

He tapped out his reply. *Thanks. Keep your fingers crossed.*

He surveyed the table again, making a few tweaks to the arrangement of tulips in the vase. Then he turned back to the narrow countertop to get the food. According to Google Maps, he had about twenty-seven minutes before she would arrive. He got down the new serving dishes he'd bought and spooned all of the rice from the cardboard takeout container into one. Into a second dish, he scooped the curry chicken, the scent of the spices hitting his nose and making his mouth water instantly. He should be totally sick of Thai food by now, given that he had spent the past two weeks sampling every Thai restaurant he could find in Austin. And absolutely, he needed a break from it after this.

But for Cass, he would eat it one more night.

There was a quart of mint chocolate chip ice cream in the freezer, too.

The plan was going according to plan, so far. Becca had told him roughly when Lauren had class at the community college so he could just happen to walk by. She gave Lauren his address and let him know that Cassidy was headed his way.

So far, so good.

But once she got here, he was on his own.

The doorbell rang. He opened the door and, if he hadn't been expecting Cassidy, he might have thought the woman framed in the doorway was Lauren—because she looked that different. Her hair was lighter from the sun, her shoulders and arms more deeply tanned, the smile gracing her lips flirtier than he remembered. She was wearing a loose green dress that was kind of wrinkled—which meant it was probably linen. (*Thanks, mom!*) Her long brown legs ended in white canvas sneakers.

He drank her in, drank in this new relaxed Cassidy. Her mirrored sunglasses reflected back at him his slightly stunned expression. She looked happy. The move had obviously been the right thing for her to do. But of course it was—Cassidy was known for making smart, reasoned decisions.

He reached out and carefully lifted her sunglasses from her nose. Yep, even her eyes were smiling.

"So how long have you been stalking me?"

She took her sunglasses back and squeezed between him and the doorway. He turned and followed her into the apartment.

"Is that curry?"

"Not stalking you at all. And yes."

She tucked her sunglasses into her purse and put on her

regular sexy librarian glasses. She squinted at him, then rubbed her jawline. "I like that sexy scruff thing you have going on there."

He rubbed his own jaw in response. "I can have a little facial hair now that I'm not working for a fire department anymore. But given how ungodly hot it is out here, I may shave it soon." He gestured toward the table. "Hungry?"

"Famished."

He pulled out a chair for her and she sat down. But she kept her purse on her lap.

"So what does everyone back home think about all this?" She looked behind him to the rest of his admittedly tiny apartment.

"Does it matter?" He shrugged. "Becca and Jack are okay with it. With this part of it, I mean." He pointed to himself and then to her. "With us." He filled her plate, then his.

As he sat down across the table from her, she reached into her purse and pulled out a sheet of paper, folded in half. She unfolded it and slid it across the table.

"I have a proposal," she said.

He picked it up and skimmed over the lines of text. It was a version of their friends-with-benefits contract. He tore it in half, then tore it in half again.

Her face fell.

"I don't want to be friends with benefits," he said.

"You don't?"

He shook his head. "I want more than that. I want to be your boyfriend. Your lover."

"You mean exclusive?"

"Yes, exclusive." He stood and pulled her up from her chair. "I meant it when I said I loved you, Cass. And I believed you when you said the same about me."

"I'm probably not moving back to St. Caroline."

"And …?"

"And you like living there."

"I liked it when the things I wanted were there. But now the things I want aren't there." He pulled her into his arms, ignoring the rumbling in his stomach. He was hungry but dinner could wait. What he really hungered for was her kiss, her soft lips on his, her arms wrapped around his chest. It had been months already since he'd had that. Even a day without it was too long.

"So you're not going back to the fire department when you finish your classes?"

He gently pushed his hands into her blonde hair. "Not that fire department. Maybe one somewhere else. Or maybe not."

"I thought you loved being a firefighter."

He pulled her a little closer, close enough to feel the rise and fall of her chest on his.

"I do. But I fell into it because it was there. It's what my family does. But there might be other things I'm better at. Or maybe not, but I won't know unless I try." He touched his nose to hers. "You made me see that I want other things, Cass." He nipped at her lips. "You even made me consider something completely new and off the wall."

She nipped him back. "And what would that be?"

"That I might be better at being a boyfriend than being a friend with benefits."

"You were pretty good at that though."

"I was, wasn't I?" He felt her hands slide down his back and settle on his hips. "I took the liberty of speaking to your dad at the wedding. Hope you don't mind."

"I think lots of people took that liberty."

Her fingers were making some sort of tapping-dancing motion on his lower back. It was making other parts of his body want to get up and dance, too. But he needed to get this out there, before he completely lost the battle with distraction.

"I spoke to him about us. I told him I was in love with you."

Her fingers stilled. "And what did he say?"

"He said, 'good luck with that.'"

She stifled a laugh by burying her face in his chest. The

warmth of her breath went straight through his shirt to his skin. He had maybe a minute of conscious, ordered thought left. Maybe less.

Then she lifted her face. "Wait … you talked to him at the *wedding?*"

Matt just smiled.

"Am I the last person to know?"

"Pretty much. Your family is good at keeping a secret, apparently." Even with several emotions struggling for dominance on her face right now—annoyance, amusement … desire—she was beautiful.

She frowned—and even that didn't mar her beauty for Matt.

"So what does my mother think of this?"

"She likes the idea of there being someone out here with you after Lauren leaves."

"So like … a babysitter?"

Annoyance was the current emotional champion, he could see. He traced his thumb over her lower lip. He had to wrap up this conversation soon because his reserves of rational thinking were almost empty.

"I prefer the term 'boyfriend.' Though we could negotiate the exact language. Later." He cupped her face with his hands and kissed her deeply. Her hands slid from his hips to cup his ass. *Rational thinking now at zero level.*

"I'd like to point out that my new digs here have a microwave," he murmured into her parted lips. "For reheating dinner." He lifted her up and hooked her thighs around his waist. "Also a new bed in dire need of christening." He carried her down the short hallway.

"Did you bring your handcuffs to Texas?"

She nuzzled his neck in such a suggestive way that he practically ran into the bedroom.

"I did. And this time, they're going on you." He gently lowered her onto the bed, grinning down at her. "Because your sister isn't expecting you home until tomorrow."

THANK you for reading TWO OF HEARTS! To find out when the next book in the St. Caroline Series is released, sign up for my VIP Reader email list or follow me on BookBub!

In the meantime, if you'd like another sweet and romantic read, pick up *Back to Us* ...

When an assignment in the Middle East goes bad, adventure journalist Colt Buchanan comes home to New York and the love of his life, beauty mogul Zee Malisewski.

The only problem? She says they broke up four years ago.

Can there be a second chance at love for a man who can't remember ... and a woman determined not to forget?

The daughter of an actress, Zee Malisewski grew up on movie sets and in boarding schools. As an adult, she's built a life away from all that—and a successful cosmetics business with her best friend—in New York City. Men? They've come and gone. Mostly gone. She's sworn off the male species anyway, after her latest boyfriend tampers with her company's new product and nearly destroys everything she and her business partner have spent years working for. Now Zee wants a home of her own and she's done waiting for Prince Charming to show up and share it with her.

Adventure journalist Colt Buchanan grabbed his own bootstraps and yanked hard—leaving the poverty of his rural hometown behind for a scholarship to a fancy east coast college and then the bright lights of the big city. But when an assignment in the Middle East leaves his interview subject dead and Colt's memory riddled with holes you can drive a bus through, he comes back to the only place that's ever felt like home—the Manhattan apartment of a pretty Hollywood princess he never had any business wanting.

Pick up your copy at Amazon.com or BarnesandNoble.com!

ACKNOWLEDGMENTS

As always, I am indebted to the generous advice and support I get from Anna James, J.B. Currie, Victoria Hanlen, and Ann Clement.

ABOUT THE AUTHOR

Julia Gabriel writes contemporary romance that is smart, sexy, and emotionally-intense (grab the tissues). She lives in New England where she is a full-time mom to a teenager, as well as a sometime writing professor and obsessive quilter (is there any other kind?). If all goes well, she'll be a Parisienne in her next life. Her books have been selected as "Top Picks" by RT Book Reviews, and critics at RT Book Reviews, Kirkus, and others have called her work "nuanced," "heart-wrenching and emotional," "well-crafted contemporary romance," and "deeply moving story-telling."

Be the first to find out about new books and more by signing up for my email newsletter!

Say "hello" on social media ...

facebook.com/authorjuliagabriel

bookbub.com/authors/julia-gabriel

instagram.com/juliagabriel.author

amazon.com/Julia-Gabriel

ALSO BY JULIA GABRIEL

St. Caroline Series

Hearts on Fire

Two of Hearts

Phlox Beauty Series

Next to You

Back to Us

The Senator's Wife

www.ingramcontent.com/pod-product-compliance
Lightning Source LLC
Chambersburg PA
CBHW071127200626
46817CB00018B/2364